# MASTER OF Secret Desires

# Other Ellora's Cave Anthologies
## Available from Pocket Books

### BEDTIME, PLAYTIME
by Jaid Black, Sherri L. King, & Ruth D. Kerce

### HURTS SO GOOD
by Gail Faulkner, Lisa Renee Jones, & Sahara Kelly

### LOVER FROM ANOTHER WORLD
by Rachel Carrington, Elizabeth Jewell, & Shiloh Walker

### FEVER-HOT DREAMS
by Sherri L. King, Jaci Burton, & Samantha Winston

### TAMING HIM
by Kimberly Dean, Summer Devon, & Michelle M. Pillow

### ALL SHE WANTS
by Jaid Black, Dominique Adair, & Shiloh Walker

# MASTER OF *Secret Desires*

S. L. CARPENTER

ELIZABETH JEWELL

TAWNY TAYLOR

POCKET BOOKS
New York  London  Toronto  Sydney

POCKET BOOKS, a division of Simon & Schuster, Inc.
1230 Avenue of the Americas, New York, NY 10020

Library of Congress Cataloging-in-Publication Data
Master of secret desires / S.L. Carpenter, Elizabeth Jewell, Tawny Taylor.
    p.cm.
    Contents: Broken / S.L. Carpenter—Six enchanted princesses / Elizabeth
Jewell—Dragons and dungeons / Tawny Taylor.
    1. Erotic stories, American. 2. American fiction—21st century. I. Carpenter,
S.L. Broken. II. Jewell, Elizabeth (Elizabeth R.) Six enchanted princesses. III.
Taylor, Tawny. Dragons and dungeons.
    PS648.E7M37 2007
    813'.6—dc22                                                    2007060084

ISBN-13: 978-1-4165-3615-4
ISBN-10:      1-4165-3615-9

This Pocket Books trade paperback edition June 2007

10 9 8 7 6 5 4 3 2 1

For information regarding special discounts for bulk purchases,
please contact Simon & Schuster Special Sales at 1-800-456-6798
or business@simonandschuster.com

# Contents

# Broken

## S. L. CARPENTER

# Dedication

This story is dedicated to Missy for supporting
and pushing my initial idea to "keep it real."
Thank you, Missy.

# Prologue

ARI'S HAND SHOOK AS she took a sip from her drink. She was nervous, scared and slightly drunk. She had finally gotten the nerve to go out again. She'd gone to a local club with a few girlfriends and they had either left with their dates or new acquaintances. Kari was letting her mind clear and finally closing the chapter in her life that was over. Enough time had passed after her heartbreak—she had set out to begin a new life.

Her new life had actually started a year ago and, because the man she'd left was an abusive, fucking bastard, she had been alone ever since. Now she fought everything she felt inside, but the burning urge to be with someone made her ache.

The darkened nightclub was almost empty. A low cloud of smoke and the scent of bad colognes mixed into a strange smell. The walls were covered in a wood-grain siding and the small stage was lit with a single spotlight. The light focused on the piano sitting center stage. A man sat down and put his cigarette out in the ashtray on top of the shiny piano.

It was a bar like most others, with the lonely looking for love in all the wrong places. The standard scumbags were scattered around the bar. She wasn't interested in anything like them. They were hunters and she wasn't going to be their prey for the night. She wanted a warm body with emotions, passion and a hard cock to take her.

Kari sighed, cleansing her tweaked mind. She needed to relax. She rested her weary eyes and was swept away by a soothing melody on the nearby piano. The chatter and clinking glasses quieted. A calm filled her body and she smiled as the tune gently played. A sucker for country music, it had the feel of home to it. Comforting yet sad.

Kari opened her eyes and turned to see a handsome man leaning over the keyboard of the small piano. He had long, dark hair that was a little messy but very sexy. He looked up and their eyes met.

*Okay, you have my attention now.*

Humming along with the melody, his low voice vibrated into the microphone and through Kari. He quietly began to sing.

"I am hiding my pain,
"Through these tearful eyes,
"This world is dark,
"And I'm all alone,
"Our house is closed,
"With my dreams inside,
"Now I must go on,
"Here without you.

"Each time I look in the mirror,

"All I see are shadows of you,

"Memories of better times,

"Memories of our love,

"Lost in the caverns of hurtful scars,

"But I'm over the pain,

"Over the loss of our love,

"And alone, here without you."

His words tore at her heart. He knew what she was feeling. Kari wanted to find out more about this man. She had found the warm body she wanted for this night.

FOR EVERY REASON SHE HAD to use this man for sex, everything only seemed to get worse.

She became irritated by the latex rub of the condom in her pussy. It felt like sandpaper against her flesh. His hands groped and squeezed hard on her now sensitive breasts and nipples, uncaring to her pain. He wasn't interested in her needs, just his own.

The void she felt became more hollow and deep with every thrust inside.

Nothing was right. His movements felt awkward. His cock didn't fill her as she wanted. He swiveled and pounded roughly into her and it did nothing except make her wish she wasn't there.

With a grunt, he moaned loudly in her ear. "Oh, fuck, baby, I'm gonna come."

Kari only wanted it over and, within seconds, it was. She felt the flexing bursts within her walls. She felt dirty and used as he pressed down against her body with his sweat smearing across her chest. Dropping his weight, he smashed against her lying beneath him.

"Oh, Tami, mmm, Tami baby, damn, you're a good fuck."

Closing her eyes, Kari felt the urgent need to scream. Tears streamed from the corners of her eyes as she pushed his slumping body off her and rolled off the bed.

An oozing wetness slimed between her legs. Reaching between her thighs, she pulled out the soiled condom that dangled from her pussy and tossed it on the bed against his leg. He hadn't even stayed hard long enough to have it stay on him.

"What's with you?"

"My name is *Kari*, you mindless fuck!" crying as her rage began to rise. "I just wanted to forget about someone and you quickly reminded me of all the things I loathed and hated."

"Hey, you picked *me* up remember? Don't get mad at me!"

"Why not?"

"Because I'm not your problem, *he* is. I was just looking for a quick fuck."

"Well, that's what we both got, you got a fuck and I got the quick part of it."

Anger and frustration welled inside of her. She felt used, degraded and cheap for letting this *nothing* fuck her like a whore. Beginning to bawl, Kari leaned into the wall and slumped down.

The man obviously wasn't sure what to do. He pulled his pants up and grabbed his shirt and other clothes, then moved toward Kari.

"Just get the fuck out of here." She pointed toward the door with her head resting on her knees, naked and cold.

He hurriedly pulled the rest of his clothes on and stepped beside her, apparently not sure whether to thank her, leave his phone number or give her a hug for comfort.

With the clunk of the door closing, Kari sighed and stared blankly out of her small bedroom window. It was a very rainy night, cold and dreary. Just like her life had become.

# Chapter One

*ESSE LEANED AGAINST THE* phone booth door. Rain was pouring over his head and falling along his face. The cold raindrops masked the tears streaming from his swollen, red eyes.

He slouched forward then leaned back, bringing the half-empty bottle of whiskey to his lips. Another long swig, another memory washed away. Jesse wasn't sure if there was enough whiskey in Seattle to cleanse the sad memories from his mind.

He was alone, drunk and thoroughly disgusted for letting himself fall into the easy trap of self-pity. He had just moved to this broken-down neighborhood after being crushed by a woman's words and lack of compassion for him or his feelings. Getting drunk did nothing more than show weakness when he should have been showing strength.

Staggering away from the phone booth, the rain seemed

to be falling harder. His body numbed by the drinking. He walked across the empty street toward someplace that felt familiar. He saw a blurry figure of a man running to a parked car. The man covered his head with his jacket and didn't notice Jesse standing in the middle of the street behind him.

Following the path his feet led him down, he walked toward a small alley behind the apartments where the man had run from. It was muddy from the constant rain. The pavement had cracks in it and a few garbage bags had been pulled from the dumpsters behind the place. Neighborhood stray dogs scattered the contents around the alleyway. Jesse stepped on wrappers as he walked. It was the same alley the garbage trucks followed.

Taking another drink, Jesse was determined to drink his sadness away. But he knew he wasn't doing anything more than hiding it. People try to escape into a bottle, but Jesse was just hitting rock-bottom. He just wanted to numb the confusion and regret, even if just for a while. Life was cruel and he wanted to just succumb to the urge to quit—but he wasn't the type to give in.

A light brightened the alley. It was from one of the apartments. It used to be an old hotel. The owner had converted it to apartments and, in these tough times, they rented quickly because they were cheap. But you get what you pay for . . .

Jesse walked toward the light. Being curious and drunk tended to be a very bad combination.

Curtains covered the small window, but there was a sliver of space that he could see through.

Looking in, Jesse saw a woman naked and stepping into the shower. She had her back facing him, then turned and let the water rinse over her. Her head hung low with the wet strands of her hair dangling down. Her hair was long and dark. She had a natural beauty to her, but there was sadness in her face and the dark smears of mascara revealed she had been crying.

Jesse began to stare at her. Her body was slightly tanned and she had an attractive but not perfect figure. She brought her hands to her face, turned around and crouched down into a ball. She finally looked up and Jesse could see she was still crying. Her green eyes were filled with such sadness and remorse.

He looked down. Jesse felt like he was invading a place he shouldn't. Something disquieting was making this woman sad. He knew nothing about her except that she was pretty, had a nice ass and a tattoo on her front hip of a heart. He may have been drunk, but looking at a naked woman brought details to the forefront for any man.

Looking back up through the window, Jesse saw the woman was now leaning her head against the shower wall, crying and letting the water wash over her.

Like him, the woman was trying to rinse away her pain.

With a final drink, Jesse collapsed in the alley in a pile of debris, hitting his head against a small, dark car.

Kari looked up from her tears, hearing the noise outside her window. She didn't care what it was, dismissing it for a dog ravaging for food in the trash. Her own sadness encased her in disgrace, letting herself become dirty. She just wanted to crawl away and hide forever. Life had been cruel to her also.

◆ ◆ ◆

"WAKE UP! GODDAMMIT! GET UP, you dumb, drunken bastard. I have to go to work!" A woman kicked Jesse, trying to wake him.

"Fuckin' bitch! Quit kicking me . . . I'll get up." Jesse was grumpy, wet, dirty and had a headache that felt like a truck had run over his head.

Jesse propped himself up and looked at the woman. Awkwardly he hung onto the car for balance so he could stand erect. His back ached and he was slightly hunched over like Quasimodo. His anger was about to erupt but, as soon as he saw her eyes, it hit him. He recognized her from the night before. Those green eyes were deep and full of emotions. He stood like a deer in headlights.

She stood, hand on hip, waiting for Jesse to speak. "I can see you're a real talker. Hey, buddy, I'm running late and have to get to work. So if you'll just move, I can get into my car and go."

He just stood there, drooling and smelling bad.

"Okay. I'll make it clear. Move your ass or I'll kick you in the balls!"

Jesse moved aside, not saying a word. He noticed she was wearing a waitress uniform from the diner around the corner from his job. The white and gold nametag read "Kari".

IN TYPICAL PACIFIC NORTHWEST fashion, it rained most of the day. Kari hadn't made shit in tips because it was a Monday— a typically slower day and just not as many people shopping around town in the rain.

*Almost five. Come on clock, fifteen more minutes.*

Kari wanted this day to end. Her feet were sore, she was cold and the next guy to comment on her nipples sticking into her blouse would get a scalding pot of coffee poured onto his crotch. She wasn't overly thrilled to be a waitress, but overall the diner was a nice place to work. Better than most she had been in. It was clean, had a long, white, marble-looking counter with a row of wooden stools lining it and the setup made serving people easier. The booths were for bigger groups and they had red seat covers, which were comfortable and easy to keep clean.

What she liked best, though, was that her boss was a fair guy, and didn't grope at the waitresses or flirt uncomfortably with them. It was a busy downtown diner. His wife was the hostess, and he was in the business to make money. If his employees worked hard, he paid them well for it. Perfect for Kari, because she busted her ass all day and the manager knew it.

*Ding, ding . . .*

The door opened and a gust of cold wind followed the man into the diner.

Kari was cleaning the table from her last slobbish customer and turned to see the guy who had walked in. He was talking to the hostess at the register and she pointed in Kari's direction.

*Oh, shit, what did I do now?*

She returned to her cleaning and wiped off the tabletop, then walked over to toss the towel into the waitress sink. Kari turned to see the hooded man plop into the newly cleaned booth. He dripped water everywhere. *Bastard.*

"My shift ends in a few minutes, sir, let me get you one of the other girls." Kari looked to the front of the diner, trying to catch Betty's attention.

"I don't want another waitress. I want you."

*Hello. All right, girls. Now it's really showtime.*

She turned and pulled her order pad out from her apron. When she looked toward the man, he pulled his hood back on his pullover sweatshirt and she recognized him.

"Well you certainly look different. At least you don't have week-old burritos stuck in your hair." She smiled and waited for his reply. She saw his dark hair was now clean, refried beans–free and combed. He had shaven, revealing the hard lines of his chin, and those eyes just made her sigh inside. He was roughly handsome.

"Speaking of burritos, what's the special today?" The stranger grinned. "I wanted to apologize about this morning. Not the best way to meet someone—lying in a pile of week-old garbage with morning breath like a dragon. First impression suicide."

Kari couldn't help but snicker. She took his order and gave it to the cook hiding behind the wall. The scent of burning oil was floating around the diner's kitchen. The cook had a bad habit of burning French fries.

While Kari finished her shift-end duties, she looked back at her latest customer a few times. She'd watch him sit patiently, except for the silly way he built playhouses with the salt and pepper packages. Then he'd create a fist and knock them down, making sounds like Godzilla. What a goofball.

After a few minutes, Kari brought him his burritos smothered in salsa and a small basket of chips. Slipping the tag under his glass of water, she turned to see the clock and sighed. "Quitting time, finally," she murmured under her breath.

"Quitting time, huh? Can I buy you dinner?" He gave her a wide grin.

Kari paused for a moment. *Might be fun to actually go out to dinner.* "Um, you're eating dinner aren't you?"

He motioned for her to join him and pushed the salsa chips to her side of the table.

"Whoa, big spender."

Kari waved to the hostess, getting her attention, then pointed at her watch. After a nod of approval, Kari plopped in the booth bench across from him.

His smile was warming. "I wanted to introduce myself— my name is Jesse Andersen."

It was a pleasant break from the usual ass-grabbing people who visited the downtown diner. He seemed harmless enough. Just an average guy.

Kari pulled the hairnet from her head and tugged out the tie holding everything up in a bun. Her hair fell loose and she rubbed her scalp, fluffing her hair. "Kari Hawkins."

Jesse stared. His weakness revealed before his eyes. Long hair on a woman made him all warm and fuzzy. It also began to make him hard because, deep in his mind, he remembered seeing Kari naked, and the image of using her hair like the reins of a horse as he pounded into her awoke his other brain. *Down boy.*

"I work at the package delivery place down the block. I'm the manager there. So if you ever want to see my package, just ask." Pausing, Jesse realized what he had said and took another bite from his dinner.

"Really. Well hopefully it's a big package and not too quick of a delivery." Kari had a shit-eating grin on her face.

Jesse held back a laugh. "I was being good. I didn't say it, but you did. I like that."

Time rolled by with Jesse and Kari talking and laughing.

The typical ten questions had been asked. Where they were from, how long they had lived in town, what new movies they'd seen. Favorite sexual position was the next question. The standard format to break the ice and get acquainted. Soon two hours had passed and it was now dark outside.

"Oh, shit, I have to go!" Kari scooted out of the booth.

"Husband?"

"No, I just have to go. I am sorry." Kari walked behind the counter and grabbed her purse.

"Boyfriend?" Jesse asked again.

"No, I am not married and don't have a boyfriend. I just need to go."

Jesse paused then asked as a last-ditch effort, "It's my cologne, isn't it?"

Shaking her head and obviously getting perturbed, Kari whipped around and leaned on the table, getting right in Jesse's face. "Relax, I just need to go home. My favorite show is on TV, I need to take a major number-two poopy and get out of these stinky clothes."

Jesse looked at Kari and his eyes were drawn downward. He could see down her body through the top of her blouse. The black lace of her bra made him swallow. Her breasts filled the cups of thin fabric. "Well, if you gotta go, you gotta go."

"It was nice to properly meet you, Jesse. This was nice. Next time let's do this at a real restaurant." With a wave, Kari walked away.

Jesse's eyes watched her movements. Each sway of her hip reminded him of why he loved a woman's body. Kari had elegance—even when unintentional. That and a nice ass didn't hurt.

After a few seconds it hit him. He slapped his palm to his head. *Oh, shit, she dropped a dinner hint and I let it go.* "You fucking moron!"

"Who you calling a 'fucking moron'?" A large, bearded man at the diner bar glared at him angrily.

"I am calling myself a fucking moron."

The man scrunched his face then shrugged. "Well you'd know best . . . fuckin' moron."

# Chapter Two

THE SOFT SOUND OF country music filled the bare apartment.

There were a few pictures on the walls and a well-used couch and loveseat in the living room. There weren't a lot of fancy things in her apartment, but it was home for her. Comfortable and clean. On the one large wall, Kari had set up her television and stereo in the entertainment unit. She loved her music to sound good and TV was her escape from life. Those two items were important. Above it hung an old, framed photograph of her parents. The entire place was painted off-white but still had a gray look. It was just an apartment.

Kari was a woman with little flash. She was single, working in a low-paying job and just getting by.

She grabbed a towel from the laundry basket in the short hallway separating her bedroom and the bathroom.

There were about a dozen candles lit and water running in the tub. The scent of cinnamon spice filled the room from the flames of candles.

She leaned over and let her hand splash at the water, checking the temperature. It was just right.

Tossing her robe off her shoulders, Kari caught her reflection in the mirror. She was a pretty woman. Not overweight, but not skinny. She had curves. A nice set of breasts that were still firm because gravity hadn't taken over. She tugged the barrette from her thick, dark hair and scratched through it and over her head, fluffing her hair. The bruises on her shoulders and the back of her arms had faded away with the memory of how they had gotten there. She smiled, knowing she had a lot going for her and out there somewhere was "The Guy".

Stepping into the water, the warmth was a blanket over her skin. After climbing in, she submerged her body and then her head, letting the bath swallow her aches and pains away.

Kari laid in the bath. The steam helped clear her head. She was sore all over from a long day and the bath was her escape. She raised her leg up, letting the water cascade down her thigh. If a company could package and sell the soothing pleasure from a bath, they'd make millions—at least Kari would pay it.

She reached for the small glass of wine she had poured. Not being much of a wine drinker, she didn't even care about the year or type of wine. It just tasted and felt right. Sipping from the tall glass, she let it coat her throat. With a sigh, Kari set the glass back down.

She was relaxed, but the emptiness of her life began to

creep in and spoil her evening. Then something happened she hadn't expected. With her eyes closed, she envisioned Jesse. Her regular fantasy men from movies and nudie magazines weren't what she wanted tonight. She wanted somebody real.

The heat of the bath water was cooling, but she wasn't. Laying her head back on a rolled-up towel, her hands began the slow descent along her body.

A low, soft moan escaped from her body with the smooth caress of her breasts. In her mind, Jesse walked into the bathroom and began to appreciate her body and touch her like a man should.

Begging for attention, Kari let her fingertips tug gently at her now hardened nipples. Being in the water made her wish she were an octopus so she could touch every sensitive area of her body.

Her mind again searched for something to focus on. Jesse's face appeared in her head. His hands caressing her full breasts. Those eyes looking down to her heated pussy. The dark brown centers, hollow and deep, staring at every movement and squirm. Kari licked her lips and slid her hand between her legs, laying it on top of her pussy.

The water surrounded and protected her in a cocoon of warmth. The edge of her fingertips slipped along her pink flesh.

She could see Jesse biting his bottom lip, his white teeth gleaming with saliva, wanting to play with the tightened lips of her swollen cunt. If her mind was playing tricks, she was falling for them. She wanted to let her imagination flow free.

Her head pushed hard into the rolled towel as she slipped her finger between the folds of flesh. The jolts of excitement shot up her spine. Pulling her leg up, she hung it over the lip of the tub. This opened her pussy wider and Kari freed her fantasy.

Things were becoming more and more real to her. Every move of his hands, his lips, his body, all the passion in his heart all encompassed her mind. She knew it wasn't reality but, damn, she could imagine it.

She could feel Jesse's wet tongue flicking over her engorged clit. Every move of her hand became Jesse's tongue. She'd always had a thing for a man going down on her since high school. Back then that had been with a French exchange student who had taken her to prom. Ever since that glorious night, having a man eat her pussy was a sure way to orgasm. For both of them.

She could mentally see them on her bed, with Jesse engrossed in the opening of her pussy. He wouldn't let it free from his mouth, and Kari moaned with the deep penetration of her fingers into her cunt.

Over and over she stroked her fingers over her clit and spread the opening wider, begging it to be filled by Jesse. The splashing of the rippling water aroused her more. She could feel her body climbing, higher and more desperate for release.

She wanted his cock inside of her. The hard, slapping sounds of fucking filled her head. That ultimate feeling of fulfillment as he came inside her convulsing walls during a mind-shattering orgasm. The vision in her mind was what she wanted and longed for. She needed it.

Her fantasy had her on the brink of eruption. She frantically rubbed on her clit, faster, faster. The water sprinkled against her hot skin as it splashed. Her breath became a pant. Kari softly whimpered then her body began to quiver.

With a rush of heat, she started to come. As her muscles constricted, she tightened and squeezed her fingers between her legs. The bath water seemed cold compared to the rushing heat in her veins. He had made her come. Jesse had become her muse for orgasm—his smile, that weird wiggle of his eyebrow and, mostly, that fierce tongue flicking over her clit.

The spasms subsided and Kari looked down at her body in the water. Her nipples were tight and hard, and the water was now cold.


THE NEXT FEW DAYS passed and each afternoon Jesse would walk by the diner and look in. A few times he got lucky and Kari saw him walking by. He'd grin and wave.

Except the one time he wasn't looking where he was going and ran into an old lady with a walker. Kari could see him apologizing, but the little old lady whooped him pretty good with her purse.

Kari would smile back. She wasn't sure why he wasn't stopping, but the attention was nice. She began to wait for it. And Jesse was there every day. Being curious, she figured she'd be a little forward the next time and ask him why he didn't stop in.


IT WAS FRIDAY AND SHE looked up to see it was almost five, then told her boss she wanted to take a late break. She finished all her duties and ripped off her apron to make sure she'd meet Jesse at the right time.

In the ladies' room, she freshened her makeup and smoothed her uniform over her curves. The blouse was tight to her skin and the pants clung to her legs and now moist underwear.

She applied red lip gloss and realized the time. *Fuck, shit, dammit, I'm gonna miss him!*

Bolting out of the bathroom, the door swung open hard. *THUNK.*

Closing her eyes and gritting her teeth, Kari reached over to close the door. She knew what had happened. She'd hit someone with the door.

Peeking around the door, she saw a scattering of daisy flower petals and a man's feet. Moving to get up, he held his hands over his face, keeping the blood inside his cracked skull. *Oh, fuck!* It was Jesse.

"Shit, what an idiot I am. Damn, I'm sorry. I . . . umm . . . I was . . . uhh . . ." Her attention changed from Jesse looking like a knocked-out prizefighter to the small bouquet of flowers bundled on the floor. "Oh, look, flowers."

Kari picked them up and tried to repair the damage from the door.

Jesse struggled to regain his wits. "Yeah, I got them for you." Blinking his eyes a few times he commented, "Both of you. Damn what hit me?" He finally gathered himself and focused on why he'd ventured into the diner.

Kari tried to change the subject. "These are really pretty. How'd you know I liked flowers?"

"A guess. I haven't stopped by lately because you said you like to go home after work and relax. But it's Friday and I figured I'd ask if you might want to have dinner or something." His nervous smile barely hid his fear of rejection.

"Well . . ." Kari paused then looked at the flowers. "I guess so. Why not? I don't feel like cooking tonight anyway, and microwave pizza doesn't sound too appetizing."

*Yess! He shoots and scores.* Jesse was elated she'd accepted his invitation to dinner, even with a throbbing head. "Is seven okay? I can pick you up at your place?"

"Sounds fine. I need to change anyway."

They walked out of the diner together and Jesse opened her door for her, a gentleman to the core.

As her taillights left his sight, Jesse finally showed how he felt. He pumped his fist into the air. *Fuck, yeah, who's the man? That's right, I am. Damn right.* He thumped his chest in approval.

He heard a rustling in the dumpster behind the diner and the man from the diner counter the other day shook his head and mumbled aloud, "Fuckin' moron."

The evening air was becoming wet and the skies were cloudy again. He needed to hurry and walk home. Good thing he didn't live too far.


SHAKING OFF THE DAMPNESS and cold, Jesse walked into his apartment.

"Yo, Rich. You here?" He looked around for his roommate.

"I'm in my office. Damn, you should see this bitch's tits. These *can't* be real." A man's voice echoed down the hallway.

As Jesse walked into the room, his gaze met a huge pair of breasts. They were spread across a wide-screen TV and reminded him of two watermelons. *"Shiiiiiit!"*

"I told you, dude. Man, I love DVD porn. You can

freeze-frame this stuff and even go in slow- or fast-motion. It's incredible. I love my job."

"Hey, Rich. I have a date. I don't know when I'll be in. Just wanted to let you know."

"Hey, Jess?" Rich was suddenly interested and stopped his DVD mid-stroke during an anal sex scene. "Is she . ... *hot*?"

"Yes, she is." Jesse took another full look at the TV. "Damn, change the scene. I'll have that image embedded in my mind all night."

"Does she have a sister?"

Jesse shook his head. "I don't know. I wasn't trying to fix you up, I was trying to get me hooked up."

"Some friend you are." Rich went back to watching his porno movies. "You're just lucky you got home late. I had this one with two women on a farm. They had this billy goat that—"

"Enough. Never mind." Jesse waved his hand, motioning Rich to stop. "Rich, buddy, ol' pal, can I borrow your car? I don't want to take a cab or have her drive."

"You fill it up with gas, it's all yours. Just don't stain the leather seats with sex juice."

"Rich, you're a sick bastard."

"Hey, Jess. If you think you're gonna get some, you may want to do a little maintenance. It's been a while since you had a date."

"Maintenance? I'm fine. No problem there."

"Okay. I'm just giving you some advice, dude. Wouldn't want to fire the torpedoes too soon. Might not even get the submarine into the dock, if you get my drift." Rich stared at his movie again, playing with the zoom function.

Jesse just turned away and went into his room.

As he closed the door, he heard Rich yelling, "Oh, man, you gotta check this out . . . You can see her kidneys with this zoom! *Aaargghhhh*—she has teeth down there!"

The vision from the DVD was stuck in Jesse's head. A shudder crept through his body. *Damn, that was scary.*

He needed to clear his mind and concentrate on his date with Karl.

*Hey, maybe Rich is right—I might get lucky.*

JESSE BEGAN TO STRAIN. His body tight and sweaty.

"Fuck, yeah, just like that. Oh, damn, you are so fucking hot." They were words spoken in the heat of carnal pleasures. This was his triumph.

Like a jackhammer, he pounded into her tight cunt. Faster and harder he punished her pussy, making her moan with lustful bliss. Her moans fueled Jesse's inferno of passion as he ferociously fucked her doggy-style.

His legs were weakening and his balls were tight as they slapped against her dripping pussy lips when he sank into her. He knew he was about to blow.

Leaning back, he slammed the length of his cock into her tight cunt. His eyes closed and began to burn. Nothing could stop the eruption into her velvety, inner walls . . .

Except shampoo seeping into the corner of his eyes.

Blinking, Jesse cussed. "Fuck, the soap's in my eyes! Dammit—*shit*."

As his cock spewed jets of seed against the shower wall, the stream of water from the showerhead caused the shampoo in his hair to trickle into his eyes and burn.

Reaching blindly for the showerhead, Jesse shot a spurt of seed onto his hand and tried in vain to regain his sight and fling it off his hand.

The burning increased, he reached up to wipe the soap from his eye and instead ended up smearing semen into his eye.

*Fuck, I know what a woman feels like to have it shot onto her face now. Shit!*

He grabbed the showerhead and rinsed everything out of his eyes. It took a few seconds because his eyelid was stuck shut, but he finally managed to finish his shower.

# Chapter Three

*K*ARI MUST HAVE CHANGED a dozen times. Her floor was scattered with blouses and skirts she had tried on. Nothing looked good.

*I need some new clothes. This is ridiculous.*

Finally, she decided to wear a red silken blouse and a tight black skirt. She loved heels and her black stilettos looked hot.

Jesse sat in the car. Parked in front of Kari's, he pondered his evening. *Be cool. Don't get too talkative and ramble like an idiot.* A quick cup of the hand over the nose and mouth. *The breath is good—clothes are clean.* He looked down at his lap. *No boner, so I can walk to the door.* He took a deep breath and climbed out of the small car.

*Knock, knock, knock.*

A moment passed, Jesse looked at the car and figured he could make a quick getaway.

The door opened and Kari stood in the doorway.

Jesse's eyes started at her feet and followed up her legs to her skirt and all the way up to her eyes. "Wow. I feel underdressed now. You look incredible." His mind had her *undressed*, totally.

"Well, thank you. I just threw this on."

"Well, shall we?" Jesse held his hand out, like a proper escort. "Your chariot awaits, my princess."

Kari blinked a few times then squinted as she saw the incredibly small car parked against the curb. "Um, you drive a Mini?"

"Actually it's my roommate Rich's car. Mine is a work-in-progress."

"I was hoping you weren't trying to tell me everything about you is small." Kari grinned and walked down the path to the car.

*Don't say it*, Jesse thought to himself—feeling the urge to show her the opposite right then.

Hitting the keyless entry button, the doors unlocked and Jesse opened Kari's door for her. She kneeled into the car. Her long legs became uncovered to the thigh before she put them into the small car. Jesse sucked in a bit of drool from the corner of his mouth.

The drive was fairly quiet. The soft tones of country music filled the car's emptiness. It was actually a soothing noise compared to the mind-numbing hustle-bustle of everyday life.

Even though she had lied to Jesse about throwing her clothes on—because after makeup, clothes, ruining three pair of stockings, picking colors of thongs and doing her nails and hair, it had taken her two hours to get ready—

nothing a woman does is just thrown on—Kari felt relaxed. She wasn't afraid, anxious or on edge. Something about Jesse eased her nerves. Except the nerve that led between her legs. That one was flickering with a steady stream of excitement. She liked Jesse, and her pussy was becoming a bit aroused in anticipation of meeting him.

"Thanks for going out with me, Kari. I have been a little out of the scene. I . . . umm . . . just, thank you." Jesse was apparently struggling a bit.

Kari turned and smiled. "My pleasure. Let's just have a nice dinner and talk. No pressure. Just friends."

*Friends? Did I just say friends?* Kari could have smacked her face silly. She'd said the dreaded "F" word.

Jesse had a different interpretation. *Friends, uh-oh. Looks like an early night. I was hoping to be more like fuck-friends. I could use a good, limitless sexual deviation into a woman like her.*

"That came out wrong, Jesse. I have been out of the so-called dating loop for a while too, and just want to take my time before jumping back into a relationship. I like you. You are, well, you make me feel good. So let's just start there and see where it takes us."

"Okay that sounds great. So a blowjob is out of the question?" Jesse teased but, apparently, Kari wasn't about to let him get away with it.

"Not necessarily." She reached over and brushed her hand along the inseam of his pants, inches away from Jesse's once again perky cock.

Jesse swerved the car a bit and saw Kari lean closer to his neck.

The wet tip of her tongue flicked against the skin. It became hot with arousal. Her hand slid upward toward his crotch and just before the red nails of her hand grasped his cock, she stopped. "Oh, look, we're here."

"Um, you want me to drive around the block a few times?" Jesse laughed and wiggled his eyebrows at Kari.

"I'm starving, let's go eat." Kari looked out the window at the brightly lit restaurant.

"I have something for you to swallow," Jesse murmured, trying to calm himself.

"I heard that," Kari quipped back.

THE MOOD OF THE restaurant was romantic. Jesse had made reservations and appeared to know the host since they were shown their table before the other couples sitting in the lobby area.

"It helps to grow up with the guy seating people." Jesse smiled and walked behind Kari. He liked watching her walk in front of him. The black skirt hid everything, but Jesse could picture that ass bouncing up and down in front of him as he and Kari fucked doggy-style into ecstasy.

Jesse held her chair back for her to sit down. His thoughts and feelings were back to normal. As were the perverse thoughts that the testosterone flowing through his mind had on him because, as Kari sat down, he envisioned his head below her as she sat on his smiling face. "Stop it!"

"What did I do?" Kari asked.

"Nothing, it's me. I'm talking to myself."

Kari shook her head. "Well as long as you don't answer back, you'll be okay."

*Listen to her. Oh, shit, I am answering back. Why does this always happen when I go out?*

The restaurant was one a few of Jesse's buddies at work had told him about, she learned. Nice, cozy atmosphere and great service. It was casually elegant. Dinner was perfect. The food was actually better than expected and the few drinks had eased their tensions. The two of them began to open up to each other.

"I just haven't been able to go out a lot. My last relationship was a disaster." Kari paused. "I don't mean to ramble on, Jesse, I just want to be honest. I decided to just take things as they come. I made a mistake a while back and now want to go slow. No one-night stands any more. I want to become friends with someone then we can have wild, incredibly fucking erotic sex."

Jesse swallowed his water. "Umm, you got me on that one." He cleared his throat. "I actually agree. Things move so fast now. The whole dating thing is scary. I had a long relationship go bad recently and, well—never mind."

"No, tell me."

"I haven't been able to go out or anything since. Until . . . well . . . until you." He took another sip of water and looked at Kari.

Warmth swept through Kari. He had said the perfect thing.

"Jesse? *Yo, bitch.* How's it going?" A loud voice bellowed through the restaurant.

The man's voice was obnoxious and Kari's first impression was, "Asshole. Maximum-strength".

"Hey, Alan. Been a long time. This is my friend Kari." Jesse introduced the two of them.

Alan instantly began to check Kari out. She could feel his eyes creeping over her like bad slime.

"Just got back from San Francisco. Business trips suck. That's the bad part of running a company, all the money but no time to spend it. That's what the women are for." Alan's bravado was bared and he was winning the verbal pissing contest with Jesse already. He was tall, dark-haired, slim-framed and acted like he was made of money and testosterone.

"Alan?"

The woman's voice made Jesse's skin crawl as it rang in his ears. He recognized the voice and all his emotions rushed to his heart and began to tear away at him—all over again.

"Alan? Who are you talking to?" The woman walked up to their table. She was everything women hate. Pretty, thin, blonde and seemed especially nice. "I can't believe it. Hello, sweetheart." She leaned over and gave Jesse a squeeze.

"I haven't seen you in a while. Been running around, taking care of all the little things. You know what I mean." Her hand lingered on his shoulder as she talked.

The woman turned to see Kari sitting quietly.

Jesse was obviously struggling to not make a scene. "Viki, this is Kari."

Kari smiled and had an uneasy feeling creeping through her body as she sensed she was being measured by the other woman. "Hello."

Kari remained quiet after noticing how the woman had instantly changed Jesse's mood. *I could probably kick her ass. There is no way her hair is naturally that blonde. Cheap dye job.* Kari felt something unfamiliar. She was becoming jealous.

"Don't let us bother you, Jesse, you have fun here with your date. We'll have to catch up sometime." Viki's hand still rested on Jesse's shoulder, making Kari a little uneasy.

"Yeah. Sure." Jesse sighed, slumping in his seat.

"Come on, Alan, our table is ready. Nice to meet you, Kari. I'll see you soon, Jesse." The woman tugged Alan away.

Kari noticed Jesse looking down into his plate. The man she had agreed to go out to dinner with had disappeared. He was now withdrawn, somewhat hidden.

"What is it? Who was that?" Kari asked.

"That was my life. Six months ago she ripped my heart apart. She left me for another guy, my college buddy Alan, and gave me no reason except to tell me I wasn't enough for her. She wanted more freedom. Things had gotten complicated and our priorities changed. It kinda fucks with your ego having a woman tell you something like that."

Kari sat in her chair. Her own life had recently been like Jesse's. "You know something? We all go through stuff like this—where you are somewhat lost or broken. You need to just . . . well . . . keep going."

Jesse looked up at Kari. In her eyes he could see she understood. And she listened—what a novelty.

"You know something? You're right. I am sorry to have this bring our dinner mood down. Did I tell you that you look incredible tonight?"

Smiling, Kari knew he was avoiding this topic.

"She must have done a helluva number on you, Jesse." Kari sipped her glass of wine and was curious as to what had happened. "You can talk to me you know. We're friends on a date tonight. I'm here if you need someone to talk to."

Jesse wasn't sure what to say. It would be nice to hear a woman's opinion on things but he didn't want to turn Kari off. However, there was something about her that made him want to open up—a comfort zone or something.

"It's really difficult getting over someone you truly

thought was your soul mate. Shit happens and you're left out in the cold. We are torn between what needs to be done and what we want. I was a wreck for a while but I'm getting better." He paused.

"I don't want to talk about this. That's the past." He held up the glass of water he nursed after the earlier whiskey shots. "Here's to something new."


THE MOMENT OF TRUTH had come. They sat in the car in front of Kari's apartment. Dinner had been good. Conversation had been good. The only blip had been having Alan and Viki interrupt a rather pleasant first date.

*Okay, Jesse, mellowww, mellowwww. The boner is hidden, let's turn on the charm. Lean over and kiss her without staring at her tits.* His inner voice was trying to get him back into his groove—or at least get him into *her* groove.

Hanging his head a bit, unsure, he started to lean closer to Kari. She opened her door as he puckered up for thin air.

*He swings . . . and misses.*

Jesse climbed out of the car and hurried to walk up to her doorway with her.

They both glanced back and forth at each other like a couple of high school kids on a date. Stepping up to the doorway, Jesse took a deep breath. *Courage*, he thought. Leaning in, he was going for a great first kiss.

Not seeing this, Kari looked into her purse to find her keys.

Jesse kissed a mouthful of hair above Kari's forehead.

*Strike two.*

Jesse wasn't going to be denied. He put his finger under

Kari's chin and raised her head. He stared into her deep eyes and moved in to kiss her red lips.

Kari held her breath, cautious to let go of her excitement and fear. She wanted this, but didn't want to seem too desperate. Her calmness all night had been a shield.

She closed her eyes with the kiss and imagined what might happen next.

As their lips met, the shield came down. The soft meshing of their lips was butter to the heat between them and melted. Her underwear felt like something else was melting in them. She wanted more, so moved forward.

Jesse had gotten his kiss and made it to first base on the lovers' scale.

Kari wanted a triple.

She pushed against Jesse. He leaned against the entryway with Kari's hands gripping his ass, pulling his torso to hers. In the dim light of the porch, Kari felt safe that they were hidden and she moved her hands around the front, feeling his cock through the fabric of his jeans.

"Mmm . . ." She moaned into the wet kiss they shared, and Jesse moaned back.

She released his lips from hers and let her tongue follow the line of his chin.

Jesse let his head fall back against the wall. He was euphoric and aroused.

Kari could tell because his cock seemed to keep growing bigger and bigger with her massaging of it.

She kissed his Adam's apple, which vibrated along his throat, and with her loose hand, she tugged his shirt down his chest as far as she could. Her other hand, stroking his cock, stayed fixated on feeling the length.

Kari felt a swelling of desire matched by Jesse's swelling. She wanted to taste more than just the flesh of his face and neck. She craved the flesh of his cock. It was all that would satisfy this mouthwatering need.

"Shouldn't we go inside?" Jesse moaned beneath his panting.

"No . . ." Kari wanted him like this.

She let her nails drag down Jesse's chest and abdomen as she knelt down before him. His clothes were pulled loose everywhere and his pants were being unfastened.

Kari paused, seeing his cock straining against the fabric of his underwear. She freed it and Jesse groaned.

Kari was hungry for a man. She needed a man. Jesse was more than enough for what she wanted.

Kneeling down before him, she kept her eyes linked with his. The swollen tip of his cock was bobbing inches from Kari's mouth. She could see Jesse wanted this too. A trickle of anticipation glistened at the tight hole on the tip. Kari licked her lips and moved forward.

Jesse rested his hand on the back of Kari's head as he entered her mouth. He groaned with pleasure as the tight moistness of her lips encompassed his rigid cock.

Kari paused, feeling the head of his cock touch the back of her throat. She struggled not to gag, letting Jesse fill her mouth. She savored the power she had. It excited her and her pussy now ached to have the same feeling as her mouth.

She began to withdraw and loosen her mouth to suck Jesse off. She could tell what she was doing had him wild with passion because his hips would thrust forward each time she slid his cock into her mouth.

Urges of passion grew in her. Kari raised her left hand up

his torso, under his shirt and could feel the heat from his body rise. Her nails dug into his flexing muscles as he closed in on his release. Kari was drooling as she quickened her movements.

Jesse began to groan and his hand grasped a large clump of her hair.

The head of his cock began to swell in her mouth as she sucked him in deep and hard. Kari knew he was about to erupt.

With a loud groan, Jesse held her head against him, his cock buried in her throat.

A blinding flash of light and an ear-numbing roar of thunder shook Jesse and Kari from their kiss. Kari's momentary fantasy during their long, embracing kiss was shattered at the worst time. She would finish this quick, erotic fantasy later. Jesse was tapping into her subconscious and toying with her head.

"I'd better get home before this storm gets nasty." Jesse gave Kari a tight hug and turned away.

*Can't you come in and we can fuck all night? I'll even swallow!*

Kari was thinking with her pussy, not her brain. People say men have two brains, one in their head and one in their cock. Women have two as well, but don't think with their other brain as much as men rely on theirs like it was a prophet.

Jesse walked to the car and heard his inner voice. *She's going to think we're gay, you asshole. We even did our little maintenance just in case. She wanted it and you didn't even give me a shot at it. I'll never forgive you.*

Jesse's other brain had a little bit of an attitude.

# Chapter Four

*T*HE NEXT DAY JUST floated by. Kari was working and in a great mood. She'd had a pleasant date with Jesse. Except for the people at the restaurant, who seemed to upset him, everything had gone well. Only one small thing missing—she hadn't gotten laid. Well, she actually hoped it was a *big* thing.

Thank God for vibrators and extra batteries. He had really done a number on her libido.

While cleaning the long counter, she could overhear a group of four women chatting at a booth near the end of the counter. They were giggling and talking like friends catching up on gossip. Not that women ever gossip, they just discuss juicy rumors in groups.

That's just a myth.

"I tell you, she is *so* evil. Even though she has a boyfriend, she keeps dangling herself in front of her ex. She has him wrapped around her finger." The four ladies all sat in the booth slowly eating their late afternoon food.

Kari had moved onto cleaning the glasses behind the counter. She could still hear them talking but wasn't really paying attention.

"Well, don't say anything, girls. But I think she may try to get her ex back for good. She has the one thing he can't be without and is going to use it." The blonde girl pulled her hair behind her ear and sat forward, patting her fingers against her chest like a heartbeat.

"Who's her ex?" one of the brunette girls asked.

The blonde smiled and said, "Jesse."

The radar was on and Kari heard *that* name loud and clear. So she set the glasses down and silently stepped closer to wipe the countertop. It was already clean but she wanted to hear better and figured it was a good excuse to get within clear earshot.

"She just plays him like a guitar. She said she saw him out last night with some woman." The blonde sipped her drink and continued. "Viki said the woman was no competition. Some low-life skank."

The first thoughts for Kari were of rather violent things to do to a woman with the new set of kitchen knives. Or peeing in the salad dressing before serving it to the ladies at the table.

The shorter brunette pouted. "That's not nice. Maybe he was just hard up." She then giggled with the others.

*Where's the salad dressing?*

"Viki's not worried. She just wants to keep him on a short leash. She says Jesse was great in bed but he is a little too clinging for her. He thought they should settle down.

She wants to live a little—nothing is going to slow her down."

Kari stopped cleaning while the girls gossiped more. The spot on the counter was going to shine like a silver platter if she didn't stop cleaning it soon.

"Whatever. Did you hear about Lucy and her sister's boyfriend getting caught screwing at the mall?" The blonde started a new line of rumors. "They were in the dressing room. Somehow, they ended up in a standing sixty-nine with her legs hanging over the door. Right when the guy blew his load he lost his balance and fell against the door. It opened and they fell on the floor. Lucy had to get her throat looked at because his weight fell on top and she gagged with his cock forced down her throat. It was a sticky situation . . ."

Kari wasn't listening anymore because their conversation changed to comparing cock sizes between the men they had all shared. Kari only glanced over when all of them sighed. A man named George was mentioned.

She didn't catch his last name. Might come in handy on a lonely night with the phone book in front of her.


THE RESTAURANT WAS FAIRLY empty. He was being a sucker, sitting there waiting for Viki. Waiting for over an hour at dinner for her to arrive. He hadn't listened to Rich, who had warned him not to get his hopes up.

After waiting, he found his way back to the bar, alone.

She had called him—emotional on the phone—saying she missed him and needed to talk. There was something important she needed to talk to him about. As usual, Jesse was being the nice guy and agreed. Another foolish assumption was in thinking she would actually do what she said and not leave him waiting again.

He was a fool and knew it, but didn't want to be alone. The wounds Viki left were deep. He'd loved her once and love tends to linger in the holes of the heart that it leaves.

A couple of drinks and an hour later, it was obvious Viki was a no-show, and Jesse was sad and starting to feel the numbing effects of the drinks. His thoughts lingered on his emptiness. He had reached rock-bottom and was so utterly sick of letting the loneliness and depression run his life. It was pathetic.

"Hey, Jesse. You okay, man? I'll get you a cab." The bartender went to pick up the phone.

"Ralph, it's okay. I'll walk." Jesse downed his last beer and tossed a twenty onto the counter.

"It's going to rain, Jesse." Ralph shrugged seeing him walk crookedly toward the door.

KARI STRUGGLED TO SEE the road while the sky opened up, drenching the city with yet another downpour. It rained a lot this time of year and today was no exception.

Her street was darker because the damned streetlight on the corner was out again. Turning toward the alley where she parked, she slammed on her brakes, sliding into a puddle and splashing a man sitting on the curb in front of her apartment building.

He barely moved, even though he was the benefactor of a shower of muddy water. It was Jesse.

Kari rolled her window down. "Jesse, what the *fuck* are you doing? It's pouring and you're going to catch pneumonia."

He wobbled and tried to stand up. The bottle he held fell and busted on the curb, scattering glass all around him.

Pulling her car around him, she parked and got out, locking the doors with the remote. "Jesse, what the *hell* are you doing out here?"

"I was thinking about getting drunk, but since I just dropped my bottle, it looks like that won't happen." Rain fell over them. Kari stood in front of Jesse, looking into his deep, sad eyes. He had been crying—and was absolutely gorgeous to her.

Falling forward, Jesse leaned into Kari and when she looked up, he kissed her with deep emotional need.

Kari sighed inside, her breath being taken away. With all his humility, fears and feelings bare, this was more real than anything to her. Her eyes closed and she fell into the heaven of his lips kissing hers.

Pulling back, Jesse looked back down at Kari. "I'm sorry, I shouldn't have done that. I'm a little drunk and probably shouldn't have picked up that pint of whiskey on the way home. If I'd drunk it, I would have been passed out, and not just cold and wet."

"No *shit* . . ." Kari felt a little drunk herself. Her knees hadn't wobbled like this in ages. "And you're soaking wet. Good Lord, Jesse, what's wrong?" She grabbed him around his waist and pulled him toward the front of the building.

He leaned onto Kari, letting her help him walk. Stagger would have been a better word.

Kari propped him against the wall. While she pushed his shoulders back, her foot slipped and she again found herself against Jesse's large, wet body. It was cold outside but her inner fires began to burn hot. And she was wet on the inside as well as the outside.

Kari opened the door and tugged at Jesse, who seemed content to lean against the wall for the night.

Jesse followed her into her apartment and mumbled something about Alaska and skinny-dipping. Like a tree falling in the woods, he dropped face-first onto Kari's couch.

Kari shook her head and stood over the heap of a man who resembled a sloth. "Couch potato, my ass. This is like a couch turd, dead and worthless."

She grabbed his feet, tugging the dripping tennis shoes off. With a clump, each one fell to the floor. She raised an eyebrow noticing the size of his feet. *Hmmm, big feet . . . big . . .*

She continued tugging wet clothing off Jesse—his mismatched socks—pushing him over to get his jacket off. She wanted to be tactful as she unfastened his jeans.

With expert care, she undid the fly and unzipped them. Pulling off pants is an art. Kari hadn't mastered it yet. Pulling at the ends, Jesse grumbled and lifted his ass up off the couch. With a final yank, his pants came off. Something else slid down too—his underwear. All the way to his knees.

Kari paused and bit her bottom lip. *Hmmm, it is true what they say about feet and cocks. It is proportional.*

Jesse blinked a few times and made a smacking sound with his mouth. "Damn it's cold in here." He glanced down and suddenly sobered. Reflexively, he cupped his cock and balls in his hands. "What the hell?"

He curled into a fetal position and sat upright. "Oh, shit, my head is pounding. Oh, shit, why is the room spinning? Oh, shit, where the fuck am I?" Reality set in. "Hell, Kari, I'm so sorry. I haven't eaten all day and the drinks hit my stomach and . . . and . . . Hey, why are you taking my clothes off?"

"Because you passed out on my couch. You're soaking wet." She held back a laugh at seeing Jesse trying to take in everything going on around him. He was still mostly naked and holding his family jewels. "And I didn't want to find you dead outside from drowning in the rain."

Kari walked over to the small stack of folded laundry and tossed him a shirt and some pajama pants. "These are big on me so they should keep you warm 'til we dry your clothes."

Holding up the shirt, Jesse grimaced. "It's pink and has a kitten on it."

"Beggars can't be choosers. You go get dressed and I'll start some coffee."

Jesse got up and waddled toward the bathroom with his underwear still around his knees.

As he passed by Kari, she smacked his bare ass. "Hurry up."

"*Hey!*" He rushed quickly to the bathroom.

Kari turned back and ignited the gas fireplace. It was the one thing that had sold her on the first-floor apartment. It was the only one vacant of the four with a fireplace.

Jesse stood in the bathroom, his cock in one hand and the other on the wall. It was surprising how long it took to pee out three beers and a shot. With a sigh and a shake he yawned, dropping his arm from the wall to scratch his ass. His head was still spinning, he was still lightheaded and his stomach growled with hunger.

Loneliness and self-pity are a bad mix. As is beer and a shot of cheap whiskey. Jesse was exhausted, cold, a disaster to look at but, mostly, he was just sad.

The mirror revealed how messed up he really was. His hair was a new-wave nightmare and he wore Kari's pink shirt and flowered pajamas. If the guys saw him now, they'd have him going to gay bars within minutes. He had a horrible taste in his mouth that resembled something out of a kitty litter box. Maybe the cute little kitten on his tight pink shirt had left it in his mouth.

Jesse saw a bottle of mouthwash on the sink. Grabbing it, he took a mouthful and gargled loudly. He accidentally slid his foot forward, hitting a nail on the floorboard of the sink and swallowed the mouthwash. Tasty stuff. It burned all the way down. He figured he had enough alcohol in his system that the mouthwash would mix well with it.

Leaning over the sink, Jesse closed his eyes, trying to regain his cool and composure. He began to fantasize what might happen next . . .

*As soon as he stepped out of the bathroom Kari met him at the door and grabbed him around his waist. Her mouth met his, kissing him with the passion of a woman tormented with desire.*

*Her tongue parted his lips and the sweet taste made Jesse ache.*

*Her hands fell to the small space between them and her tiny appendages caressed the stiffening length of his cock. Falling against the hallway wall, Jesse was overwhelmed. Her kiss became more aggressive and firm.*

*She kept one hand stroking his cock through the pajama bottoms and her other brushed his face as her lips moved to his neck.*

*Jesse was beside himself in pleasure.*

*With a deep growl, Kari kissed his Adam's apple and let her fingers follow the neckline of his shirt. She dropped her hand and pulled the shirt up his chest, keeping her other hand firmly gripping his thickened cock.*

*His chest was wet from the perspiration of Kari's actions and was* raising the heat in his body. Jesse was squirming, gritting his teeth with pent-up desire.

Kari began to lick around his neck, teasingly biting his skin. She released her grip on his cock through the pajamas.

With a sigh, Jesse caught his breath, only to have Kari suck on his nipple and put her hand inside the pajama bottoms, feeling the warmth of flesh to flesh.

Jesse rested his head back against the wall with a thud and kept his eyes closed. He was savoring this fantastic fantasy come true.

Kari began to kiss down his torso. Each touch of her lips brought her closer to Jesse's now throbbing cock. She would stop to kiss and lick the indentions of his flexing abdomen, making him more and more crazed.

With a quick tug, the pajamas and boxer shorts fell to his ankles, and Kari saw Jesse in full glory. He stared into her eyes and was close to exploding. This was what he had dreamed of since they had met.

Kari looked up at Jesse and licked her lips.

Anticipation bubbled through him and the shiny tip of his cock glistened with his urges.

When her lips met the tip of his cock, Jesse wanted to see it filling her mouth . . .

So when he opened his eyes to see his reflection in the bathroom mirror, his fantasy was still only in his mind.

He walked out of the bathroom, hopeful to reenact what his mind pictured. Kari was stretched out on her couch in front of a nice fire. His clothes were hanging over a metal screen beside the fireplace. Even in a drunken stupor, it felt like home.

Jesse plopped down on the couch with a thud. The flames flickered and Jesse sat, watching them dance. It was warm and peaceful. Unlike his apartment where Rich listened and watched porn movies like a cocaine addict.

Kari had a bottle of wine on the small table in front of the couch. She was sipping a glass. "Mmm, this is nice. I love coming home from a long day and just laying here watching the fire."

There was a cup of steaming hot coffee, an obvious choice for Jesse's blurry head. Jesse looked at Kari. She had her eyes closed and was so at ease. He was spinning in a haze of confusion. He didn't like where his life was going. Kari was the one stable thing in it. She was comforting and consistent. She was also attractive and lying on a couch beside him.

Jesse leaned forward and picked up the cup of coffee. It warmed his body, as did Kari. It wasn't dinner but would probably mix well with the mouthwash.

"So you going to tell me why you were sitting in the rain outside my place half-drunk and crying?"

Jesse looked down. "I am a fucking idiot."

Kari paused. "Okay, that part's already obvious. Talk to me, Jesse."

"I spent three years with someone. You get used to the person being there, even when they aren't. It's the knowledge that they will be. We had . . . we had something special to me. When it's gone, you want it back. I just haven't come to terms with the fact that I'll be alone for a while." Jesse sighed.

Kari was quiet for a moment then replied, "That is the biggest load of shit I have heard in a long time. Jesse, everybody gets his or her heart broken. Everyone has rough times. It happened six months ago. Get over it."

"I'm sorry. I'm pretty pathetic tonight." Jesse rested his hand on Kari's feet, which were next to him on the couch. "Damn, your feet are cold!"

"Yeah, I should put on slippers or something, but they get sore after working all day. I like to air them out a bit."

Jesse turned a bit sideways on the couch. He took Kari's foot in his hand and slowly began to massage the sole. "I remember my mom coming home from work. She was the manager at a supermarket. She'd be exhausted and my dad would rub her feet at night. I never really saw the point in it, but my mom *loooved* it."

Kari was in heaven. She wasn't a foot-fetish type, but having a man massage her feet was a total turn-on. His fingers would stroke against the arches and send shivers up her legs, directly to her crotch. "Your dad did this every night for your mom?"

"Yep. She asked him to a lot of times."

Kari tightened her legs and Jesse moved his hand under her calf, massaging the muscle. "How many kids were in your family?"

"Six. Why do you ask?"

Kari smiled. "Just wondering. If your dad did this every night, I'm surprised you didn't have more." Kari began to squirm as Jesse switched legs and continued massaging her feet and calves.

"Umm, Jesse . . ." Kari needed a break. She was going to pounce on him if his fingers inched any higher up her legs. She needed a time-out. "I have to go to the bathroom—all this wine is going right through me." She got up and walked away.

Jesse watched her. He admired a woman's body and how simple moves were all sexy and seductive, even when unintentional.

Jesse paused. He knew he should get going because he

had some things to do at work early in the morning. Kari had been nice enough to help him out. The coffee and company were great and he didn't want to ruin it. He wanted her. His boner was proof of that.

*Don't fuck him. Don't let it happen. Things are going too good, and I can't mess it up by acting cheap and fucking him into oblivion in every position I can imagine and a few I haven't thought of yet. Make him wait. Yeah, I'll make him earn it.*

Kari was talking to herself while relieving her bladder of the wine.

Jesse tugged his pants from the rack in front of the fire and stood up.

"Shit, that coffee really has a caffeine kick in it." He wobbled and tugged off the pajamas. His legs were cold again as he pulled up his jeans.

The term "hot pants" fit perfectly. The fire had warmed the jeans to a nice, toasty temperature of one-hundred-and-fifty degrees Fahrenheit.

Kari walked into the living room to see Jesse cussing, blowing and fanning the front of his pants as they scorched his nuts. "Fuck, shit, dammit, these are hot, hot, *hot.*"

"Should I leave? I feel like I'm interrupting something." Kari shook her head and laughed.

"These pants are hot." Jesse held his head. "Damn, I am still drunk."

Kari rushed over to Jesse as he staggered away from the fire. "Watch it. You're not too sturdy yet."

"Let me go to the bathroom. I'll throw some water on my face and join the land of the sober. I am sorry, Kari."

She helped him toward the hallway—he held the walls and stopped.

Kari stepped into the bedroom. She was going to grab her keys to give Jesse a ride home. He was in no shape to walk, and the rain was pouring outside.

She had set her purse on the other side of the room. When she dug inside the bag for her keys, she heard a loud *THUMP* behind her.

Turning around, she saw Jesse face-first on her bed. She'd finally gotten a man into her bed who she wanted, and he was passed out with his clothes *on*. She couldn't win.

With a couple of pushes, Jesse was on one side and lying on top of the covers. Kari smiled and grabbed a small blanket from her closet and covered him up as he snored.

Kari went back into the living room to straighten things out and close the fireplace screen. The fire glowed now as the flames died down. Kari stared at the orange embers for a moment. She too raged with fire until time had cooled her to a steady, mellow burn.

Undressing, she imagined Jesse watching her and felt aroused by her thoughts. She pulled on a black nightshirt with her favorite band emblem on it that had always felt comfortable to her. 'Course she also thought the guys in the band were pretty hot. Kari had others with lace and frills, but those were for naughty nights. A snort and grumble later she was back to normal and tugged at the covers to climb in beside him.

There she was, in bed with Jesse, and wasn't even worried that he might try something. In reality she wished he was awake, sober and on top of her—them making love with the sounds of moans and pleasure echoing through the room.

Instead, he was passed out and snoring.

As she drifted to sleep in the dark, her body began to

warm with the thoughts filling her mind. She inched back against Jesse, snuggling into his heat, letting the scent of him surround her. Her small frame fit into him like a piece of a puzzle. Her head against his chest, her ass round against the bend of his torso, they fit together perfectly. Her own needs for comfort were being met by him. She had found someone she liked and she had him right where she wanted.

Except he probably wouldn't remember anything in the morning.

# Chapter Five

IT WASN'T QUITE MORNING. The rumble of thunder woke Jesse from a deep sleep.

A few seconds passed and he realized he wasn't home. He also realized he wasn't alone.

On nights like this, a man wonders how drunk he really was. This was the measure of how desperate he had become for a female. Drinking also lowered one's standards, regardless of the sex. Which explains why there were so many pretty women with ugly-ass guys.

A glance around the dark room and a peek over Kari's cheek reminded him of where he was. He settled back into the bed beside her.

Jesse breathed in the sweet fragrance of Kari's hair. Her body was warm against him. His memory of being in her apartment was vague. The numbing ring in his brain was a reminder of what he had done. The taste of mouthwash in his mouth relieved the morning-breath smell. Ending up in bed with her was even more clouded, but he didn't care how he had gotten there. He was just happy to be with her.

Kari was in her nightgown under the blankets.

He was on top of the bedspread with a small blanket barely covering him. Clothed and having a major problem with his underwear twisting against his cock.

Jesse moved his arm up to hold her hip.

With a sigh, Kari snuggled against Jesse, her sweet ass moving slightly.

He breathed in again. Letting the fragrance of her fill his lungs. His chin nested into the small gap between her shoulder and neck.

Jesse closed his eyes and began to gently kiss the soft skin below Kari's ear.

It seemed so natural, so pure. Mostly, it was arousing the hell out of him.

With a moan, Jesse knew Kari was feeling something also. He could tell by how her ass pressed harder against him and her legs were tightening. Now his underwear was beginning to strangle his thickening cock. But he didn't want to move.

Tracing up her ear with his tongue, Jesse was on a quest to explore the woman lying next to him.

Kari felt Jesse's warmth. She also felt a swelling against her ass that made her ache. She was attracted to Jesse and the way he made her feel. They had a friendship. Was it right to take it to the next level?

"Oh, God, you feel so good." Jesse's deep murmur answered her question.

The sheets and her thin rock band nightshirt were the

only barriers between them. Her shirt clung tightly to her body like a layer of skin. Jesse's lips continued caressing her neck making her body cold from the rush of blood between her legs.

The tips of her nipples begged to be toyed with as they protruded out through the fabric.

"Jesse, don't tease me." Kari was dying to have him be with her. The comfort she felt with him was as refreshing as it was seductive.

"I just want to be with you. Just you." Jesse reached his hand upward over the sheets to cup her breast.

His breath was instantly followed by a gasp from Kari. Snuggling back against her neck, Jesse massaged the breast filling his hand. A muffled growl vibrated down Kari's back as he kissed the back of her neck.

*Oh, fuck, this is incredible.* Kari's thoughts raced in her euphoric mind.

Kari reached up and rested her hand on Jesse's. He was so in control and knew what her body wanted and ached for. Each touch sent emotional jolts to her heart and now moist pussy.

Jesse pulled away from Kari's breast and moved his hand beneath the blankets, feeling the heat from her body. When he brushed against the bare flesh of her thigh, Kari jerked. He followed the line of her body and back up to her breasts. The thin hair on his arm tickled Kari's sensitive skin.

His warm palm caressed her full breasts, letting the aroused nipple poke between his long, thick fingers.

"Oh, Jesse." She spoke, breathy and quiet. She closed her eyes, letting the warm flow of her blood soothe her shiver.

"My God, you are so beautiful, Kari." Jesse lay astride her, admiring how her body reacted to his touch.

"Say my name. Say my name." Kari became swept into the ocean of pleasure Jesse began to stir. Her insecurities washing along the beach and disappearing.

"Mmmm, Kari, Kari . . ." His words muffled into a mumble as his mouth found her breast.

The flicking of his tongue toyed with her through the fabric. Jesse tugged at the shirt, pulling it up her hot flesh and bunching it below her neck. Time stood still as Kari waited for it. She wanted to feel it.

Jesse gave her what she craved. Now exposed, he smothered her breast with his lips. Hot bursts of breath scorched her tightened nipples.

Kari was awakening in so many ways. All the dormant sensations in her body sparked to life and she became enthralled by the fires.

Jesse closed his eyes and let his body tell him what direction to go. As usual, his body wanted to go downward. Following the curves of her soft skin. Tracing the indentions of her squirming body to the heated center of her soul.

Jesse let go of her breast and dragged his index finger down Kari's shaking body. She sighed when he rested his hand against the wet silk of her panties.

"Oh, my God." Kari arched upward, her breasts begging for his mouth not to abandon them when he began the slow descent down her tight, flexing stomach. She didn't dare open her moist eyes because this much-desired fantasy was evolving into reality. She wanted this feeling to stay with her.

"Mmmmm." Jesse's sounds vibrated through her stomach and caused her to shudder. He was so close.

He was right there, so close to her clit that Kari could feel it trying to leap to his tongue. Her breath was shallow and she wanted to scream. She lay on the bed, grasping the sheets with her fingers, and her feet digging hard into the mattress. She was ready to explode.

Moving closer, Jesse pulled off his pink nightshirt with the kitty on it and tossed it onto the floor. Kari saw how his muscled body was tight and sweaty.

Kari chirped with pleasure as Jesse stroked his finger along the silk of her worthless underwear. The silk was soaked and Jesse could see the lips of her pussy parting in anticipation. Wet and hot, just inviting him for a closer look.

Jesse rolled off the bed and kneeled at the foot of it. Looking down on Kari's semi-clad body, he felt a hunger grow within him. He couldn't help himself, he needed to explore Kari more. He wanted to take his time discovering her body.

His clothes were tangled. Breathing a sigh of relief, he unfastened his jeans and undid his zipper. "Kari, you have me so horny my cock hurts. It's all twisted inside my pants and throbbing."

She looked down his silhouetted frame, salivating at the thought of him. He loosened his pants and stopped.

"But first, I . . . I need to . . ."

Jesse lowered his head to Kari's legs, resting his arms on each side of them. He nuzzled his face between her thighs. His breath blew across Kari's pubic area, cooling the moisture between the lips of her pussy.

When he pulled up, Kari opened the space between her legs. The only thing between Jesse and Kari's hot pussy were her panties. He traced the line of her underwear with his finger, touching the sensitive skin of her inner thighs.

Kari was trying to contain the depraved sexual urges she had. But she wanted Jesse to unleash her. She rolled her head to the side and widened her legs, easing Jesse's descent into her soul, falling into a pillow of clouds.

His finger pulled the thin fabric from covering her puffy, wet pussy. With a deep breath, Jesse filled his lungs with the fragrance of her desire. In a smooth fashion, he pulled the thin, wet fabric from her legs, leaving her exposed and free.

Leaning back, he saw the slick folds of her pussy glisten in the dim light of the room. The sight was so tantalizing it made him growl.

Kari gasped when Jesse slipped his finger between her pussy lips. He knew it wasn't just the sex, but the buried feeling of desire. When his mouth finally kissed her cunt, he glanced up to see that she had closed her eyes.

Jesse became lost in the succulent taste of Kari. Like a ripened peach, her juices burst with each suckling of the folds. Jesse's cock was swollen and the thump of his excited heart made it throb. But his thoughts all concentrated on the savory fruit he was eating.

His tongue found her clit and Kari began to arch, thrusting against his face. Jesse slid his hands beneath her ass and raised her cunt further against his face, grinding his mouth against her.

Kari panted, grasping her breasts with need. It was as if she wanted every essence of her body fondled at once, and her nipples were screaming for attention.

Jesse moved his hands beneath her ass and let his thumbs part the lips of her pussy, opening them wider, exposing her throbbing clit more.

Kari was beside herself with need. It had been so long

since she felt so vulnerable, so bare. Feelings washed over her. The hollow shell she had been for so long was full of feelings of passion. Desire crept through her heart. Jesse was doing more than giving her pleasure—he was giving her dreams to hold on to. A fantasy to rekindle the woman within her.

A long, smothering lick sent Kari over the edge and she came. Her mouth hung open and her eyes squinted tightly as her body began to convulse in orgasmic spasms.

Jesse buried his face harder between her legs, sucking on her wet flesh and fighting against Kari's legs trying to close together. She knew he wasn't going to let this pass until she was spent.

He let her legs loose and she rested them on the bed. Moving up, he rested his head on her stomach. He let his finger draw images on her skin. The thumping of her heart slowed—she was calming. Jesse sniffed as if he was breathing in the scent from her aroma of arousal and licked his fingertips, then smiled as he wrote a note on her tummy.

"What's that?"

"Jesse was here." He playfully placed kisses on her skin.

Jesse got up from lying on her and said, "I just wanted to see this vision of beauty blossoming before my eyes."

A wicked grin crossed her lips and Kari opened her eyes to see Jesse standing up at the end of the bed. "That's a definite three-pointer on the brownie points scorecard." He was pulling his shirt off and she stared at him. The muscles of his stomach flinching as he struggled to get the tight shirt over his head.

Kari sat up and scooted to the end of the bed in front him. There wasn't too much space in her bedroom. The queen-size bed filled most of it. She had a few family photos scattered around on the nightstand and her dresser top, which were also littered with makeup and numerous beauty products.

Reaching forward, she grabbed the waistband of his pants and pulled him to her. Looking up, she saw Jesse smile.

She could see he was aroused by the strain of his cock against his loose pants. Tugging at the legs of his jeans, she let them fall to a bunch at his knees.

"I thought you'd be a boxer kind of guy," she joked. She hadn't mentioned it earlier.

"I don't like it when it hangs out the bottom of the boxer legs." He smiled.

"Bragger . . ." She pulled the underwear out and off his cock, then paused. "Okay, maybe not bragging."

He was sprung forward and the moistened tip showed his excitement. Kari leaned forward and let her tongue brush over the tip of his cock. She enjoyed her new control of the situation. Parting her lips, she rested the head between them. With a slow, steady glide, she let his cock move smoothly into her mouth. Inch by inch, she took him, savoring the feeling.

Jesse moaned with pleasure—the warmth of her mouth enveloping him. "Oh, fuck. You don't know how . . ."

Kari began pulling back and forth. Her tongue licked along the base as she tried to keep a steady sucking on his cock. She was like a piston, going faster and faster. He was her food and she was starving for him.

"I can't—I can't handle this, Kari." Jesse began to breathe quickly. He was aroused to a feverish point.

With a pop, Kari freed him. She crawled back up her bed

and rolled onto her side. She rummaged through the top drawer of her nightstand, finally finding what she wanted.

"Here, use this." Kari handed Jesse a condom and laid back on the bed, waiting for him, longing to feel him.

"I haven't seen this brand for a while. You know I . . ." He paused, seeing her lying there amongst the sheets. "Fuck, you are so damn beautiful, Kari." Jesse rolled the condom down his cock and pulled his pants and shorts off his feet.

Crawling up Kari's body, Jesse began to growl like an animal viewing its prey. His tongue stopped at her navel, leaving a trail of saliva up her torso as he stopped to suck on each of her nipples before meeting her face-to-face.

They didn't need to talk. There was no need to ask questions. This was true. This was right.

Lowering his weight to her, Jesse let his lips meet hers and, in a sensual kiss, he lowered his cock into her wet, tight pussy. He moaned when their bodies melded together.

Kari could finally breathe again. She exhaled and brought her legs up to wrap around Jesse's hips. Not wanting to let him go. She wanted this feeling to stay—this feeling of want. The way he made her happy to be a woman.

As he pulled back, she arched upward, not wanting to let his cock leave its newfound home.

Then he lowered back in. Easing her worries. Over and over again, he eased her worries.

Their movements became more frantic as Jesse began closing in on his peak. "Oh, God, I'm . . . I'm . . ."

Kari wrapped her arms and legs tight around Jesse's sweaty body as he struggled to control his release. "It's okay, just let go."

Her words freed him, and with a final plunge, he came. Gushing his seed in spasms.

Kari closed her eyes, letting her pussy feel the throbbing spasms of her man inside.

Jesse pushed his weight off her and looked down upon Kari's smiling face. "I'm sorry. I wanted to come with you. I just couldn't hold it—"

"Shhh, don't worry. We have *allll* night." Kari rolled Jesse onto his back, climbing on top of him.

# Chapter Six

K ARI AWOKE TO A shimmer of light through the blinds over her eyelids.

The scent of a new day filled the air and she had an instant smile when she felt the ache between her legs from having them spread apart most of the night before. She was warm and content and rolled over in bed to feel Jesse next to her. Problem was, he was gone.

At first, she was shocked at his leaving without a word. *Not again.*

Looking around the room she saw a piece of paper stuck on her mirror, which fluttered in the wind from the window cracked open slightly for fresh air.

Tearing the sheets loose, she waddled to the mirror like a wrapped burrito. After grabbing the note, she jumped back onto the bed on her stomach and opened it.

*I lay here in bed watching you sleep and don't have the heart to wake you.*

*Last night was—well—incredible.*

*I had to get to work early but wanted to thank you for showing me the pleasure of a real woman.*

*A woman with compassion, heart and a really cute . . . ummm . . . you know.*

*I'll come by your work later and will be thinking about you all day.*

*Jesse*

THE NOTE WAS SHORT but said volumes. Kari became warm and her pussy moistened at the memory of last night. Jesse might not be Mr. Right but this was a great start. He'd done everything right last night and that reminded Kari of the good things a partner could bring into her life.

Kari did the natural thing. She pumped her fist in the air and said, "Yesssss."

Falling onto her cloud of a bed, she felt the urge to stretch. "Ouch, ouch, my leg is cramping, shit, *shit*."

JESSE WAS SITTING IN HIS dark leather chair at work. He was warm, extremely relaxed, tired and sleeping on his hand. A trickle of drool rolled down the corner of his mouth to the side of his hand holding his head up.

*Wham.*

Jesse's hand slipped from his chin and he whacked his head on his desk. The swirling stars blurred in his scrambled skull. He shook his head and got up from his chair. He winced in pain and grabbed his groin area. Fucking pulled muscle. *Damn Kari about killed me.* He looked down and breathed deep. His boss quickly opened the door, hitting him square across the forehead. Jesse was knocked-out cold.

"Kari, I don't want to eat marshmallows in my macaroni and cheese," Jesse mumbled as his boss kneeled above him.

When Jesse came to, he looked up to see a blurred image close to his face. He puckered up and laid a wet kiss on his boss—and it wasn't even raise time.

They both spit and coughed for a moment after realizing what had happened. Jesse was embarrassed and dumbfounded as what to say.

His boss knew what to say. "Jesse, you need to shave, I've got stubble burn."

"Fuck, Don, I'm sorry, man. What happened?"

Don yanked Jesse up by the arm and told him. "You must have bent over in front of the door right before I opened it. You were knocked out like a prizefighter getting nailed with an uppercut."

Jesse rubbed his head, feeling the swelling.

"Who's this Kari? A new girlfriend?" Don asked as he sat in the chair in front of Jesse's desk. Jesse sat back in his chair and continued to rub his head.

"Kinda. We've seen each other a few times. She's really great. She works at that diner on the corner of Fifth and Daniels Street."

Don wrinkled his eyebrows thinking for a second. "Ohhh, Wow. I think I know the waitress you mean. She has blonde hair and the biggest set of titties, and always has her top buttons open . . ." Don waved his hand like fanning himself from a hot flash.

Jesse thought for a second. He didn't remember seeing *that* waitress there. He made a mental note to go more often—just for research purposes. "Um, no. She's a cute brunette."

"Oh. Well I know you've been through a lot of shit, Jesse. If you like this woman, make sure you treat her right, bud. I've been through three wives, so if you need advice, just ask." Don seemed to think that being married so many times had made him an expert.

"Thanks, Don. I'll remember that. But, I think I have it covered. I have some special things planned for her." Jesse had a plan, and if he had to listen to this three-time loser's advice, he would definitely do the opposite of what he said.


EVERY DAY JESSE WOULD go by the diner after he was off and put a flower on the hostess's easel with a note for Kari. Some days he'd see her and wave. On Wednesday, she met him by the door and gave him a hug and a kiss before he could run off. He seemed in a hurry to go and it caught Kari's attention, but she figured he had things to do.

Each day she started looking forward to the note attached with three lines of words. If she caught him in the act, she would ask what the next note would say, but Jesse would change the subject as he laughed and teased her.

Jesse was being careful to not rush things. He'd call at night around ten and they'd talk a little, but he knew she worked hard and said she liked to cool down and rest after work. His other brain wanted to spend more time with her. Like spending every night buried in her tight, wet pussy.

It was Friday and the bell above the door rang around five as usual, as Jesse walked into the diner. This time he didn't hold a note. Instead, he held a red box with a card.

Kari bolted toward the door, brushing against Ally and leaving a draft behind her as she rushed by. "Hello, Jesse."

"You didn't have to run. I would have waited."

"It's okay. You want something to eat?" Kari grabbed a menu and was going to take Jesse to a seat.

"I wouldn't mind eating *you* for dinner." The wicked smile showed his intent. "But I came here to give you this for now."

Clearing her throat, Kari smiled and replied, "Well, we'll talk about your . . . ummm . . . dinner order later." Kari looked at the red package and the small handmade card on top.

The girls in the restaurant were all moving closer to get a look and some clue as to what Jesse had given Kari.

"Awwww, this is cute." She leaned over and gave Jesse a hug then opened the little box. "Mmm, yummy. How'd you know I liked chocolate truffles?"

"I took a guess. So you said you get off early tonight—come by around eight. Is that okay?"

Kari sighed. "After giving me this, you'll get off a few times tonight." Kari looked around not realizing she was talking out loud. The giggles from the girls made it obvious she'd said it loud enough for others to hear.

"Well, I'll let you go. I'll see you later." He grabbed her hand and gave it a nice squeeze.

If he had asked, Kari would have given him a blowjob on her break. He made her feel so good about herself. He also made her hornier than a minx.

As he walked away, Kari watched how his jeans fit his

ass. The girls behind her sighed right along with her. What a bunch of sluts.

Kari was thrilled Jesse was being a gentleman. She liked that he wasn't pressuring her or smothering her. She needed her time alone and Jesse seemed to recognize it. Most men began relationships with wanting to be together every waking minute they could. It got overwhelming.

Kari's own body was warming in a central location. Bluntly, she was getting hot and needing to get sexed-up.

"So, Kari, the girls want to know. Umm, who is this Jesse guy?" Ally was the diner spokesperson. Actually, she was more like the workplace busybody.

Kari blushed. "He's my new friend."

"Friend? A friend doesn't send flowers and poetry. What does the poem say? All the girls are going crazy." After a pause Ally continued. "Does he have any brothers?"

Kari pulled the other notes from her inside pocket and arranged them in order.

> *You remind me of a rosebud,*
> *The petals are your blanket and veil*
> *They keep you hidden when life isn't fair,*
>
> *But beneath them is a flower*
> *Ready to break out and be free,*
> *As the sun shines over you, each day you open up more*
>
> *I have seen this glory,*
> *And long to see it more*
> *Longing to watch you spread your wings*

*Because if I can peel away the petals that encase you,*
*If I can shed away what hinders you*
*I know the flower inside will bloom*

THE ROOM TURNED A nice shade of green as the girls all grew envious of Kari. Some had been married for a while and life had settled down to the point of redundant patterns. Other girls had nobody to share their life with and meeting some- one new was a distant desire. Most just remembered the times in their lives when the relationship was new and every- thing was all so wonderful.

Kari was ecstatic that she was the one getting the atten- tion instead of being the girl on the outside looking in.

*Sucks to be them*, she thought.

KARI ADJUSTED HER THONG, which was more like butt-floss. She was more a lace panty kind of girl, but the thongs hid the lines on her tight skirt. The price women pay for their looks . . .

She did a quick check. *Shirt looks nice, bra isn't showing through, shoes match skirt. Hair is . . . oh, shit, my hair is a mess. What the hell am I doing here? Fuck it.*

Before knocking on the door, Kari leaned closer and heard a muffled moaning sound. She couldn't really make out what it was, but it was definitely a female tone of voice. Maybe she was at the wrong apartment. She checked—it was apartment 22.

*Knock, Knock, Knock.*

A voice yelled from inside, "Come on in, it's open."

Kari took a deep breath and opened the door.

There before her were two incredibly hung black men double-penetrating a petite, young blonde girl. Both holes were being stretched apart and, from the look on her face, it wasn't the most comfortable position to be in. She looked like an Oreo cookie.

The wide-screen TV was filled wide all right.

"Jesse? Are you here?"

"He's going to be a little late. He said he needed to pick up a few things on the way home. You must be Kari." The man's voice echoed through the room but Kari didn't see anyone.

"Ummm, okay. Who am I talking to?"

"My name is Rich." The movie suddenly paused on a money-shot with the blonde girl getting cream-filled. A head popped up over the back of the couch and scared Kari. "I'm Jesse's roommate."

Kari moved toward the couch to be polite, and as she walked around the side she became aware that Rich was a midget. "Hello, Rich."

"Sit down. I like being eye level with people. Being this short sucks sometimes, but slow dancing with sexy women and being behind them in elevators does have its advantages." He smiled and winked at Kari. "Unless they have gas."

Flattening her skirt, she sat down and crossed her legs. Kari hadn't realized how short the tight skirt really was.

"I apologize. I have to get this work done before my deadline." Rich was scribbling notes on a pad and hit the play mode on the movie.

"Work?" Kari looked up at the screen and raised an eyebrow as the scene ended with the two black men pulling their clothes on. Dialogue wasn't important—seeing them zipping up jeans with no underwear was.

"I am a reviewer for *Virtualporn Magazine*. I do reviews of porn movies. It may sound pretty skanky but after four years of college, it was the first job in journalism I got and I've built up a reputation for critiquing porn. Now I'm rambling. Another curse I have."

Kari looked over at Rich. He was fairly handsome. He had dark hair, screaming blue eyes and seemed to be pretty smart. He was the kind of guy some of her girlfriends would like—other than only being three-feet tall.

"You want a drink or something?" Not wanting to assume anything, Rich asked another question. "You mind if I call you Kari?"

"Yes and no."

"Okay, hopefully it's yes to the drink and no to the calling you Kari. I have some wine coolers—you like strawberry?" Rich hopped off the couch and headed to the kitchen area.

Kari could barely see him from over the couch. "The drink sounds good. Those are sweet-tasting. You know when Jesse's coming home?"

The refrigerator door closed and Kari heard Rich coming back. "He'll be here anytime. Something about a customer bitching to the senior manager and Jesse had to be the middleman." Rich handed Kari the red bottle.

Kari leaned back as Rich sat next to her on the couch.

"Jesse hates me working in the living room. I have my TV setup in the back room, but his has the better sound and the better DVD." He played with the remote and picked up his pad again.

Kari kept shaking her head as the movie continued.

"Kari? Does watching this stuff make you uncomfortable? I'm curious." Rich glanced over at her.

"Not really. Honestly, I'm not a big porn fan. I think a lot of them are unrealistic. Look, take this girl. She has fake tits, a shaved pussy and pigtails like a virgin. I mean get *real*. When I was a virgin and on my first time, it hurt like hell and I wasn't going to do six positions and take it up the ass like this. It isn't realistic. That's why I like the softer-edge stuff." Kari paused, she wasn't sure if she was babbling like an idiot.

"Please go on. I don't get a lot of female perspective on this stuff. Most of mine is from guys whacking off to it." Rich made the typical male motion of jacking off.

"The cable channels show the sexy movies but not the close-ups and penetration stuff. I like a sexy movie and looking at a sexy guy. I am a woman and admire good beefcake but—I don't know—a lot of the pornos I watched in college with my boyfriends were all about the guy getting off." She stopped and took a sip of her wine cooler.

Rich was fascinated by Kari's honesty and actually making a valid point about something most of the women he talked to just scoffed at as sick stuff or had starred in a few home pornos themselves.

"You know something, Kari? I already like you. You are honest."

"Ahhh, I just tell people what I think sometimes. You asked, so I told you."

Rich smiled and looked at Kari mischievously. "You want to see the porno movie I was in?"

After almost coughing up a mouthful of wine cooler and air, Kari was flustered for a moment. Should she be watching her new boyfriend's roommate naked? He was in a movie so it wouldn't be like she was seeing him naked, up close and personal. Anyway, she was curious about the whole size of a midget's penis in comparison to his stature.

"What the hell. I've never met a porno star." Kari giggled.

"Well, I'm not the star. The star is, well, his *stage* name is Wide Wade. His real name is Melvin Kowalski. He is a total asshole. I had a small part." He paused. "No comments about a *small* part. I can tell you were going to say something."

Kari blushed. "Well, you said 'small,' not me."

Kari sat with Rich and they were laughing loudly as Rich goofed around with the fast-forward and slow-motion buttons.

After a fast scene lasting about twenty seconds Kari blurted out, "That reminded me of my ex-boyfriend on a good night."

"Check this out, Kari . . ." Rich hit the pause with a woman spread-eagle, open for business. He walked up and put his face over it. He flicked his tongue a few times then said, "Now you know what guys see when they are down here. At least it doesn't smell like fish." He laughed and was quickly quieted by a pillow hitting him in the face.

"You deserved that, Rich. That's not true." Kari laughed.

They both sat back and kept making comments about the acting and how not all men were created alike.

Rich sat upright and got excited. "Okay, here it comes."

JESSE FUMBLED WITH HIS keys at the apartment door. He'd had a long day and it'd ended on a bad note. His date with Kari would be a great plus to his day.

Leaning against the door before opening it, Jesse heard a voice yelling.

"Oh, Kari, I'm coming right now."

*What the fuck?* Jesse pushed the door open to see Rich on the TV.

"Would you like sausage on that pizza ma'am?" He whipped his cock out and set it on the pizza. Kari's doubts about proportions were answered.

Kari clapped. "Wow, Rich. I'm impressed. A part in a porno. You should have asked her for salami, not sausage."

She laughed then turned her head to see Jesse standing at the front door. "Hey, Jesse, Rich was showing me his *big* part in the porn world."

"Well I hate to brag about size. But, it's true." Rich puffed his chest out.

"I'm going to have to introduce you to Mona. She'll love you. You'll like her, Rich, she's a borderline nymphomaniac and loves pizza."

"There's more, Kari. You want to see the whole scene?"

Jesse interrupted. "Um, Rich. Let her dream, all right? She's seen the goods, now let her leave with that. I can't believe you showed my girlfriend your porno movie."

"It's okay. We had fun waiting for you."

"Give me five minutes to get changed. I have the reservations all set." Jesse walked to the back of the couch, grabbed her hand and gave it a squeeze. He let it go and walked into his room.

# Chapter Seven

THE RESTAURANT WAS VERY elegant. There was a smooth, jazzy mood to it. Soft music soothed edgy nerves. There were a few people milling around the dance area—it looked as though someone was going to do live music.

The tables were all round and spaced enough apart so when anyone stood up, they didn't bang into the person behind them. Candles reflected against the red tablecloths, setting a romantic ambiance to the dinner chatter. Kari sat at the table glancing over the dessert menu.

Jesse had stepped away because in typical male fashion, he'd spilled spaghetti sauce on his white shirt. What a graceful guy.

"Hey, Lisa? Or is it Teri?"

The man's voice brought a queasy feeling to Kari. It was the singer from a couple of weeks ago.

She turned to see him in all his egotistical glory. "It's Kari."

"Sorry, Kari. How are you? Haven't seen you since . . . well . . . since that night."

Kari held back the urge to barf on him. "I've been keeping busy."

Leaning in closer to her, he smiled and asked, "I only have one set here tonight. You think we might hook up again after the . . ."

"Hey, what's going on here?" Jesse walked up to the table. The spot on his shirt was now bigger and orange.

"Oh, sorry. Didn't know she was spoken for."

"She is. So beat it." Jesse motioned with his thumb for the guy to leave.

"Touchy, touchy. Maybe another time, Teri." The guy turned and walked away.

"Who was that clown? He didn't even call you by the right name."

Kari sighed. "He was a mistake. A very bad decision on my part. He was just bugging me, but no big deal. You want to get out of here?"

"Sure. Oh, crap, I left my jacket hanging in the bathroom. One second. Sorry." He hurried toward the bathroom.

Kari shook her head. He was such a goofy guy.


JESSE WAS LOOKING AT the stain on his shirt as he walked into the bathroom. He didn't even notice the guy standing next to him as he stepped up to the sink for another try at getting the stain out.

"Nice pick of a date, dude." The guy who Kari had been talking to was next to him. "She's a sure thing. I ought to know."

"Shut up, asshole. Just leave me alone." Jesse finished washing his hands and turned to dry them.

"Well someone must have gotten kicked down. I had her once and I'll tell you, she didn't move much but was a good fuck anyway." He preened his hair and smugly talked.

"You must be deaf and dumb because you don't listen or know when to shut the fuck up."

"Aw, did I hurt your feelings? What did you think? That she was a virgin? What are you going to do anyway? Fuckin' pussy."

Jesse returned to the table with his jacket on and the stain still on his shirt. He pulled Kari's seat back for her to get up.

"Oh, God—Jesse, your hand is bleeding? Are you okay?"

Jesse looked at his hand. "I'm fine. It's not my blood." He wiped it with his napkin and motioned for them to go.

Over the loudspeaker, the restaurant owner's voice echoed through the place. "We apologize but there will be no live piano singer tonight. There was an accident in the restroom and he's had four teeth knocked out."


THEY WALKED OUT OF the restaurant and into the parking lot. Kari's car was parked toward the back of the lot and there was very little light. She held tight onto Jesse's arm as they walked. He had defended her honor and was everything she liked in a man. He was just so *normal*. Flaws and all.

"I shouldn't have hit that guy. But, damn, it felt good. He was such an asshole." Jesse was proud of himself for sticking up for Kari, but he usually ignored anus-licking idiots like that. His hand began to throb. Funny how pain creeps up after the fact.

"Shit, my hand is starting to hurt now." He shook it, wringing out the pain.

"Let me see it . . ." Kari looked at his rough hands and saw the swollen knuckles. There was heat radiating from his hand and Kari wanted to feel it. She pulled his hand to her mouth and gently kissed each knuckle. One by one, she believed the kisses would ease his ache.

"Um . . . uhhh . . . this is making me lightheaded. All the blood is going to my head . . . this head." Jesse grabbed the front of his pants to make his point.

Something about his hands began to excite her too. It made her wet and the more attention she gave his hand, the more she wanted it to be touching her body. Kari licked her lips, pulled his index finger outward and let it rest on her lips. Imagining it was something else, she let his finger slide between her lips and moaned in a whispery tone.

Jesse flinched his shoulder because he could imagine something else sliding between those soft, red lips.

Kari was seducing Jesse in an open place and was working her own sexual desires to a frenzy. One thing on Jesse that stood out to her—other than his cock—was how much she wanted him, and this was the most natural of ways to have him.

Kari rested her hand on Jesse's shoulder. Slowly she lowered it down his chest as she spoke. "You know, I have had to endure watching porn with your roommate, dealing with an asshole reminding me of mistakes made and, worst of all, sitting across from you, wanting to jump you in your chair all night."

Her hand fell to the front of his pants and she squeezed his cock firmly. "I don't feel like waiting 'til we get home to have you fill my pussy. Let's go."

Kari pulled Jesse by his belt toward her car.

Jesse went to open the driver's side door but, instead, Kari yanked him to the back door and hit the locks. Before he could reach the latch, she kissed him.

Her tongue was hot and wet as it slid into Jesse's mouth. Kari's pussy was already hot and was now becoming wetter by the moment as his hands fondled her body.

This was passion at its peak.

Jesse pulled the car door open and Kari pushed him onto the backseat. He laid across the leather and watched as Kari slid her panties down her legs. Jesse was dumbfounded. He'd never seen this side of her and there was no way he was going to complain.

Kari dragged her fingers up his legs and grasped his groin. She wanted him and apparently didn't care why.

She roughly unfastened his belt and jerked at his zipper and pants, trying to free his cock.

Jesse let his head lay back on the door armrest.

Kari's mouth encompassed his cock, bringing it to life. Her mouth was warm and she sucked hungrily on him.

"God, I thought you were full from dinner. Oh, my . . ." Jesse moaned, feeling her pull up.

With a pop, Kari let him free from her tight lips. Panting, she answered back. "It's not this pair of lips that are hungry. It's these."

She climbed up Jesse and reached back to close the open car door.

With a clunk, Jesse whimpered. "That was my leg." He bent his knees and Kari tugged the door closed.

Kari dug into her purse on the floorboard. She smeared her juices along the length of his cock resting between the lips of her pussy. She was straddling him and, as she tore open the condom wrapper with her teeth, she wiggled her belly, rubbing his cock.

"Shit, Kari, you're on fire."

"Damn right. I am so fucking horny, Jesse. I'm about to pop." Kari moved down a bit and rolled the condom over Jesse's cock.

Jesse reached his hands down his sides and grabbed Kari's thighs.

She smacked his hands away. "Don't touch me. I want to fuck you. No touching—just fucking."

With a mutual groan, Kari lowered herself down Jesse's rigid cock.

Jesse closed his eyes. He was oblivious to everything around him, just the rocking motion of Kari riding his cock. He could feel the juices from her pussy trickling between his balls. She was moaning loudly with each time she let him sink into her cunt.

Her fingers dug into the top edge of the leather seat as she tried to keep fucking him. She drooled, falling further over the ledge of her desire. As she sucked in the saliva on the corner of her mouth, she felt the first quiver of her orgasm shooting through her pussy. She was going to come.

Jesse began to thrust his hips upward to meet her grinding. Her chirps of excitement were met with his grunts. Her other hand held his hands above his head but as she climbed her mountain of pleasure her grip loosened.

Jesse felt her body beginning to tighten and flex. He couldn't hold back anymore, feeling her pussy squeezing tighter and tighter around him.

"Oh, *fuck* . . . Kari, I'm going to . . . oh, *shit* . . ."

Kari pleaded with him breathlessly. "Not *yet*, hold on for . . . oh, yes, now, *now*—oh, *fuck*." She sat straight up, raised her hands to the roof of the car and came. Her back was arched and Jesse saw her erect nipples poking into the fabric of her blouse.

He couldn't control himself. "Shit, damn—damn, I am too." Her convulsions milked Jesse as he came with her, popping like a champagne bottle inside her.

"Oh, damn. My leg's cramped in the edge of the car seat."

They began to laugh as they untangled themselves in the back of Kari's car.

"We need to do this in an American-made car. These imports have backseats that are way too small," Jesse joked.

THEY WENT TO HIS place and talked until they were tired of talking. Then they talked some more. The friendship that had started between them was becoming stronger—as was the attraction.

Jesse was becoming "Jesse" again. He liked how it made him feel. The insecurities and baggage a bad relationship left had always clung to his heart. Kari had finally broken down some of those feelings and replaced them with warmth and trust. He felt whole again. And damn, she made him horny.

The flickering lights of the TV flashed in the front room of his apartment.

Kari and Jesse had fallen asleep watching some boring movie that was a critics' choice and the TV had come on after the movie ended.

Kari lay across Jesse, resting quietly. His chest rose and fell with his breathing. The thumping of his heart was her rhythm to live this night by. She was content, relaxed and finally at ease. This was home. A loud, droning snore fully woke her.

Blinking a few times, she raised her head from Jesse's chest and looked at the TV. *Football highlights. Figures*, she thought. Her arm was wedged along the back of the couch pillows and tingling. It was asleep and lifeless. It was late— she was now awake and bored. She looked at Jesse and the boredom turned to feeling frisky. His jeans were unsnapped as he was stretched across the couch under her.

Scooting downward, she didn't wake him but had a better vantage point to ravage him. Kari slowly tugged up on his T-shirt with her good arm. She revealed his stomach and belly button, which she was happy to report was an "inny."

Her lips became moistened from the swipe of her tongue across them. She moved herself lower on the couch and began to kiss Jesse's bare skin. There was something about his smell that aroused her. It wasn't a cologne or aftershave. It was just him.

Each kiss added to her arousal. She licked the indentions of his muscles and crept lower and lower until she was teasing at the soft hair just below his tummy, but not below the waistband of his underwear. She was seducing a sleeping man and her kisses were awakening a sleeping giant as Jesse's cock seemed to gradually move on its own. Kari slid her fingers below the elastic band of Jesse's underwear and stroked her fingertips across his cock.

Jesse smacked his lips and opened his heavy eyelids. *Hello!!!* Jesse cleared his throat and was now awake. So was his other brain. He looked down his chest to see Kari's hand in his pants and could feel the warm skin caressing his cock. What a way to wake up.

With a firm grasp, Kari held tight onto Jesse. She could feel him growing as she squeezed him. Her own fires were beginning to burn. She'd had him earlier, but something about him intoxicated her desires to be free. Kari rolled her hand around his cock and her movements lowered Jesse's zipper as his pants opened up to her.

She was twisted against the couch and could only use one hand, but had her teeth. Biting his underwear, Kari tugged them down, exposing his now hard cock to her eyes. With the head swollen and free, Kari held on to the hardened shaft and lowered her mouth to the tip.

Jesse just breathed deep. He could see the head of his cock peeking out, and Kari's red lips were so close that he was tempted to place his hand on the back of her head to guide her. Jesse laid his head back and closed his eyes. Feeling so aroused and screaming to feel those wondrous red lips he had kissed earlier wrapped around his cock, he waited painfully for her. The cool air from her breath only added to his wants.

Kari let the tip of her tongue lick the salty split of the head of Jesse's cock, causing him to groan. Her hand held fast to the shaft, ignoring the subconscious thrusts of Jesse's hips. Her pussy began to ache and the need made her squirm. She wanted to savor this.

Parting her lips ever so slightly, she let the wide tip spread her mouth open. Jesse's groans signaled his pleasure and the throb of his cock showed both heads were wide-awake.

Inching him into the warmth of her mouth, Kari felt the urge to devour Jesse. He was a nourishment to her weakened state of mind. Her throat twitched as the head hit the back of her throat and she struggled not to gag. Jesse tightened his pelvis and groaned again.

God, she wanted to fuck him right there. Just feeling him split her in two with a ferocious passion. To have him take her as his woman and not let go until they were both spent and exhausted from quenching their thirst for each other.

Her mind was a blur of thoughts. Her mouth sucking and slobbering over Jesse's straining cock. She couldn't get enough of it and wanted it deeper. The initial seepage of his seed made her want to feel him erupt in her mouth. Kari wanted his climax. To give him the pleasure he gave to her.

She struggled to get loose from the pretzel-like entanglement of their limbs on the couch and ordered him to "Stand up!"

With his cock sticking out, dripping with Kari's saliva, Jesse stood in front of her. Kari leaned into the tall back of the fluffy couch and caught her breath. Her arms were back to normal and everything was free. She looked at Jesse, sucked in the drool between her teeth and reached her arms forward, grabbing at his legs.

Tearing down his pants and underwear, they crumpled at his knees. Kari grabbed the cheeks of his ass and drew his swollen cock back into her hot mouth.

Jesse hung his head and again closed his eyes as she began to take him to the brink once more. He didn't even hear the jingling of keys at the door or it opening.

"Hey, Jess, what's up?" Rich bellowed out as he entered the apartment.

Jesse fell forward, grabbing the top of the couch and hiding his waist down from Rich's sight. "Oh—just woke up. Watching some TV."

He was hoping Kari was going to straighten things up real quick to hide what was happening. At least that was Jesse's hope.

Kari had let Jesse lean straight into the warm confines of her mouth and throat, and didn't want to waste it. She let her tongue slide along the base of his cock as he tried to keep a conversation going with Rich.

"So you went to the movies, huh?" Jesse tried to maintain his composure. "Ohhhhhhh, that sounds good. I'm—*uhhhh—ooooohh*—I'm going to stay here for a bit watching the TV. *Mmmmm*, okay."

Rich looked at Jesse and raised his dark eyebrow. "You okay, man? You look like you're straining or something?"

"Burritos. You don't want to be in here. I'm going to—uh—uh—*uhh*—*mmm*—blow any minute."

Rich shrugged and went down the hall to his room. Jesse stepped back, pushing Kari away. "You don't play fair."

With a pop, she let him free. "Fair? Who says things are fair? Damn, Jesse, you . . . *mmm*. You drive me crazy." Kari was beside herself. She had a wet, hot pussy and a hunk of a man in front of her with a hard-on. It was fucking time. "Hey, come on, let's fuck. Come on. I *want* you, Jesse."

Looking around Jesse started to speak. "Let's go to my room."

Kari hiked up her skirt and tugged her underwear downward, letting them tumble to the floor. She was revealing her naked pussy and pointing. "No, right *here*. *Now*. Look, Jesse." She rubbed at her pussy with her finger, showing him how ready she was. Something had awoken in her to make this typically subdued woman feel like a raging slut. She needed to be lusted after. A burning need, which Jesse fulfilled as he stared at her toying with the outer lips of her slippery cunt.

Jesse sat back on the couch and grabbed the TV controller. He turned the sound up and motioned for Kari to climb on top of him.

Kari smacked his hand aside and turned away from him. She unfastened her skirt and let it fall to the floor. The sound of the football highlights on the TV drowned out her soft voice. "I want to ride you. So shut up, sit back and hang on."

She dumped her handbag across the end table and found an old, regular condom. No ribbed, extra-lubricated or flavored one. This was an old school, emergency kit, sex condom. Tearing the wrapper open, she rolled the latex down his hard cock and smiled. *Party time.*

Straddling his legs, Kari lowered her wet cunt over the top of Jesse's hard cock. She grabbed his knees and began her ride as he slid deep into her heart and soul.

The only sounds came from the TV in the room and the commentators of the football game.

*"Well, Bud, it's almost the end of the game and it's been a tense one to say the least. It has been a seesaw battle for control with the red team controlling the action.*

*"You can see the offense has taken over and they're methodically running the clock out to a fantastic climax of the game."*

Kari rolled her hips and fucked Jesse. Her mouth opened and she panted with each penetrating stroke into her. Her hair swung forward as Jesse thrust upward into her and the smacking of her ass on his thighs made them burn. Her cunt milked his swollen cock with each stroke. She pushed hard on his knees to keep the deep, hammering thrusts going, but her arms and legs were giving out.

*"Have you ever seen anything so beautiful, Bud? It's poetry in motion watching this team move. When they aren't passing the ball into gaps, they pound it in over and over until time runs out. It looks like another win for— It's a FUMBLE!"*

Kari whimpered and threw her head back in pleasure. She was enjoying the roller coaster ride she was giving Jesse. His cock was riding along the thin hood of her swollen clit and shocks of pleasure cascaded up her spine. Her body would jerk and writhe in joy. By accident, she had stretched too high and Jesse's cock fell free from her body, and when she sat back down, she bent it.

After the initial pain, he wiped his tears and groped at Kari. Jesse was beyond his boundary to stop but wanted to be in control.

*"Well the ball has changed hands and the blue team is on offense now.*

*"They aren't wasting any time. They are in the hurry-up offense and already spreading the field open. This guy really knows how to run this offensive play. Look at how he handles the ball . . ."*

Jesse pulled Kari onto the couch and had her grab the back headrest, keeping her knees on the cushion as he stood behind her. Toying with her pussy, he tapped the head of his cock at the opening.

Kari turned her head and stuck her tongue out at him. With a hard thrust, he sank back into her hot oven.

*"These guys aren't going for the tie here, Bud, they're going for the win. Look at how they're pounding the holes for extra yards. It's like they don't care about time, they just want to score."*

*"Well the other team has been playing with them all day, Bob. It looks like the blue team is going to score no matter what."*

*"Uh-oh, look out. They brought in the extra tight end for the goal-line play. They've been penetrating this defense all day. Things have stiffened here near the end and everyone knows that the blue team wants to bust this game wide open."*

Kari was panting and out of breath as Jesse arched back with every stroke into her dripping cunt. They were both nearly there and needed to jump over.

"Oh, God, Jesse, I'm going to come, I'm . . ."

Kari held her hands against her chest. The muscles in her back tightened and she swore her mind popped as she arched back. Her pussy could feel the pulsing seed spurting through Jesse's throbbing cock. His moans of pleasure only excited her more.

*"There's the snap . . . It's a quarterback sneak and he plunges into the hole and . . . and . . ."*

Jesse winced as his jets of seed spewed inside Kari's constricting pussy. Like a volcano, he erupted into her with gushes of lava. The walls of her pussy wrapped tight around him like a sanctuary. The built-up lust was unleashed. Kari's toying with his aching cock had Jesse climbing the walls and now he had fallen off the ledge.

Jesse wished he could stay inside of Kari for hours. This relationship was becoming more than a simple fuck-friendship. They were both beginning to have the long-buried feelings for each other that they swore against. Broken hearts mend slowly and the pain is just too much to take again.

He kissed the back of Kari's shoulder and staggered backward, falling free from her. The full condom hung loose, and Jesse grabbed some tissues from the end table by Kari's scattered purse to clean up the best he could.

Kari felt warm and tingly through her body. Her core was hot and full and the spastic contractions had stopped. She was content. Kari fell to the couch in a ball with a smile on her face. "So who won the game?"

Jesse fumbled with his pants as he turned to look at the TV. "They're tied and going into overtime."

"Mmm. Overtime, huh? Sounds like fun."

# Chapter Eight

RIIIING, RIIIIING, RIIIIIING . . .

The phone continued to ring and Jesse continued to sit, head in hand, oblivious to the echoing sound of the phone sitting on his desk beside him. He was thinking of Kari. He was thinking of her naked. He was thinking of spreading whipped cream over her and licking it off. He was getting a boner and didn't even realize it.

A loud *bang* scared Jesse back to the real world as his boss slammed his hand on Jesse's desk. "Answer the fucking phone, Jesse. What's wrong with you, man? You've been spaced-out all day. You get laid or something?" His boss was both joking and serious at the same time.

For all the times Jesse had sat at work worrying about *woulda, shoulda, coulda,* he now had something to think about that actually had possibilities. It was good. But it sucked for his concentration and sitting at a desk with a hard-on is terrible if a guy needed to stand up.

Life tends to have a terrible way of leveling out. Just when things seem to suck more than a hooker on a Friday night, something shines a light into life to bring happiness. This wasn't a some*thing*—Kari was a some*one*. Her calm demeanor contrasted Jesse's worried soul. She was his balance.


JESSE STRUGGLED TO TALK. He was breaking his date with Kari because of a call from Viki. It wasn't fair to him or to Kari. "Look, Kari, I told you I'm sorry. Something came up. We can go out tomorrow. I need to take care of this tonight." Jesse was irritated and scared because Kari wasn't taking his apology well.

"You know, Jesse, just be honest with me. No more lies—no bullshit—just the truth. You're standing me up because of Viki. I hear things and I'm not *stupid*." Kari knew she shouldn't accuse Jesse, but she was hurt and her insides told her he was hiding something. She had lived this lie before—believing the love she'd felt could withstand anything. Her life had crumbled around her. She'd been wrong and wouldn't let that pain happen again.

Jesse was full of emotions ranging from terror to rage. "I don't want to lie, Kari. There are things I have to do that started before we got together. This is more important than—"

"More important than our trust? More important than *us*?" Kari blurted it out as she felt her heart pounding in her chest. She was ashamed to admit she was acting a little childishly. All the memories from the past crept in and her jealousy raised its evil green head.

"I can't let Viki leave my life." Jesse knew the words would hurt Kari, but he had to be honest. "You wouldn't understand. It's complicated."

Kari's fragile confidence was shredded by his words. She had built-up the courage to let a man back into her life and he was breaking down every wall of confidence she'd rebuilt to escape from this feeling of anguish. Her heart was now being broken by the man she'd thought was different from the rest.

"Kari, please understand. I want to be with you." Jesse paused.

"But? There's always a *but* in these sentences. To me, you are acting worse than a butt. You're being a fucking asshole!"

The loud clang of the phone hanging up hurt Jesse's ear, as did the feeling of betraying Kari in his heart. He was acting the part of a fool.

"*Fuck!* I can't keep doing this anymore! I have *had* it." Jesse was yelling. Both at himself and the situation he was in.

Rich walked into the kitchen area and saw Jesse standing red-faced and mad. "What's hangin', studly?"

"Everything is fucked up, Rich. Kari is mad, Viki is fucking with me and—and we're out of beer."

"Out of *beer? Shit* this is *terrible*." Rich rattled through the fridge mumbling.

"Dude, didn't you hear me? I said Kari is mad and Viki is messing with me!" Jesse became perturbed at Rich's lack of compassion for his problems.

"Well I have my priorities right. I'll get some beer later." Rich whistled, grabbed the jar of peanut butter on the countertop and a handful of celery as he passed Jesse.

"What should I do, Rich? Tell me, please."

Rich plopped down on the couch and sighed. "You ever try being honest with Kari? You know, tell her everything?" He began spreading the peanut butter across the celery and listened to the silence. His feet hung over the edge and he pushed his shoes off with his feet.

"I can't—"

"Well then don't ask me for advice. You've dug yourself a hole and the way out is right in front of your face. Just *tell* her, Jesse. Shit, dude, she's smart, kind and is *hella* fine. Not a lot of babes like that will hang around if you keep being a turd and sitting around. Just *talk* to her."

"I know, Rich. I should tell her everything, but I don't want her thinking I am a fool. I have a record, things have gotten all fucked up. I screwed up and don't want her to know what a real idiot I am."

After taking a bite, Rich laughed. "You're past the idiot stage. Hell, man, she's great."

"Shit, I hope it'll work out. I can't think straight. I have to go. Viki said we were going to talk tonight."

"Whatever, man. That bitch is nothing but trouble. She's ruining your life because she can't stand the thought of seeing you happy. Go tell her to get a body cavity search from a football team or something." Rich was obviously getting mad at how his best friend was being used and not even fighting it.

"You know I have to keep things cool between us, Rich. I have no choice."

Coughing his celery across the couch as he spoke back to Jesse, Rich replied, "Bullshit. We all have choices. You make your mind up, Jesse. I'm your friend, dude, and you need to take control before Viki ruins your life again." As he paused, he could see Jesse's confusion in his eyes. "Just take care of what you need to. Don't let her play you, buddy. Don't let her play you. I swear, Jesse, if she pulls what she did last time, I'm going to go there and kick her in the shins."

Jesse smiled at Rich's comment and grabbed his jacket as he walked out the door.

As the door closed, Rich swiped another glob of peanut butter on the celery. "It's like I'm talking to myself sometimes. He doesn't listen to anything I say."

Sitting alone in the living room, Rich looked around the room. "Why am I talking to myself?"

"Why am I answering?"

He popped the last bite of celery in his mouth and sat upright letting his gas loose.

*Pffffft.*

"Excuse me."

"It's all right."

"Why am I excusing myself when I am alone?"

"I don't know, but this is scary."

"*Echoooo.*"

"Fuck it, I need some porn!"


AFTER A LONG, DEEP SIGH, Kari looked up from her mental funk as the bell on the diner door rang. Looking along the line of young businesswomen at the lunch counter, she didn't see anyone and went back to wiping up. The lunch rush was over and the ladies sitting at the counter were just finishing their coffee mochas and whatever other caffeine stimulants they were downing.

She was still upset at Jesse for calling at the last minute to cancel their date. His avoidance of her question about

Viki made it obviously true. She'd let him into her heart and, as usual, the man she'd opened up to hurt her.

"Is this where all the hot waitresses work?" A man's voice echoed at Kari's end of the bar.

Looking up from the countertop, she saw nothing.

"Hey, Kari, turn around."

As she turned she didn't see anything except a hand waving back and forth in front of the bar and the top of a man's head.

"Yo, baby, it's your Porn-Daddy!"

Smiling, she knew who it was. Rich had come by the diner to see her. She reached behind the counter and grabbed a couple of cups and a freshly perked pot of coffee. She motioned to the hostess she was taking a break and sat in a booth with Rich.

"Why'd you come here, Rich?" Kari knew he must have had a reason to suddenly stop by.

"Jesse." Rich shuffled in his seat and leaned on the table. "He was all jabbering and upset last night. After he calmed down, he told me you and he had had an argument."

Kari didn't want to say anything. She was still angry and upset over the whole event.

"He's such a tool. I swear, there is more drama with him than a group of teenage cheerleaders. He's a mess some-times. But, he's my buddy so I just thought I'd come by and see you."

Kari was torn. She didn't know what to say but needed some answers. So she asked.

"What is all this shit with Viki? It just eats at me, and I know it's the wedge between Jesse and me. She is gone but still fucking with his head. We can't go any further until he lets her go. I can't be with him if it's going to be like this, Rich. Not like I was before. Always scared. I just . . . I just *can't*." She stopped talking and slumped in her booth bench.

"I won't lie to you, Kari. Jesse will have Viki in his life for a long time. There's nothing you or I can do about it." With a sigh he continued. "Jesse has a daughter with Viki. Her name is Natalie and she is Jesse's pride and joy."

Stunned, Kari sat in her chair, her mind an absolute blank for a minute or two. She spoke the first words that popped into her head. "Why didn't he tell me, Rich?"

"He's a fucking idiot. He's embarrassed and doesn't bring it up unless he has to. He thinks a woman doesn't want to deal with a guy who has a kid. I told him it isn't a big deal. Nowadays it's probably more common than not." Sipping his coffee, Rich shrugged his shoulders. "Kari, he really likes you. I mean *reeeeeeallly* likes you."

Blushing, Kari suddenly felt good inside. The wall between her and Jesse had suddenly been broken down, and she now understood a few things she hadn't before.

"I should talk to him." Kari looked into her coffee, wondering what she should say.

"Don't tell him I told you, Kari. He'd get pissed off. Viki is a fucking witch to him. She has custody of their daughter and uses Natty to get money and fuck with his life. He gets drunk sometimes to just ease the pain, and I can't say I blame him. She dangles that little girl in front of him and he cracks. He only sees her right after work for an hour at the day care center and has to leave before Viki gets there. I— I just can't help him with this."

"Can't he get joint custody or something?" Kari wanted to help.

"Jesse caught Viki fucking some guy in Natty's bedroom. He went off. I mean he really blew up. He beat the guy up really bad—put him in the hospital. Viki tried to pull Jesse off the guy and in the confusion he accidentally hit Viki's side, knocking her off balance. Viki fell down and Natty's crib got knocked over, and with the police and the hospital . . . it was a real mess. They both filed assault charges. She threatened to never let him see Natty again, so he signed the paperwork releasing custody to Viki."

"I thought she left him for this Alan guy?" Kari remembered the restaurant.

"Alan is just an old friend of Jesse's who Viki has been with for a while. He's a scumbag." Rich laughed. "Coming from a porno reviewer, calling him a scumbag is pretty fuckin' low."

"You may be an—" Kari pretended she was straightening a tie and cleared her throat "—*adult film critic* but, Rich, you're a lot nicer than most men I know." She reached over and held his hand as it rested on the table.

"So I guess a blowjob would be out of the question?" He laughed as he sipped his coffee.

"*That's* where Jesse got that line. You little shit—he tried that line on me on our first date."

Rich wiggled his eyebrows. "Did it work?"

"Nice try, Rich. I don't suck and tell."

Rich did all he could to stop himself from spitting his coffee on the floor, holding back a laugh.

Kari winked at him. "I'm going to have to introduce you to Mona."

"Mona? Mmm, I like that name." Rich smiled ear to ear. "*Moooooona . . .*"

"Rich, thank you. I know it took guts to tell me some of this because you and Jesse are friends."

"Look, Kari, I've known Jesse for twelve years. We've been through a lot. Jesse and I worked together as teenagers, we've been in fights together, even got thrown in a Mexican jail together. With me being a midget, a lot of times people say bad shit, you know? He has always watched my back, and I watch his. You are good for him. I see that. Viki was bad, but I kept my mouth shut because he loved her."

Rich paused for breath. "If I can help him keep a good woman and not fuck it up, then I'm happy. He'd do the same for me."

Kari squeezed Rich's hand then opened it. She smiled as she pulled the pen from behind her ear and scribbled on his palm.

Rich tried to see what she was writing. The pen tip tickled his skin.

"There you go. That's Mona's number. Give her a call. She doesn't work tonight. You two will get along great— she's a pervert just like you."

Rich smiled like a schoolboy. He held onto Kari's hand tight, giving it a gentle squeeze. "Don't worry, things have a way of working themselves out."

"I won't say anything to him, Rich, but until he can be honest with me, I'm not sure I can stay with him. I've been hurt before and just want the truth. I just want to know where I stand." Kari sighed, and her eyes moistened with sadness. "I'm scared, Rich. I am scared to let myself love someone again. I've been through this game before and can't go through it again, not with Jesse. I couldn't bear it. Tell him I care for him more than he can imagine, but the next move is his."

# Chapter Nine

JESSE WALKED TOWARD HIS apartment in a fuzzy daze. Everything was flying around in his head. His life was a constant disruptive mess. He was tearing himself apart trying to figure out what to do and one more hit from any of his life's burdens might do him in.

He worried about everything, but so many things seemed out of his control.

Walking up to the door, he heard a loud shriek. Jesse leaned toward the door to listen.

"Oh, yesss, fuck, fuck, yeah, baby—lick that pussy, lick my cunt, ohhhh, *yessss.*"

*Dammit, Rich. I told you to watch your movies in your room. The neighbors will complain again.* He was talking to himself as he looked for his keys.

"Mmmm—yes, *fuck* you can eat pussy, you little bastard . . . Oh, God, right *there*, right *there*—oh, shit . . .

ahhhh—*mm*—*ahhhh*—" The woman's voice echoed in the room as Jesse opened the door.

Jesse looked up and the TV was off. He scanned the room and jerked back when a woman's head popped up from the couch.

"Who the hell are you?"

"Mona. My name is—*ohhh*—*Mooona*." Her eyes closed and as Jesse stepped closer, he saw she was topless.

"Sorry, I didn't know you were . . . umm . . . why are you . . . umm . . . naked?" Jesse looked away to be polite, but not before he got a peek at the tight nipples on her perky breasts.

"I'm a friend of—*oohhh*—friend of Rich's—" Again she closed her eyes and her face flushed red.

"Where's Rich?"

"*Mummmgrr, mmmeeermuummphhh . . .*" Jesse heard a mumbling sound followed by a smacking sound, like lips eating something. "I'm down here, dude." There was a pause followed by a deep moan from Mona. "Give me about fifteen minutes."

Mona looked up at Jesse, eyelids fluttering. "Better make it twenty."

Jesse walked down the hall toward his room. Now he had another awkward thought in his mind. His best friend was eating out a woman on the couch. It wasn't the oral sex thought as much as the visual that Rich probably looked like he was being birthed.

With a heavy sigh he fell across his bed. He needed to think. Everything was crumbling around him. He pulled his hands over his head and looked up at the ceiling fan spinning. It was peaceful and quiet except for the noises from the living room.

The walls in the apartment were paper-thin and not much help in muffling sounds from room to room. Jesse could hear a buzzing sound. As the noise got louder, the lights dimmed and brightened in relation to the buzzing. The whimpering moans from the front room still filled the apartment.

"Oh, baby, you are so fucking hot." Rich's deep voice was opposite of Mona's higher chirps of pleasure. "Those porn chicks have nothing on you, baby. I've never done it in this position before."

"Oh, Rich, this is incredible. Ouch, ouch, your foot is poking me in the ear. Ahhhhh, there, *that's* better." There was a short pause then Mona spoke again. "Oh, Rich, you have such a big cock. I guess all men *aren't* created with size-proportioned anatomy."

Jesse covered his face with his hands, forcing the pictures out of his mind. It was bad enough that he was upset and confused about Kari, now he was witness to his friend getting all freaky with a woman. And she was making more noise than a cat in heat.

"What the *fuck* are you doing with that rubber chicken, Rich?" Mona sounded scared.

Jesse sat upright, perplexed by the image in his mind, wondering what the hell Rich *was* doing with a rubber chicken.

"*OH, MY GOD. OH, MY GOD.* I'm coming again—oh, shit—fuck me—*fuck me harder*—" Mona was screaming in uninhibited sexual passion.

Jesse heard Rich groan loudly. "Cock a doodle *dooooo*."

◆ ◆ ◆

THE APARTMENT WAS QUIET again and Jesse finally relaxed. Closing his eyes, things seemed to calm. The tranquil silence helped his brain settle and his thoughts seemed less chaotic.

*Knock, knock, knock.*

Jesse sat up. "Come on in."

Rich opened the door and walked in, dressed in a towel and strutting like a king. "What's up, dude?"

"Where's Mona?"

"She hopped into the shower. She was all sticky. Damn, dude, that woman is hot. I thought those porn chicks in the movies were sex-crazed. This woman wants the whole enchilada. I think I'm in love."

"Where'd you meet her?"

"Kari gave me her number." Rich had slipped up and he obviously knew it.

"When did you talk to Kari?" Jesse became upset and concerned.

"I only *talked* to her, dude. She really cares about you and you're fucking things up, Jesse. I just don't get you, man. Here's this great woman, she doesn't pressure you, she is nice, pretty damn hot-looking and a normal person. There's no bullshit with her. Pull your head out of your ass and take control, dude." Rich shook his head as he saw his best friend struggling with things. "I love ya, Jesse, but I'm not afraid to tell you when you're fucking up the best thing you have."

Jesse looked at Rich. "Second-best. Natalie is the most important thing right now."

"But, dude, you can have both if you get the balls to take control of the situation. Be the Jesse of old. Nobody fucked with you before. You ruled."

Jesse knew Rich was right. He needed to take control

and quit acting like a broken man. He had a good woman and his life wasn't ruined by circumstance. He needed to live with the deck of cards he had been dealt. He could still see Natalie every day. He needed to go to Kari and tell her the truth. She deserved to know everything from him.

Rich walked toward the door.

"Rich . . ." Jesse paused. "Thanks."

"No problem. Now I want to go get in the shower with Mona and show her what a midget does with soap on a rope."

The phone rang and Rich grabbed it off the dresser by the door. "Yeah, he's here. Just a second."

Cupping the mouthpiece, Rich handed Jesse the phone. "It's Viki."

Swallowing, Jesse knew he needed to move forward. He had to tell Viki he wanted his life and daughter back. "Hello?"

There was a long pause and Rich saw Jesse's eyes begin to swell with moisture. Something was wrong. "Okay. We'll talk later."

He set the phone down, brushed a hand across his eyes, slicked his hair back and looked at Rich.

"Viki is moving to California with Alan and taking Natalie with her. What the hell am I going to do, Rich?"

KARI SAT ON THE STOOL in her kitchen sipping a cup of hot tea. Life was getting more complicated and her daily ritual of clearing her mind with hot tea and silence always brought her peace.

Jesse hadn't called or contacted her for almost a week.

Their relationship was up in the air after her talk with Rich. Now, instead of being a friend and lover, he was a father, a liar and he had been with another woman.

She knew Jesse had been with Viki. He'd told her that. But here was physical *proof* that he had been with her. It sounded strange, but it was reality. What was going to happen next, she had no clue.

Kari stared blankly into the tea as the steam rose from it. Breathing in the aroma of the raspberry eased her nerves. She wasn't going to dwell on things. Life goes on and she was going to let things fall where they may.

*Knock, knock, knock.*

Her calm was broken as she walked to the door. Opening it, she saw Jesse standing there. He was in a suit and looked rather handsome. He had actually shaved and was wearing a nice, musky cologne. Kari was quiet and just looked at him.

With a heavy breath, he spoke. "Kari, I'd like to introduce you to the other woman in my life." He pulled his hand from behind his back and a little girl was holding his finger. "This is Natalie. My daughter."

A moment passed as the three of them looked at each other.

"Daddy, I need to pee." Natalie looked up at Kari and wobbled side to side, crossing her legs at the ankles.

"Come on in. I'm sorry. The bathroom is right down that little hall." Kari watched as Natalie ran by, her little blonde curls bouncing with each step.

Jesse picked up a blue-flowered bag and walked into Kari's apartment. "These are her toys."

They heard a flush and a few splashes of water from the

sink, and Natalie sighed as she walked out of the bathroom. "Thank you. What's her name, Daddy?"

"This is Kari. Remember I told you about her?" Jesse smiled as he talked.

"Oh, yes. I remember now. She *is* pretty, Daddy. Just like you said. Can I color now?" She reached for the bag Jesse held. He looked at Kari and she nodded. Natalie tugged the bag to the small table in front of the TV.

"Please—sit down, Kari. I need to talk to you." They both sat at the kitchen table as Jesse mustered the courage to talk.

"Firstly, I want to apologize. I should have been totally up-front with you, but I was embarrassed and scared. I did something really stupid and didn't want to explain my ignorance in a fit of rage, so I never told you about Natalie. For that I am sincerely sorry."

He was visibly trying to control his emotions. "Secondly, there's Viki. She and I had a long, bad relationship. We were involved—she became pregnant and everything went downhill from there. The only bright spot in those years was Natalie. She is my inspiration and my bright star. It sounds mushy, but I just want her to have what I didn't." Jesse began to struggle a bit for words. He wasn't the emotional type but this was hard for him.

Kari reached forward and put her hand on his. She was still angry at him, but could feel his remorse.

He swallowed. "I'm not asking you to marry me. That's something that might happen later. Right now, I just know I need you in my life. I am not asking you to be Natalie's mother. She has a mom. But I may ask for some help with things that I don't know about."

"Like dressing her." Kari smiled at the little, wrinkled lace blouse and mismatched color pants.

Jesse smiled back and continued. "Kari, I can't promise to be a perfect man. I have flaws. But I *can* promise to be honest with you. If I could take back putting that guy in the hospital and knocking Viki into the crib—I never meant to hurt Viki, I swear. She tried to pull me off that guy and I hit her flush with my elbow. It was an accident and I still thank God Natalie hadn't gotten hurt. I could never forgive myself for that . . . well that's another story.

"You and I started out as . . . *friends*. I can talk to you, Kari, and you make me feel good. When I'm talking to you, I am better. You make me a better man. I let my insecurities and my stubbornness make me stupid."

Kari interrupted him. "Well, you're right about the stupid remark."

Her thoughts wandered into what *could* be and what *might* happen. Everything was different now. She was seeing a side of Jesse that was raw and exposed. She'd seen his body exposed and bare, but that was different. Before her was a man. He was pouring his heart out in front of her and showing her the way things could be between a couple. His daughter was his number one priority now, and she wasn't sure if she could be second in his life.

Kari turned to see Natalie coloring. She was innocent and naive to what was going on.

"Kari, Viki will be a part of my life for a while. She's Natalie's mother. But after Viki called and told me she was moving away and taking my daughter, I knew I couldn't live with that situation. I asked Rich what I should do. He told me that I knew what I needed to do and to grow some balls and do it."

"Rich does have a way with words doesn't he?" Kari smiled, easing Jesse's mood a bit. "What did you do?"

"I went to Viki's and told her she couldn't take Natalie from me and that I'd fight her tooth and nail if she tried. She's moving away and using her to get money and revenge on me. I told her that Nat belongs with me, not her and Alan. They can start a new life together and have twenty kids for all I care, but Natalie needs *me*. Her father." His face was reddened with emotion and compassion for his daughter. "I just got back from court and Viki gave me custody of Natalie as long as she could see her whenever she came to town. So she's mine now."

"Jesse—where do I fit in all this? We've only been together for such a short time." Kari had to ask the obvious.

"I want another chance to make us work right. I want a clean slate. No more bullshit."

"Daddy said a bad word!" Natalie yelled at Jesse, scowling at him.

"Sorry, sweetheart." He smiled then looked to Kari. "I want you in my life for however long I can. A month, a year, whatever I can have. So what do you think?"

She wasn't ready for an instant family. But she cared for Jesse, and his commitment to his daughter showed her a lot about his character. Being good in bed was a plus, but sex wasn't the only reason to have a relationship. It helped but . . . She shook the sex thoughts from her mind and concentrated on what was in front of her.

For the first time in a long while, Kari was at a loss for words. She wanted Jesse, wanted happiness, needed security in a partner and he could provide all that for her. Before she spoke, Natalie walked up holding a DVD in her hand and gave Kari the words she was looking for.

"Can we watch a movie together?" She handed Kari a box with the title *Lady and the Tramp* on the front.

"You like this one?" Kari asked, looking at the cover.

"Yep—even though everything gets broken and messed-up, they're still all together and happy at the end."

Kari looked at Jesse, then at Natalie. "You're right. I'll make some popcorn and the three of us can watch it together."

# 6 Enchanted Princesses

ELIZABETH JEWELL

# Chapter One

"YOU MUST UNDERSTAND, Mr. Fitzcairn. This is a matter of great urgency. I need it taken care of as soon as possible."

Patrick Fitzcairn folded his arms over his chest and regarded his soon-to-be client coolly. "*You* must understand, Mr. Collinwood, that some things take time."

Collinwood regarded him through narrowed eyes, unfazed by Fitz's warning. "This matter needs to be settled as soon as possible. I find the whole situation vastly troubling."

Fitz could understand that. But he had a feeling rushing pell-mell into this case wasn't going to accomplish anything. "Mr. Collinwood, you've given me all the pertinent information. Let me take it home and do some research. I'll get back to you tomorrow."

"Tonight would be better."

Fitz stood, picking up the little notebook where he'd

scribbled all the pertinent information. "I'll see what I can do."

The butler led him out. At least he assumed the man was a butler. He certainly looked like one, all stuffy and grim. Fitz tried not to gape at the house on the way out. He'd barely managed it on the way in. Anthony Collinwood lived in a palatial estate just outside of Chicago.

Fitz wasn't very good at judging square footage by eye, but just the entryway was bigger than his apartment. The decorations, too, were sumptuous enough to make his eyes water. He didn't understand why some people had so much for no good reason. Collinwood could have donated the money to Third World countries or something; instead he'd used it to buy weird little knickknacks and spread them all over his big, glittery, ugly house.

Even the air felt overdecorated. Finally back outside, he drew a long breath that felt clearer, less cluttered with arrogance.

Then he saw the girls.

They were walking—no, sauntering—up the long sidewalk toward the front of the house. Six of them, with flowing black hair, dark eyes, long legs. They all wore bikini tops, their hips wrapped in long, colorful towels.

Just back from poolside, Fitz assumed.

They meandered by, mind-bogglingly identical, hips swaying, breasts challenging the Spandex in their bikinis. The one in front lowered her sunglasses as she passed Fitz and pursed her lips at him. They were beautiful women, no question about it, and the way they moved and swayed and jiggled gave a man unrighteous thoughts. Especially when they looked at you like they were picturing you naked.

Forcing his thoughts back to work, Fitz continued to his car. A sharp pain lanced down his right leg as he climbed behind the wheel.

Eyes clenched shut, half in and half out of the car, he waited for the agony to fade. The pain writhed up and down the old scar that twisted from the inside of his thigh all the way to his knee. This was more than just a twinge. By the time it finally faded, giving one last, hard wrench to his knee, he was lightheaded and could feel cold sweat on his forehead.

He put both hands behind his knee and lifted the leg, depositing it inside the car. He pulled the door shut and put his head on the steering wheel, recovering his strength. It would be a couple of minutes before he could concentrate again.

One thing, now, was certain. Something he'd suspected the moment he'd walked into the Collinwood estate. He had no choice. He had to take this case. Because he was the only P.I. in the Chicago area he knew who could handle the magic involved.

ALL P.I.s HAD SOURCES, but most P.I.s had to call them to get information, instead of having them show up at their front doors exactly when they were needed.

"Hey, Lily," said Fitz, sticking his key in the lock.

The woman leaning against the wall next to his door grinned. "Hey, Fitz. You're taking the case?"

Fitz pushed the door open, gesturing for Lily to precede him into the apartment. "Why do you bother asking when you already know the answer?"

She shrugged, sweeping into the apartment. She wore a

sumptuously purple cape-coat whose tails fluttered behind her as she walked. "Formalities. You seem to like them."

"Some of them." He closed the door and tossed his keys on the coffee table. "I take it you have an opinion?"

Pulling off her coat, she draped it over the back of the couch and sat. "This place is a shit-hole."

"This place has always been a shit-hole. You only just now noticed?" He pushed dirty dishes out of the way, looking for the coffeemaker. "You want some coffee?"

"It'd probably kill me. What's growing on that cabinet, anyway?"

"You got something to tell me, Lily?"

"There's more to this case than you realize."

"I know. My leg went ape-shit when I was heading out."

She nodded. "I thought you might get some kind of a warning."

He'd found the coffeemaker by now and was rinsing it in the sink. He really needed to wash some dishes. "The single advantage to having been wounded by a fairy blade."

"There should be at least one." She peered soberly at him over the top of the couch. "Are you taking the case?"

"I already took it."

"Then don't forget where your friends are. I have a feeling you'll need help with this one."

"Thanks, Lily." He grinned. "Now, am I gonna get a good lay before this night is over, or are you going home?"

She stood and smiled. Usually she met such comments with humor, but now he swore he saw a hint of regret in her eyes. "I'm going home."

"Too bad. Tell your husband hi."

"I will."

Lily gathered her purple coat and left, locking the door behind her. Fitz made his coffee. He missed his occasional tumble with Lily, but she belonged to someone else now. He couldn't regret it too much, though. She was still a trusted friend, one of very few he had.

It was a shame, though, in a way. They'd been really, really good in bed.

With a pot of coffee at his elbow, Fitz looked over the notes he'd made during the interview with Collinwood. The six daughters had been somehow sneaking out of the estate at night, coming back just before sunrise. No one seemed to know where they went, or how they managed to get past the Collinwood estate's ample security. And none of the sisters seemed willing to give up any information.

He tapped the file folder thoughtfully. Some kind of magic was involved. Possibly harmless, but given the streak of pain down his leg earlier today, probably not. Whatever these girls had gotten themselves into, he doubted they had the wherewithal to get themselves out.

There was no other choice. He picked up his phone, called the Collinwood Estate, and made arrangements to come back in the evening.

"So THERE'S NO OTHER way in or out of this room that you're aware of?"

The bodyguard—Fitz was pretty sure he'd called himself Bo—nodded. He was big, black and bald. Very bodyguard-like. "I've been over the original blueprints seven or eight times. Plus we've been through this whole room, knocking on the walls. I got no clue how they're getting out."

Fitz nodded soberly. "Somebody needs to sit right in the room with them."

"And then they'll just stay put."

"Yeah, probably."

"Good luck getting the okay from the old man to be in his daughters' bedroom while they're in it."

Fitz had suspected as much. "He seems a little . . . over-protective."

"That's not the half of it." Bo took a step closer and lowered his voice. "Between you and me, the guy went off the deep end when his wife died."

Fitz nodded. He'd come to that conclusion himself, after reading Collinwood's bio.

"Those girls haven't left the grounds in ten years. Private tutors—and not many of them lasted more than a few months. No boys, very few girlfriends, and those have been handpicked by Mr. Collinwood." He shook his head.

"I'm surprised he doesn't insist on eunuchs as body-guards." Fitz grinned.

Surprisingly, Bo grinned back. "Not quite. But we're all gay."

Gay and muscle-bound, Fitz noted. He'd noticed something else, as well. "There are no cameras in this room, are there?"

"Nope. Gay or not, he doesn't want us watching his girls on the monitors."

"Some kind of surveillance would be a help. Maybe I can change his mind."

Bo shrugged. "Go for it, but I doubt you'll get very far."

◆ ◆ ◆

Bo was right. Collinwood turned stony-faced when Fitz brought up the idea of a camera in the girls' room.

"I'm paying you to protect my daughters, not ogle them," he said, his voice flinty.

"You've had bodyguards standing outside the door for months and nobody's accomplished anything. The next logical step is either to install a camera in the room or for me to hide in a closet and observe from there."

"If you can't do the job within the parameters set for you, then perhaps I should hire someone else."

A dull ache began in Fitz's leg, echoing the one growing in his head. "How many P.I.s have you hired already for this job, Mr. Collinwood?" He'd thought about asking that yesterday, but had decided against it. Until he'd found out about the magic. Now, no more pussyfooting.

"That is none of your concern, Mr. Fitzcairn."

"How many have died, then? Is that my concern?"

He met Collinwood's glare without flinching. He was sure more than one man had crumpled under that glare, but Fitz had faced off with worse. Much worse.

But Collinwood wouldn't budge, either. Finally Fitz said, "At least one, then." He stepped backward, toward the door. "I don't intend to be added to that list. If I see you're not willing to cooperate, then I may just drop the case. And I'll tell you right now, there's not another P.I. in the state of Illinois who can handle this case."

Collinwood opened his mouth, then, to Fitz's surprise, shut it again.

"It's why you called me, isn't it?" Fitz said. "You knew."

Collinwood glared at him, a veneer of cool arrogance barely hiding the fear in his eyes. "Do your job, Mr. Fitzcairn."

"I'll do what I can." He twisted the doorknob hard in his frustration.

"If there are no results tonight," Collinwood said, just as Fitz was about to walk out the door, "talk to me tomorrow."

Fitz nodded. Not much of a concession, but it was something.


"SO, HAVE YOU SEEN the new bodyguard?" Catherine Collinwood said.

Her sister Annabeth ran the brush through Catherine's long, thick, black hair. "He's not a bodyguard. He's a P.I."

"That's worse," said Lisl.

"Not necessarily." Annabeth gathered Catherine's thick, silky hair into a ponytail and tied a ribbon around it, then turned around to let Catherine return the favor. Catherine took the brush from Annabeth's hand. "I'll take care of him."

"Like the last one?" said Deirdre.

"The last one ended up dead," put in Missy.

"That was not our fault," Annabeth added firmly.

She tipped her head back, giving Catherine better access to her dark, flowing hair. She, too, felt some guilt over the death of the last P.I.—she'd never even been told his name—but he'd had no idea what he was meddling with. He'd assumed the sisters' situation could be handled by normal means, and had paid the price for his ignorance. If the same thing happened to this one, that was none of her concern.

"So what do we do tonight?" asked Greta, busy combing Deirdre's hair.

Annabeth shrugged. "We go."

The other girls giggled happily.

"I'm so glad," said Greta. "I wanted to try something new tonight. Two sprites at once. Do the rest of you want to watch?"

"Two boy sprites?" asked Missy. "Or a boy and a girl?"

"Or two girls?" suggested Lisl.

Annabeth's mouth tightened. They could think of nothing else but their sprites, of the nightly orgy and what new kink they could try tonight. They had no idea what else happened in that place. They had no idea the price she, Annabeth, had paid to keep them all alive.


FITZ SETTLED DOWN ON the floor in front of the door to the girls' bedroom. Bo and the other guard, Mitch, had been scheduled for duty tonight but Fitz had sent them away. He had a feeling the two wouldn't have much trouble making alternate plans, giving one disadvantage to Collinwood's all-gay bodyguard plan. These two, at least, seemed to be pretty thoroughly distracting each other.

Without permission to enter the girls' room, Fitz had loaded himself up with the best possible surveillance equipment. Even with that, though, he could do little more than listen through the door.

Or maybe not. He'd just finished setting up his listening equipment when the door opened just a crack, and a dark head poked around it.

"Good evening," the girl said.

He should have known they'd realize he was here. He supposed there was no point hiding the surveillance equipment, either, even if he could.

"Good evening," he replied.

"I'm Annabeth."

Digging through his memory, he came up with what he knew about Annabeth. She was the oldest—inasmuch as there could be an oldest, since the six girls had been born on the same day. In any case, she'd been the first baby delivered, by C-section, as well as the largest of the six and the first to come home from the hospital.

"I'm Fitz," he told her. He didn't trust the look in her eyes. She looked like she was up to something. "What can I do for you?"

Annabeth pointed over Fitz's shoulder, toward the security camera on the wall behind him. "See that?"

"Yeah."

"And it sees you. Unless you go over there." She pointed to the end of the hallway. "If you stand exactly there, none of the cameras can see you."

"Are you sure?" Of course the security system was likely to have blind spots. What surprised him was that Annabeth knew where they were.

"Absolutely. We know a great deal about this house."

"What's your point?"

"Go stand over there, and I'll tell you."

"Won't that look suspicious?"

"Leave that to me." She ducked back into the bedroom, closing the door behind her.

Fitz went, mostly out of curiosity. A moment later, Annabeth joined him, coming out of another bedroom door.

"How—" Fitz started, stopped because Annabeth had grabbed him. He couldn't talk with her tongue in his mouth. This was certainly an interesting twist. He tried to focus on what might be his next step, but she pressed hard into him, her full, soft breasts mounding against his chest. One hand slid into his hair, the other slid down his body.

*What does she want?* He forced his mind back to a relevant question. *What is she trying to distract you from?* Then her hand slid between his thighs.

For a girl who'd been locked away for ten years, she had a remarkable way with her fingers. It had been a long time since a woman had touched him that way, and his cock responded with more than its usual enthusiasm. Her fingers teased the steely length through his trousers while her other hand combed through his hair.

He drew her closer, kissing her hard and deep, plundering the heat of her mouth.

She tapped him on the temple and he dropped like a rock into unconsciousness.

# Chapter Two

"MR. FITZCAIRN."

Fitz blinked himself awake. He lay sprawled on the floor in front of the girls' bedroom, and his mouth tasted like someone had washed their feet in it. Grimacing, he rolled over to look up into the decidedly unhappy face of Mr. Collinwood.

Of course.

Collinwood's jaw worked as if fighting to restrain the vitriol with which his words desired to emerge. "Mr. Fitzcairn, this is a disgrace."

"I can explain—" Fitz started, and then realized he really couldn't. What was he going to say? *Mr. Collinwood, there's a perfectly reasonable explanation. Your daughter started to seduce me, then zapped me with what felt like a fairy thorn?* Oh, yeah. That would go over just great.

Fortunately, Collinwood had already heard more than enough.

"It's not possible for you to supply me with an acceptable explanation for this behavior. Nevertheless, I will give you one more day to show some progress on this case. After that, if you continue to prove incompetent, your employment will be terminated."

He spun on his heel and departed. His nose wasn't actually in the air, but he gave that impression.

Fitz sat up, rubbing the back of his neck. Behind him, from the other side of the door, he heard giggling.

Suddenly furious, he lurched to his feet, grabbed the doorknob, and shoved the door open.

The six girls looked up. They were sitting and standing around the room, in various stages of dishabille. They were all laughing. Fitz felt his face go red, whether with anger or embarrassment he wasn't sure.

Annabeth looked straight at him, eyelids lowered. Her full, round breasts were bare, and Fitz fought to keep his eyes on her face. She shifted, arching her back, pushing her breasts out and up, and he lost the battle. Her soft nipples rose and puckered under his gaze.

"Is there a problem, Mr. Fitzcairn?" she asked quietly.

Fitz's mouth thinned and he glared at her, right into her eyes. "You have no idea what you've been fucking with. You think it's all a lot of fun, little spells and magic and whatever the hell else you're doing at night, but it'll change. Any second now, you'll find yourself holding the sharp end of the blade."

For a split second, he thought he saw a flicker of fear in

Annabeth's eyes, but she quelled it, turning her gaze to blue steel. "I think it's time for you to go, Mr. Fitzcairn."

"Fine." He spun on his heel and stalked out the door.


LILY STOOD OUTSIDE HIS front door. This did not surprise him. As he struggled under the weight of his surveillance equipment, she took one of the cases so he could worry a key out of his pocket and open the door.

"How's it going at the Collinwood place?" she asked as he staggered in under his burden.

Dropping his equipment on the couch, he looked at Lily. Had he detected an edge to her voice? If so, what had it been? Fear? Surely not.

"Not so well," he answered. "Collinwood's restrictions are making it difficult, not to mention the girls . . ." He told her about last night's misadventure. She laughed and shook her head.

"A girl touches your dick and your brain just goes bye-bye, doesn't it?" she said.

"What can I say? I'm a guy."

"Yes. I remember." Again, there was that faint sense of wistfulness. He wondered what was going on, if she had some reason to be unhappy in her marriage, but he wasn't sure it was his place to ask.

"Those girls don't know what they're doing," he said instead. "They have no idea of the danger."

"Are you sure about that?"

Fitz shrugged. "How could they? They've been locked up in that house for ten years."

"Then how did they get involved in the first place?"

He hadn't thought about that. "I don't know. How do these things usually happen? Screwing around with a Ouija board? One of those old demon-summoning books they have in all the horror movies?"

"Where would they get one?"

"Maybe there was one stowed in the attic or something."

Lily gave him a sour look, something she'd rarely if ever done, not even when they were a couple. "I don't think *you* even know what's going on, Fitz."

The brittleness of her voice surprised him. He met her disapproving gaze full on, trying to find some clue in her eyes. "Do *you* know?"

Unexpectedly, her eyes slid away from his. "I don't know anything more than you do. Not really."

"Then can you help me?"

"I can. Tomorrow."

Suddenly she seemed bruised and fragile, not like his Lily at all. She gathered her purple cape close around her and headed for the door.

"Lily," Fitz said, the words carried on impulse more than thought.

She turned, and for a moment her eyes were bleak. "Yes?"

"How's John?"

Lily lifted her chin. "He's fine, Fitz. He's fine."

The door made a little too much noise behind her as she closed it. Fitz, frowning, wondered.


HE REQUESTED A MEETING with Collinwood for the afternoon, but by three p.m. he'd heard nothing. So he gathered his surveillance equipment and headed for the estate.

By the time he got there, he had a plan. He left most of the equipment in the car, taking only a small listening device he could carry in his jacket pocket.

Collinwood was no help, so screw him. If he expected Fitz to deal with his daughters, then he was going to have to trust Fitz a little further. Tonight he was going to do just that, whether he knew it or not.

Walking up the long sidewalk, he saw the girls lounging poolside. Annabeth was smearing sunscreen over Deirdre's shoulders—at least he thought it was Deirdre. The others were engaged in other poolside pursuits, reading or napping. One—Fitz thought it was Lisl—was actually in the water. As he passed, Annabeth looked up and caught his gaze under her floppy straw hat. Thinking suddenly of her breasts, partially hidden by her swimsuit, he clenched his teeth and looked away.

The doorman let him in without question. "Will you be seeing Mr. Collinwood this evening?" he asked.

"No, I will not," said Fitz, and went on his way.

"Very good, sir," the doorman called to his retreating back.

Yesterday the bodyguards had shown him the security room, where they monitored the cameras placed throughout the house. Fitz headed that way, surprising himself when he actually walked straight to the correct door.

Bo sat inside, watching the cameras. "Afternoon, Mr. Fitzcairn."

"Afternoon, Bo. I saw Mitch outside. He said to tell you hi."

Bo perked up immediately, according to plan. "Just now? Is he still there?"

"Maybe. I can stand in for you here for a minute if you want to go check."

"That'd be great, Mr. Fitzcairn. Thanks."

And, just like that, Fitz found himself alone with the bank of security cameras.

It took him only a few minutes to adjust the cameras outside the girls' bedroom. Annabeth's talk of the security system's blind spots had put the idea into his head. The door to the girls' room looked the same as the door to the bedroom next to it. He switched the equipment so the same image fed into both cameras, leaving the girls' bedroom door unwatched. With luck, no one would notice until it was too late.

He had just finished up and double checked the settings when Bo came back. "I must have missed him, but thanks anyway, Mr. Fitzcairn."

Fitz relinquished his chair. "Not a problem. Oh, by the way, I won't be surveilling from inside the house tonight, but I'll be setting up some equipment here and there."

"Trying some alternative methods?"

"Something like that."

"Well, good luck."

"Thanks."


THE GIRLS GENERALLY RETIRED about ten p.m., so at eight, Fitz slipped into their bedroom, undetected due to the camera switches.

He hadn't paid much attention to the room yesterday. With his eyes riveted to Annabeth's naked breasts, he'd registered little more than the fact the room was huge. Now he took a closer look.

It *was* big—it had to be, for all six beds to fit—but the ceiling seemed low, giving it a looming, oppressive feel. Each bed had its own gauzy canopy in a different color. One wall—the common wall between this room and the one next door—was completely occupied by a closet with mirrored doors. The rest of the room was surprisingly plain—a few generic watercolors on the walls between the beds, and a plush, plum-colored carpet on the floor.

As he'd suspected after Annabeth's performance yesterday, there was a small doorway in the back of the huge closet, hidden behind a display of shoes. A lot of shoes. It had been crudely but cleverly made, with a panel that slid in and out.

Never underestimate the ingenuity of prisoners, he thought, because that was exactly what these girls were. Carefully, he slid the panel out. It led to the bedroom next door, and in that closet was another, leading to the bedroom at the end of the hall. So that was how Annabeth had gotten to the blind spot at the end of the hallway.

He made his way back. Maybe another secret door could explain their nightly disappearances, but he doubted it. They were on the second floor, after all, so it wasn't as if they could have tunneled through the floor and ended up in Chicago or something.

But he checked, anyway. The second closet, the attached bathroom, under the six beds. Nothing.

Until he looked more closely at the last bed. And even then he wasn't sure what he'd found.

He was relatively certain this was Annabeth's bed, but that didn't explain what he was looking at. The headboard was intricately carved with vines and roses, in exquisite cherry wood. Among the carvings he found places his fingers fit, where he could barely feel tiny latches just out of reach of his thick, man's fingers.

There was something there, then. Something magical that he could probably activate if he knew how.

Fitz looked at his watch. Nine-thirty. Time to take up his post and prepare for the arrival of the six sisters.

ANNABETH KNEW HE WAS there. She wasn't sure how she knew, but the minute she walked into the bedroom, she sensed Fitzcairn's presence. A moment's "sniffing" while her sisters giggled and flopped down on their beds, told her exactly where he was—lurking on the other side of the secret door in the closet.

She said nothing to the others. Her silence didn't disturb any of them—they were used to her moodiness. And none of them were quite perceptive enough to realize the difference between her usual moods and this.

What was it about Fitz? Something strange. Something that reminded her of Eoin. Or the way Eoin had been in the beginning.

Something else the other girls didn't seem to notice— that Eoin had changed. Fitz had been wrong. They weren't about to find the sharp edge of the blade. Annabeth had already grasped that blade. But she didn't know how to rescue them. Maybe Fitz did. She'd done everything she could, but it hadn't been enough.

She looked around, at her five beautiful but somehow

dim sisters. It wouldn't be fair to say she, Annabeth, had been given all the brains, but she'd received something. Some kind of extra level of perception. Certainly they lacked the sense of foreboding that had plagued her even before she'd been forced into the dark pact with Eoin. They thought everything was just a game, and couldn't see the places where the magic had begun to darken.

Suddenly coming to a decision, she said, "We're not going tonight."

The sisters stopped talking almost in the same breath, staring at Annabeth.

"What?" said Catherine.

"Why?" said Lisl.

"I'm tired," Annabeth said. "I need sleep. Don't you?"

"But Eoin—" Greta protested.

"Said we should rest two nights out of every seven. This is one of those nights."

Missy shook her head. "Shouldn't we get his permission?"

"I know how to handle this. Leave it to me."

They accepted this with slow nods. Catherine and Deirdre seemed to mull over it for a short time, then they, too, returned to their pursuits of meaningless chatter and brushing of hair.

Annabeth gave them a few minutes to become completely absorbed, then went to the closet. She made her way silently to the back wall and moved the shoes.

"Hello, Fitz."

Fitz stared up at her in surprise, still holding his listening device up to his ear. "Who's Eoin?" he finally said.

Annabeth slipped through the door and closed it behind

her, sitting down next to him. "I'm surprised you could hear anything through all the shoes."

He lifted the listening device proudly. "This is a highly sophisticated and effective piece of equipment."

"I see." She hadn't answered his question and didn't intend to. "So you heard. There's nothing for you to do tonight. We're staying here."

"Yes. So I gather. Who's Eoin?"

"So you can go home. You're not needed."

He studied her face, and she saw something in his blue eyes that gave her a sudden reason to hope. She wasn't sure why, though. It was the strange intuition again, the sixth sense that had led her to Eoin in the first place.

"Why did you decide not to go?" he asked gently.

She might have told him if she knew the answer herself. But she wasn't sure. "Just . . . a feeling I had."

He nodded. "What kind of a feeling?"

"A feeling—" She broke off, unsure. "The feeling you might be able to help."

"How can I help if I don't know what's going on?"

"But you do. You said so this morning. The sharp edge of the blade. It's already come. I can see it but the others can't. I might survive it but they won't."

"So who is this Eoin?"

"I don't think the question is so much 'who' as 'what'. And I can't answer that."

Fitz reached out to touch her face, gently moving a strand of black hair away from her eyes. "Whoever he is, he's more than half fairy, and he's marked you."

Annabeth's eyes widened. "How did you know?"

"I can feel it. He marked you hard and I'm betting he

hurt you with it." He paused, studying her face. She swallowed, trying to keep her expression from betraying her. "I'm right, aren't I?"

"Yes."

"You never should have gotten mixed up in all this."

She nodded. "I know. But it was a place to breathe. You don't know what it's like . . ." She broke off, feeling the tears building behind her words and unwilling to shed them in front of this man she barely knew.

"Your father's an asshole," he said, and she laughed.

"You don't know the half of it."

"No, I probably don't." He brushed her hair back again, as if enjoying the feel of it. She liked the way his fingers moved in her hair. "The question remains, though—how can I help you?"

The answer came to her suddenly. It frightened her, but somehow she knew it was the only way. "Mark me."

Something in his blue eyes went hard. It was almost like fear. "You have no idea what you're asking."

"No, I think I do." She knew what it would take for him to mark her—to put a claim on her that would challenge Eoin. She also knew—or had some idea—what Eoin's response would be.

"He could kill you for it," Fitz said carefully. "He could kill me."

"Is there any other way to break free of him?"

Fitz considered. "There are ways. None quite so immediate or direct."

"So do you have any better ideas?"

"There are procedures. Rituals to sever this kind of binding. I could get the tools and we could do it tomorrow."

"It's a spell?"

"More or less."

It would be an easier way, and it tempted her. But she had learned some things, by paying attention while her sisters cavorted and exerted the illusory power Eoin allowed them. "It's my understanding, though, that such magic can only be countered by like magic."

"That's correct. But you could still make the statement."

He didn't want to do this, she realized. She didn't want him to, either, but she needed him to. "If the mark isn't completely countered, I'm still vulnerable to Eoin's control. You can't leave me in that position. It's even more dangerous than countering the mark in the first place."

Exasperation rising on his face, Fitz shoved both hands through his short-cropped, sand-colored hair. "I'm trying to spare you—"

"I know what you're trying to spare me from. Don't bother." She started to unbutton her blouse, chagrined to see her fingers trembling.

Fitz laid his hand on hers, stopping her. His voice was earnest and gentle. "You're right. It's the best way, the quickest way, and the most thorough way. But I don't know if I can do this to you."

She jerked her gaze up to his, too aware of the tears trembling against her eyelashes. "Of course you can. He did."

His hands moved to her face, cupping her cheeks. A tear escaped and he found it with his thumb, brushed it away. "It won't be the same."

"I hope not."

Even in the extra, unused bedrooms, like the one they

were in now, the closets were big. He led her that way, took her in and closed the door.

"Is it too dark?" he asked.

"No." The dark was better. As Fitz took her shoulders in his hands she was suddenly flooded with memories of Eoin and her body clenched up, influenced by a fear so primal she could barely feel it.

He put his arms around her from behind, pressed his lips against her ear. "It's all right. I'm not him."

She took a long, careful breath and let her body relax in his loose grasp. His breath moved against her ear and another primal urge rose, bringing her skin to life with arousal. He slid his hands down her body, outside her shirt, cupping her breasts, her belly, moving down until the edges of his hands rested against her thighs.

"Are you sure you want to do this?"

"No, but I'm sure I have to."

He let his hands move back up, retracing their path up her body. She shivered at his touch. His hands were big and gentle. She whimpered a little, unable to hold it back. She wasn't sure if it was fear or need.

"Why did you let him do it?" he whispered.

"He told me the other girls would die if one of us wasn't completely under his protection."

"He sensed your power." He was unbuttoning her blouse now, slipping his hands along her bare stomach. The warmth of his fingers trailed over her skin, soft. "He wanted control over that."

"Do you?" She tensed again, not as much this time, realizing it was a valid question.

"No. And I can mark you without owning you." His

hands had moved upward to cup her breasts. He had gone this far, explored her this much, and had yet to hurt her. Maybe she could trust him. Maybe this time her instincts had been right.

"He didn't offer that option." She was having a hard time now, making her voice heard. It wanted to stay in her throat and mewl and weep with the gentleness of his hands.

Fitz turned her nipples in his fingers, through her bra, and she jumped a little but didn't pull away. It felt good. He had magic hands even without the magic. "No," he said. "He wouldn't have. Because what he wants is what's good for him. He cares nothing for you."

"You can't care for me. You don't even know me."

"I'm here to protect you. Remember that."

His fingers slipped under the light, stretchy fabric of her bra. He found her nipples again and this time she gasped. It was even better without the barrier of the fabric. She could feel her heart pounding hard in the back of her throat, could almost taste its pounding. A heavy, demanding ache had settled between her legs.

Fitz's lips touched her ear. "I was right, wasn't I? He hurt you."

"Yes."

He muttered something she couldn't quite hear, but she was pretty sure it was, "fucking bastard." Then his lips teased the back of her ear again. "I won't hurt you. It has to be hard and fast, but it doesn't have to be brutal."

She nodded, still caught between fear and anticipation. Fear because the memory of Eoin's violation remained all too clear. Anticipation because Fitz's hands had already aroused something in her she'd never felt before. Something she wanted. And this was her choice, not a decision she'd been forced into by threats against her sisters. Taking a long breath, she made herself relax.

Fitz slid her shirt off her, unfastened her bra. His hand slid gently down her back. She flinched, though it didn't hurt. But she heard his intake of breath as he saw the rune Eoin had put there. He had hurt her that was certain. She'd screamed when he'd drawn the mark on her. Fitz would have to replace it with a new mark. She wondered if it would hurt this time, as well.

"It's okay," Fitz said. Gently, he pushed her forward as he unfastened her jeans, sliding them down. Moving to her hands and knees in front of him, she heard his zipper open, felt him shift behind her as he shed his own jeans.

He didn't take her right away as Eoin had. His hands grasped her buttocks, kneading gently, easing her. Her fear began to fade as her body responded to him. The heavy heat between her legs had become almost unbearable, but it wasn't pain.

It was need, she realized. She hadn't felt this before, and she wanted to hang on to it, experience its power. While her sisters had been happily cavorting with the fairy sprites, she had been raped and claimed by their master. No happy sex for Annabeth. Just pain and humiliation. Until now.

His fingers slipped down, touching the folds of her sex, sliding between. He slipped the ends of two fingers inside her and separated them a little, spreading her open, then slid more deeply, then again. She gasped, swallowed. Too much noise would not be good—her sisters might hear through the wall. But this was good. This was very good. She wanted more. More width, more depth. She felt like she could take his whole hand inside her.

He slid his fingers out. She made a sound of protest, to no avail. Other noises came from behind her—rustling and a soft grunt from Fitz. Unsure what they meant, she started to look back at him, but just then his cock pressed against her. She felt the full, hard length of it against her buttock, then he shifted. The thick, warm head pressed her sex open again, as his fingers had, and he paused there, just for a moment before sliding his full length deep into her.

She tensed automatically, clenching on him, but instead of hurting it felt better that way. More intense. She could feel every millimeter of his length, hot inside her. She moved her thighs a little apart, almost surprised to feel her body accept rather than reject him.

"Oh, God," she breathed. It actually felt good. Better than good.

"Are you okay?" he asked.

"Yes."

"Okay."

He seemed to want to finish it quickly, undoubtedly assuming she wanted it over and done with. But she found herself rocking back into him, meeting his thrusts as her body demanded more. Faster, deeper, harder—fire grew inside her and she wasn't sure she was allowed to let it go. Instinctively she reached back along her own body, let her fingers explore between the wide-open folds of her sex where she could feel his long shaft sliding, thrusting—

"Fitz—" she managed, her voice thick.

"Yes," he said. The gentleness of his voice surprised her. "It's all right."

So she let her instincts guide her, her fingers finding her clit and making circles around it until the pleasure grew so fiery hot she thought she might die with it. She'd never driven herself this high before, not in her own experimenting, not even with the sprites. Certainly not with Eoin, who had wanted only to hurt her. It felt so good she wanted to scream out her joy, but here silence was necessary so she had to content herself with a muffled, moaning keen.

Then the heat exploded inside her and she could no longer think about sound or silence or anything else. Fitz came too; she could feel him pulsing inside her. As he did, as she soared high, his hands moved on her back.

She was too involved in the spiraling orgasm to quite realize what he was doing, but suddenly a hot tingling covered her back as he swept his hands down it, then a sharper heat as he traced a new rune. But no pain. In fact, the sensation he brought with the spell took her that much higher, that much farther, and she could no longer hold back. The sound that came from her wasn't quite a scream, or a shout, or anything she'd ever heard out of her own mouth before, but there was no denying it was loud.

Fitz pulled her close, clapping a hand over her mouth, and they both collapsed to the floor. To her own surprise, Annabeth started to laugh.

"Good God, you're gonna wake the dead, much less your sisters," Fitz hissed, but there was more amusement in his voice than anger.

"I'm sorry. It's just . . . it was so different."

She turned toward him, and in the vague light could see a shadow of pain on his face.

"I should hope so," he said.

Suddenly uncomfortable, she drew away from him. Her body protested with a pulse of orgasmic aftershock as he slid out of her. Shuddering with it, she pulled her jeans back up, hunting down her sweater. She could barely think past the shivering of her own body. "What do we do now?"

"There's not much we can do until tomorrow night," he replied. "By then I should have some additional tools."

"What kind of tools?"

"Something that will let me go with you." He touched her, slid a gentle hand over her shoulders. "Are you all right?"

She nodded, but the hope that had been building in her suddenly found itself awash in skepticism. Because it was hard to believe he truly had answers when he seemed so unsure of what they might be.

# Chapter Three

FITZ WISHED HE COULD have given Annabeth a better summation of his plan, but he couldn't. He wouldn't even know for sure what he would be able to do tomorrow night until he saw Lily.

He thought about this as he drove home in the magic-thick hours of predawn. All the powers most of the human world knew nothing about gathered themselves to retire as the sun came up. He could almost hear them, if he concentrated hard enough. From time to time he could see them out of the corners of his eyes, fairies and nymphs and such skittering away to bed.

He wondered whom, exactly, this Eoin was. A fairy-type, he would guess, hitched into dark powers. His rune on Annabeth's skin had been branded on her rather than drawn, black and puckered and obviously inflicted with pain. Certainly he'd raped her in the process of marking her. That much had been obvious.

Whoever he was, Fitz wanted to kill him already. He didn't need to meet the man—seeing his work was enough evidence for judgment.

Eoin would be after him now too. He would know his control over Annabeth had been broken. Which meant tomorrow night would be unbelievably dangerous for both of them. He only hoped Lily would have what he needed to counter that danger.

At home, he collapsed into bed and fell almost immediately asleep. His dreams were dark and uncomfortable, but when the ringing of his doorbell interrupted them, he could remember only vague, shadowy images without details.

The bell had rung three more times, with increasing urgency, before he managed to stagger to the door and open it. Lily stood on the other side, holding a large box. She looked tired, dark circles framing her eyes.

"Are you okay?" Fitz asked.

"Good morning to you too." She sauntered past him into the apartment and laid the box on the couch. "Long night?"

"You have no idea." He pushed thoughts of Annabeth out of his mind, focusing his attention on Lily. "What about you?"

Her lips tightened, but the shadows in her eyes told him she wasn't going to tell him much. "The same."

A realization popped into his head. John. John was doing this to her. But what, exactly? He saw no bruises on her face, sensed nothing from her body—and he'd been well tuned to her body once, when they were sleeping together. If there had been bruises beneath her neat clothes, he would have known it. He also knew, somehow, that he needed to leave it alone, at least for now. Somehow, she was handling it.

So, reluctantly, he changed the subject. "Do you have something for me?"

"In the box."

He picked it up, laid it on the kitchen counter. It was wrapped in brown paper, tied with string. Patiently, he worried the knots loose. They weren't very tight, but it still took longer to untie them than it would have to hack through the string with a pair of scissors.

But when he pulled away the string and then the paper—carefully, without tearing it—Lily nodded her approval.

"Good. It likes to be treated carefully."

And such was the magical world, where you had to rely on some strange, sixth sense to figure out how to open a package without pissing off the contents.

The contents, in this case, proved to be a trench coat. Nondescript, tan, knee-length. It would make him look like a government agent.

He cast Lily a curious look over his shoulder.

"Put it on," she said.

He shrugged and did so. It fit as if made for him. He shifted his shoulders, letting it fall naturally down.

"How does it fit?" Lily asked.

"Perfectly."

"Good. It likes you."

He smoothed his hands down the front laps. The cloth was of exceptional quality. "So what does it do?"

"Go look in the mirror."

He quirked an eyebrow, then headed for the bathroom.

"Are you going?" Lily asked.

"Yes," he said, wondering at the ridiculous question. He was walking straight for the bathroom. Couldn't she see that?

But apparently she couldn't. Because when he positioned himself in front of the mirror, he couldn't see himself at all.

"Are you there?" called Lily.

"Yeah." He turned back and forth, but could see nothing in the mirror except the wall behind him.

"Where are you?"

"The bathroom." Fitz heard her footsteps heading toward him. "This is awesome, Lily. Where'd you get it?"

"It was my dad's. I've had it for ages. I had to get it out of storage. Do you think it'll help?"

"How could it not?" He took the coat off, watching himself reappear in the mirror. The illusion only worked on outside observers—he could still see himself, but the mirror couldn't see him and neither could Lily. "How does it work?"

"Something to do with light refraction."

"I'll take it tonight."

"Yes. Do as much as you can to finish this tonight. It can't go on much longer."

Folding the coat over one arm—it didn't seem to work unless he was properly wearing it—he studied Lily's face, the apprehension she was trying to hide. "What's up, Lily? Does this all have something to do with you?" He'd promised himself he wouldn't ask, but he couldn't stop the words once they'd started.

"Just leave it alone. That part of it, at least. Do your job and the rest will fall into place."

"Is it John?"

Her lips tightened. "I said leave it alone."

He nodded slowly. "All right. Thanks, Lily."


WHEN HE ARRIVED THAT night carrying the box, Annabeth was waiting for him. She sat by the pool, wearing a demure white pantsuit. She seemed awkward, no longer flaunting her sexuality.

Was she afraid of him now?

She beckoned him over to join her by the pool, watching the dying sunlight paint orange sparkles on the clear water. The air smelled vaguely of chlorine.

"What's in the box?" she asked.

Fitz glanced at it. It looked innocuous, still wrapped in brown paper as it was. "A trench coat."

"What for?"

"It's an artifact. It makes me invisible."

She nodded soberly. "You're coming with us tonight."

"Yes. I don't think your sisters need to know."

"You're right. They don't."

She looked toward the orange-streaked western sky. The expression on her face reminded him of a woman walking stoically toward her own death.

"I'll scope out the situation and figure out just how much trouble you're in, and what I need to do to get you out of it."

She nodded. "And what will I do?"

"Whatever you would normally do."

"That might not be possible." Her shoulders moved, the motion so small he almost missed it.

"Yes, he'll know I've overridden his mark, but there won't be anything he can do about it, particularly not while I'm there. His was a controlling mark. Mine is protective. It takes a much more powerful magic to override a protective mark."

She eyed him narrowly. "Just how powerful are you?"

"Powerful enough to save you and your sisters." He smiled wryly. "I hope."

She looked away, blinking rapidly. "Don't joke about it."

"I'm not." Hesitantly, he reached out to touch her shoulder. She flinched at first, but didn't pull away. "It'll be all right," he said.

WITH THE OVERCOAT ON, he followed her to the house, up the stairs to the girls' room. It was, he thought, handy not to have to answer any of the awkward questions that might have come up. Better yet, he didn't have to worry about getting Collinwood's permission to do what he was doing.

In the bedroom, Annabeth sat on the edge of her bed—the ornate one with the intricate, mysterious levers hidden in the headboard—and slid off her shoes. She looked toward the bedroom door, squinting as if in an attempt to see Fitz.

"Are you there?" she said.

"I'm here."

"You could take the coat off for a bit. We have an hour or so before the others come."

He nodded, then realized she couldn't see that, and shrugged out of the overcoat. Visible again, he hung the coat over the footboard. For whatever reason, the footboard didn't disappear. Magical artifacts were fickle in more ways than one.

She watched him as he reappeared, then looked away, her hands folded primly in her lap. She looked so young. Young, vulnerable and wounded. He hadn't thought of her as a child since he'd first laid eyes on her, but she suddenly looked her age, reminding him she was only twenty.

Her gaze shifted, fixing on the wall opposite where he sat. Fitz looked that way, as well. She seemed to be staring at one of the watercolors on the wall, a landscape painted in misty pastels, but he could tell by the look in her eyes that she didn't really see it.

"What would you ask of me?" she said. Her voice was so soft he wasn't sure, at first, that he'd actually heard it.

He shrugged. "Nothing right now. I'll need your help later. Your support—" Then he saw the bleakness on her face and suddenly understood what she was asking. His heart wrenched inside him. "Annabeth—nothing. I told you, it was a protective rune, not a controlling rune. And if I could have marked you in any other way, I would have done it. It's just the power in the sex—"

She flinched and he stopped. Anger rose bitter to the back of his throat. He wanted to kill this Eoin. Obviously he was a magic user of some power and no scruples.

Tears had risen in Annabeth's eyes and he wanted to touch her, but didn't want to seem to be forcing himself on her in any way, even one as trivial as a comforting touch to the shoulder. She had been wounded too deeply for him to be anything but utterly cautious.

Gathering her courage, Annabeth looked at Fitz. She

hoped she'd understood his meaning—that what he'd done to her had actually constituted freedom for herself, rather than trading one master for another. It seemed he did mean that, though. She felt no compulsion of any kind from him, no intrusion. In Eoin's presence she'd sometimes wondered if he controlled even her breathing, the beating of her heart.

So he would ask nothing of her. She wondered, barely bold enough to form the thought, if she could ask something of him. But if she asked and he said yes, would she be able to go through with it?

She swallowed hard. "May I ask something of you?"

His answer came without hesitation. "Of course."

She opened her mouth but couldn't make herself speak the words. Her mouth snapped closed and she closed her eyes, gathering herself. Perhaps it would be easier to speak to the backs of her eyelids. As she struggled, Fitz remained silent. She wished she could reach out to him, take hold of his solid strength for support, but even that was too hard right now.

"I—" she started, then swallowed again, her mouth so dry it was a wasted effort. "I've never been made love to before. There were the sprites, of course, but only a few times, until Eoin—" She broke off. He knew what Eoin had done to her, which was a relief, since she didn't want to have to tell him.

But to go on, to ask the rest of it . . . She gripped her hands together tightly, until she could feel her own pulse beating in her fingers. "I need that, I think. To be truly free from him, I need that. Lovemaking. Not magic making." She forced herself to open her eyes and look at him. "Can you give me that?"

He considered, his expression gratifyingly sober. "You said we have an hour?"

"At least."

"Then yes, I can give you that."

He reached out and touched her cheek, and for a moment she thought he would kiss her, but he drew his hand back. "You need to lead this," he said. "It won't be right for you unless you're in charge."

"I don't . . . I don't know what to do."

"Of course you do."

She felt tears rising and wasn't sure if she was afraid, embarrassed or just overwhelmed. She blinked them back, biting her lip.

He took her face gently between his hands. "It's okay. It's okay."

Annabeth closed her eyes. It *was* okay. She made herself think back, returning to the times when this had all felt like a game. When it had been about getting away from the cage their father had forced upon them, and not about the other kind of slavery imposed on them by Eoin.

The skin on her back grew warm suddenly. She stiffened at first, then remembered the rune there was no longer Eoin's controlling mark. The other mark's heat had always felt sick, like an infection growing under her skin. This was liquid warmth, alive, like the comforting warmth of the sun, or the stimulating warmth of desire.

As the warmth grew, she opened her eyes, trying to shake free of its intensity. Then she looked at Fitz, and realized the growing warmth would take her exactly where she needed to go.

She let it carry her to him, let it guide her mouth to his.

At the firm press of his lips, she melted into him, caught as thoroughly in the heat as she'd ever been caught in Eoin's compulsion. But she wanted this. Wanted it more than she'd wanted her own freedom. Or perhaps wanted it because it *was* part of her freedom.

She pressed more deeply into him and he responded, his tongue thrusting hard into her mouth, his hands coming up to pull insistently at her shirt. Impatient, she ripped it off over her head herself, tossing it across the room.

He peeled off her bra and she simply—let go. Something inside her recognized him as a safety zone. She lost herself in a burning flood of lust, tearing at his shirt, his jeans. His skin felt hot under her hands, against her own skin as she pressed her bare breasts against his chest. The rough textures of his hair against her nipples brought them tautly erect. Desire shot from their tips straight down, pooling between her legs. She shifted back and forth, letting the hair on his chest further stimulate her. His hands slid down her body, pushing her pants down. She took a quick, sideways step out of them.

Freedom, she thought vaguely. This was what it really meant. To be somewhere completely safe, and to allow yourself to let go. Even her voice had been freed, rising and falling with the movement of her desire, wordless but the most expressive utterances that had ever come out of her mouth.

Fitz let her lead, but not at a loss of his own responsiveness. She tore at his jeans, wedged the button free and jerked the zipper down. His cock lunged forward into her hands as she pulled him free from his clothes. The hot, steely erection slid through her fist. She dropped her head and tasted it.

Heat, and salt, a sticky drop of fluid that slicked under her tongue. She dipped her head and took it all, all of his cock in her mouth, until the hair that ringed the base of it tickled against her lips. She held there a moment, listening to his harsh, guttural breathing, feeling the hard length of him jut against the back of her throat.

She controlled this. All of it. Smiling, she let him move, up and down, in and out of her mouth. She shaped her lips and tongue to the movement of his cock, wringing the deepest, most torturously aroused sounds out of him that she could.

There must have been something to the bond they'd made last night, because somehow she knew, from a sound in his throat or from a hitch in his breathing, when to let him go. She ringed thumb and forefinger behind the head of his cock and squeezed gently. Looking up, she noticed the tips of his ears had gone red. He had his eyes clamped shut, as if on excruciating pain. She smiled.

The color in his ears faded after a moment and he opened his eyes. "Go."

She lifted herself over him, spread her legs across his thighs and took him inside her. A long, shuddering moan came from her as he drove deep. He echoed the sound.

She couldn't comprehend the intensity. It brought tears to her eyes. She was neither possessing nor being possessed. She was taking him in as he accepted the gift of entry. This was such power, she thought. And like the magic, she'd stumbled into some part of it without understanding what she did. This was the real thing. It humbled her. If she had only known this was the thing to pursue, this joining, melding. Not just as a symbolic escape from her father's control.

Blinking back tears of realization and sheer ecstasy, she moved on him, lifting, falling, feeling his deep penetration, the hot friction of his withdrawal. Sensation rose and spiraled within her, forming a tight, spinning knot just above the place of their joining. Faster and faster, hotter, spinning in violent red and orange until it exploded and crashed through her body. It took her so hard she could make no sound, though her mouth came open in an "O" of startled joy.

He had been there too, she realized, when the endless, rising moment finally descended. Tears rolled hot down her face and she smiled at him.

"Was that what you were looking for?" he asked, his voice a satiated murmur.

She nodded. "It was beautiful."

They still had time. Fitz would have loved to spend the entire hour making love to her, but she had curled up against him, head against his chest, and was obviously in cuddle mode. So he decided on another approach.

"How did it happen?"

She shifted against him, nestling. "We wanted out so badly. Out of here. It was awful. Before Mother died, we went to school, played with our friends, then suddenly we couldn't anymore. We were already broken up about losing Mom . . ." She trailed off. He waited. He heard nothing from her—no weeping, not even a hitch in her breath, but she was still for a few minutes before she went on. "Then I started seeing him. Dreaming him."

"Eoin?"

"Yes."

It was Fitz's turn to still himself, reining in his anger.

What Annabeth described was a horrendous misuse of power. Eoin could be executed for it, if anyone could manage to put him on trial. That was the tricky part. No one in the magic-using community ever wanted to pass judgment on anyone else. It was a free-for-all world, and its inhabitants liked it that way.

To his surprise, Annabeth said, "Are you all right?" She was more attuned to him than he'd expected, or perhaps the rune had gone deeper than he'd meant.

"I'm fine," he said, after taking a long breath to be sure it was true. "Go on."

"He told me things. At first I thought it was just a dream, but then he started daring me to try things. He would demonstrate a spell and dare me to perform it when I was awake. Small things. How to make the bodyguards hear strange noises in another room. Picking locks. Calling birds to the window and charming them to sit still in my hand. Harmless enough. Then he asked if we wanted to meet him."

"Did any of your sisters have these dreams?"

"No. Everything came through me. He said I was special, that I had power."

"You do."

She looked up at him, frowning. "Then why wouldn't the others? We're identical."

"Which is extremely unusual, if you didn't know already. Most fertility experts would say impossible."

"Obviously not impossible. We're here."

"Most fertility experts don't take magic into account."

"No, I suppose they wouldn't."

His hand slipped over her hair, fingers combing gently

through it. He convinced himself it was to comfort her, but it was more for him. Because he wanted to touch her, to experience her textures. Because the soft silkiness of her hair between his fingers calmed him.

"I've seen this kind of thing before, but usually with twins or triplets. Some kind of magic influences the development of the fetuses—often that's what causes the egg to split in the first place. But for some reason the magic attaches to only one of the resulting children, leaving the others with little or no ability."

"So magical ability isn't inherited?"

"It doesn't seem to be. It seems to be more of a random, free-floating kind of thing. Though I'm more inclined to believe the direct intervention theory."

"Direct intervention?"

"A developed magic user uses his or her power to affect an unborn child. Or infect, depending on how you want to look at it. Some powerful users have been known to set up breeding programs, causing little protégés to be born here and there." He paused, letting his implications sink in.

"So Eoin—" She didn't finish the thought. He didn't blame her.

"It's entirely possible. He sounds like the type who would."

"But why us?"

He considered his answer, decided on the truth. "He probably sensed potential in you shortly after conception. He would have been looking for someone like you, and when he found you, he spelled your mother. The splitting of the original single embryo was undoubtedly an unplanned side effect. These things can be tricky."

Annabeth was silent for a time. When she spoke again, it was to resume her story.

"We decided to meet him. He told me how to set up a doorway, and I did as he said."

"The little levers on your headboard."

"Yes. And we met him, and he showed us such wonderful things, and then—" She stopped.

"Then he made you his captives, and you were back where you started."

"Basically."

He tightened his arms around her, kissing her forehead. "Don't worry. I'll do everything I can."

If she noticed he hadn't actually promised anything, she was kind enough not to point that out. But her hand strayed down his body to touch the deep, ugly scar on his thigh.

"It didn't kill me," he said, "and I saved her."

She eased her hand back, but not without brushing his cock on the way. It was ready for more action, but there wasn't time.

"That was all I wanted to know," she said.

# Chapter Four

B Y THE TIME THE other girls arrived, Fitz was sitting on the floor next to Annabeth's bed, securely wrapped in the trench coat. The mirror on the opposite wall reassured him that the coat was functioning properly. While Annabeth tweaked the covers on her bed, which they'd remade together, he waved his arms and made faces at the mirror, unable to see any of it.

"I can hear you flapping," Annabeth said, and just then the bedroom door flew open, admitting the other five girls. Fitz hurriedly crossed his arms over his chest and held still.

"Are we going tonight?" Fitz wasn't sure which sister this was. Catherine, maybe.

Whoever it was, she didn't seem to see the bleakness in Annabeth's eyes. "Yes. We're going tonight."

The other girls, equally oblivious, clapped and giggled and ran for the closets. Moments later an argument broke out between Lisl and Deirdre over a sleek, strapless, pink gown.

"All they care about," Annabeth muttered. Fitz heard her—he doubted the others could. He wanted to take her hand, to comfort her a little, but didn't dare in his current state.

"All right," Annabeth said then, louder this time, and with an edge of anger. "Hurry up. We don't have all night."

Her fear was apparent on her face, at least to Fitz, who saw it in her compressed lips and the thin line down the middle of her brow. She, too, went to the closet, but pulled out a dress from the far end, where the other girls weren't wrangling. The dress was straight and black, the kind every woman was supposed to have in her closet.

She held it up a moment, looking at it, then turned around and tossed it on the bed. With a glance over her shoulder at her sisters, who were arguing now over a filmy blue garment, she peeled her shirt off in a sleek, fluid movement. She hadn't put her bra back on after they'd made love, and her breasts bobbed back into place, firm and pink, the nipples pouting.

Fitz drew in a breath. Annabeth wasn't looking at him but her lips curled in a satisfied smile and he knew she'd heard him.

She took off her jeans in the same fluid way, but more slowly. Her gaze was fixed somewhere on the floor, but awareness of her audience colored every movement.

Easing the jeans down her hips, she exposed the triangle of her lavender silk panties. Then she turned her back to him and pushed the jeans to her ankles, bending over until her fingers touched the floor.

"God, you're killing me here." Fitz mouthed the words, not even daring to whisper. She'd cocked her thighs just so, giving him a clear view of her silk-covered sex. He couldn't help imagining himself sinking into it from behind. All the way. Pumping . . .

His hand had strayed to the steely lump in his own jeans and he snatched it away. If there was one thing he had no time for right now, it was jacking off.

She turned toward him again, stepping out of her jeans, reached for the dress and dropped it over her head. With sleek, sinuous movements, she wriggled her way into it.

The dress was long enough to cover the essentials, but only barely. He could have bent her over a table and taken her without moving the miniscule skirt at all. But, he realized when he dragged his brain back out of his crotch, that wasn't why she'd chosen it. Though the neckline was sedate, the back dipped down into the curve of the small of her back. The rune was completely exposed.

Across the room, the other sisters had finally agreed on wardrobe choices. They, too, were undressing now, Fitz noticed. Funny, he thought. They were identical, down to the last detail as far as he could see, but only Annabeth drew his eye.

When they had all changed, they gathered in a clump next to Annabeth's bed and waited for guidance. Realizing they would be leaving soon, Fitz got to his feet. Good thing he was invisible—that way he didn't have to worry about hiding his boner.

"Is everybody ready?" Annabeth asked, her voice trembling.

"Are you okay, Annie?" Greta asked.

Annabeth seemed surprised. Fitz understood why—her sisters weren't the most perceptive women in the world.

"I'm fine. Great," said Annabeth. "I'm just tired, that's all." She looked at Fitz. He nodded automatically, encouragingly, forgetting she couldn't see him.

She must have sensed something from him, though, for she squared her shoulders, firmed her mouth and knelt in the middle of her bed.

He couldn't see what she did, exactly, but he felt the graduated release of power as she manipulated the levers on the headboard. A blue, glowing oval grew above the bed. A portal. The color and the feel of the power told Fitz they would be traveling into the depths of Faerie. He'd suspected as much.

When the oval had reached its full height—a few inches over six feet, and nearly touching the ceiling—Annabeth turned to face her sisters.

"I need to go just ahead of you tonight," she said. "Wait fifteen seconds before you follow."

She gave no explanation, but there was no question or protest. Fitz had a feeling she could have told them to wait a full minute, then walk through the portal backward on their hands and the reaction would have been the same.

But he knew what she intended. She threw him another look before she stepped onto the bed and through the blue, shimmering light. Immediately, he followed her up onto the bed and through the portal.

The precision and power of the magic surprised him. Whoever this Eoin was, he'd obviously been efficient in his directions to Annabeth. Based on what she'd told him, she'd constructed this portal herself, with his guidance. Eoin had probably reinforced it from his end after the initial construction, but for that to work well, the channels had to have been clearly and cleanly made in the first place. It was impressive work. Pity a man with such skill chose to use it for evil.

It begged the question, though—how the hell was he, going to defeat someone with this kind of ability?

The magic of the portal enveloped him, everything around him becoming one with its crystalline blue. It pulled him forward, like a moving walkway in a tunnel of clear sky. Ahead of him he couldn't quite see but could sense Annabeth. She was so frightened. He felt that suddenly, like a wash of cold water against his face. She was terrified.

Then he saw the dark at the end of the bright tunnel, saw Annabeth silhouetted against it for a moment, then he, too, had reached the end of the blue light. He took a last step forward and he was there. His feet on solid ground again, the surroundings no longer blue but brown, gray, red, orange. And smoky.

One of the other sisters arrived behind him and he moved quickly out of the way to stand on Annabeth's other side. He had to stay alert. It would be too easy to forget his invisibility and accidentally give himself away.

Annabeth looked back toward him, toward her sisters, her eyes narrowing as Lisl, the last, appeared out of the portal's back door. The blue oval shrank, then, to a circle barely larger than Fitz's head.

"Just follow me," Annabeth whispered. "Don't mind the others."

As the blue light faded behind him, Fitz saw that they had exited the portal in a sort of alcove along the edge of a wide, open room. It looked as if it were supposed to be a dance floor, but little, if any, dancing was going on.

Or perhaps that depended on your definition of dancing. Bodies tangled with bodies all over the wide expanse. Standing, prone, supine, or leaning against the walls, but none of them alone. The whole place reeked of sex.

The five other girls, giggling, ran out to join the fun, but Annabeth stayed with Fitz.

"So this is the place," he said, trying to keep the distaste out of his voice. From their vantage point in the alcove, he scanned the room. It was about fifty feet wide, surrounded on all four walls with alcoves similar to the one they stood in now. Some of the alcoves had doors. He wondered if any of them led out of the room. It could make a difference, if he had to defend himself or any of the girls.

The walls were ornate, with richly colored, heavy curtains decorating the empty walls between every other door. Some kind of generic, elevator-type music played in the background, barely audible over the sounds of the general orgy. And the orgy, he noticed, had its limits. There was a wide, circular area in the middle of the room where no one went. Odd.

Annabeth's lips were thin, her nose slightly scrunched, as she said, "Yeah, I'm afraid so."

Fitz had seen this kind of place before, of course. He didn't think there was a magic-user on the planet that hadn't. It was the best sort of sex club, because there was no danger of any sort of attachment. Because none of the sex partners were real.

They looked real enough. Human in every detail, sight, smell and touch, and he knew this from firsthand experience. A long-ago experience, but still an experience.

Fitz couldn't help looking as Annabeth led the way across the wide room. It was hard to tell which member of each couple was human and which wasn't, just by looking. Fitz, in those years of his misspent youth, had learned to tell by something not quite smell, not quite telepathy. It was important to develop that skill. Because heaven forbid you should find yourself actually fucking a human being.

He stepped gingerly among the writhing couples, careful not to compromise his invisibility by stepping on anyone. It was hard not to be distracted. Here he could simply watch as a fairy sprite's long cock plunged in and out of the slick, open pussy of a human woman. On the other side, another sprite squealed with pleasure as a human man sucked greedily at her clit.

Then there was the four woman chain, tongues and fingers doing things to red and pink labia that even Fitz had never thought possible. And the inevitable man-on-man coupling—three or four of them tonight that he could see, plus a threesome near the opposite wall. That he didn't care to watch.

Annabeth seemed intrigued, though, and he caught her watching the nearest male couple as one enthusiastically penetrated the other, who moaned with equal absorption. It made Fitz wince just to think about it, but Annabeth's face had flushed red.

"Where are we going?" Fitz said, mostly so she would quit looking and he could quit thinking about what she was looking at.

She jerked her attention away, but didn't seem embarrassed by her interest. "I'm going to see Eoin. I want you to come with me."

"He'll go nuts when he sees the rune."

She shook her head. "He won't hurt me. Not yet."

"Why not?"

"He'll want to use me to get to you."

It made sense. "Don't forget—I'm there if you need me."

"I won't." She hesitated, her gaze drawn again to the action around her. "Fitz," she said suddenly, and this time she did seem flustered.

"Yes."

"Would you do that for me?"

He looked where she was looking. A heterosexual couple this time. The man was handcuffed to a pole, one of a cluster on one side of the wide room. He hung there while a woman knelt in front of him. She traced her hands up and down his body, her fingernails trailing over his skin. She was casting magic, the movement of her hands leaving lines of glowing power behind.

He threw his head back. He looked tired, drained, yet when she cupped his flaccid cock in her glowing hands, he bucked and moaned and smiled as his erection rose again.

Fitz had assumed the man was a sprite, being used by a human woman with fantasies of domination. But, watching, he suddenly realized the man was the human. The female sprite, who had now taken his cock into her mouth and was in the process of driving him to what appeared to be the edge of his endurance, was doing exactly what the man wanted her to, no more. Because that was what sprites did.

The sprite let go of the man, his cock bobbing out of her mouth, and turned her back to him, bending over. He looked down at her with a fierce grin and pumped himself into her. Hissing with pleasure, the sprite rode herself backward onto him until he came with a howl.

Fitz swallowed, not bothering to fight the huge erection he'd just developed, since no one could see it, anyway.

"Would you?" Annabeth prodded.

He looked right at her, and for a moment it was as if she could see him. "I would do anything for you Annabeth," he said, his voice thick with desire. "Anything you asked me to."

She held perfectly still for a moment, seemingly overwhelmed by his answer. Then a small smile curved her lips. Holding herself with just a bit more firm confidence, she went on.


IT WAS STRANGE, ANNABETH thought, to know Fitz was with her and yet not be able to see him. She could sense his presence, almost, in a strange way she didn't understand and wasn't sure she believed in. But she couldn't *see* him.

Still, as she approached Eoin's rooms at the back of the orgy room, she felt different than she ever had before, making this trek.

She didn't feel afraid. Perhaps it was the knowledge of Fitz's presence, the not quite tangible sense of him that seemed to linger in a vague pressure at the base of her skull. Or the equally vague warmth low on her back, where he'd placed his mark.

Or maybe it was just because of what she knew now that she hadn't before—that Eoin was evil, that he had used her and continued to use her. That he was a poor example of what magic could be. And that she herself had power, and someone now whom she could trust to help her use it. Who would help her and her sisters escape their current predicament.

Annabeth forced her attention away from the rutting couples on the floor. There was a lurid fascination there, as well as a desire to join them, but it came countered with revulsion. Tonight the two warred within her.

Then she remembered what she'd shared with Fitz and both desire and revulsion changed to pity. The humans out there, impaling and being impaled by fairy sprites who were no more real than the air, had missed the most important aspect of sex. The human aspect. The part that connected one soul to another.

If she'd known that six months ago, if her father had allowed her to live her life instead of locking her up and forbidding her human contact of any kind, she wouldn't be here right now. She could have avoided Eoin's snares, seen them for what they were. But her father, trying to protect her, had instead left her vulnerable, a victim of her own ignorance, her own curiosity, and her own stubborn need for freedom.

She could blame it on her father all she wanted, she supposed, but that didn't change the fact that she was here, now, in need of rescuing. And that, by sheer coincidence, her father's continued meddling had provided her with a rescuer.

She paused at the door, laid her hand on the knob. She could sense Eoin's presence behind the door, but that sense was a shadow of what it had once been, and a shadow to what she now felt from Fitz. She drew a long, slow breath, allowing herself a moment to bask in that realization. Eoin no longer held power over her.

Fitz's invisible hand slid softly over her shoulder. "Go on," he whispered. "I'm here. You'll be all right."

She tossed a glance over her shoulder, aware somehow of exactly where his eye line was even though she couldn't see him. "I know." She tightened her hand on the knob, determined. "Thank you."

She pushed the door open. Eoin stood on the other side, lighting a cigarette. A red ember came to life on the tip of it as he cupped it protectively with his hand.

Annabeth came in and stood just inside the door, looking at him. She'd never felt like this in his presence before. She actually felt her chin rise, haughty, and a small smile curved her lips.

Eoin's black eyes narrowed. He pulled at his cigarette, exhaled a cloud of gray smoke.

"If you would close the door," he said quietly.

Annabeth did, but not before making sure Fitz was in the room. Gently, clicking the latch, she turned again to face Eoin.

He still intrigued her baser senses, even now that she knew who he was. He was tall and lithe, his body like a dancer's, his hair and eyes black, his mouth framed by a neatly trimmed Vandyke beard. His long black hair was tied back at the nape of his neck in a careless ponytail.

"I know," he said, his voice still soft and without menace. "I knew as soon as you came out of the portal."

She said nothing. It seemed unwise to provoke him.

"Whatever possessed you?" he went on. "You were safe under my protection."

She spoke without thinking. "You hurt me. He didn't."

He let out a short bark of laughter. "A man of character."

He took a drag on the cigarette. The tip glowed and its small, orange light felt suddenly menacing. "In this place, character is rarely an advantage."

"I'll tell him you said that."

"Please do. Tell him also that I look forward to seeing him tomorrow night. He has taken what was mine and I intend to take it back." His voice thinned and lowered as he spoke, reflecting the anger and affronts that now lurked in his eyes. "Your sorcerer friend has no idea what he's gotten himself into."

*Oh, but I do believe he does.* She said nothing, only inclined her head to him, fighting the thin smirk trying to curve her mouth. She knew her cockiness was premature, and he proceeded to prove it to her.

"Before you go, I should like to take a look at his handiwork," Eoin said. He set his cigarette down in the ashtray on the table and came toward her. She could feel Fitz's mark on her back again, more intensely even than she had before. Each separate line seemed to burn into her skin, yet the sensation wasn't really pain. It was more like an intense awareness. Much as it had been when Fitz had placed the mark on her in the first place.

Eoin stopped mere inches away from her, so close she could smell the stench of smoke on his breath. He lifted a hand and trailed his fingers down her cheek.

"I never counted on losing you," he said, his voice quiet and seemingly without anger. "I never dreamed you'd go out and find yourself a protector. I didn't think you had that knowledge."

Silent, she held herself still against the assault of his careful touch. He couldn't hurt her, she was certain of that.

Never again could he do to her what he had done before, trying to break her spirit, her will, trying to gain control of the power she hadn't known she had. This was the only thing she understood about the situation—that in that way, at least, she was safe.

His fingers trailed down her face to her throat, down to the edge of the neckline of her dress, down, until he cupped her breast. She shrank from the touch. She'd thought—hoped—he could no longer touch her in that way. Holding herself rock-still, refusing to let him see her revulsion, she tried to will his fingers to burst into flames. What good, after all, was this supposed power if she couldn't do useful things like that?

There were no flames forthcoming, but an odd expression appeared on his face and he drew his hand away.

"A strong protector too, it seems, or at least a knowledgeable one." His voice remained calm but she detected a hint of displeasure in it. Disappointment.

Then, abruptly, he flattened his palm against the small of her back, pressing hard, so that she lost her balance for a moment and took a half step forward into him. His chest pressed against her breasts, and she could feel the jut of his cock pushing into her stomach.

She wanted to strike him, or at the very least to push away, but the memory of his power over her stayed her hand. The expression on his face reinforced this decision. His hand shook against her back, and she could feel each line of the rune picked out, clean and hot, on her skin. As she watched his face, from far closer than she'd hoped she'd ever have to be again, pain spread through his features. Suddenly, he jerked his hand away. She stumbled backward, catching her balance after a few steps.

"Get out of here," he said, his voice a low growl. "Get out of here now. Next time I see you, I want to see him with you."

Obediently, she left the room. Somehow she knew Fitz was with her, knew he slid out the door just ahead of her when she hesitated there, oh-so briefly, the door open, as if she'd considered saying something but changed her mind at the last moment.

Just outside the door, she felt a hand close on her wrist. Startled, she looked down and saw nothing. Fitz's voice whispered in her ear, "Did he hurt you?"

"No."

"Is there someplace we can go? Where we won't be seen? I need to talk to you."

Annabeth smiled a little. Anywhere they went, he wouldn't be seen. But she knew what he meant. It might look strange if she stood out in the open, apparently talking to herself. "This way."

Along the back wall of the big room were a number of doors, leading to small rooms. Occasionally a couple—or a threesome or foursome—would use one of the rooms rather than join the vast orgy. Annabeth had never really under-stood why. It seemed a bit silly to look for privacy here. But if two humans hooked up, for some reason they often chose to retire to one of the side rooms. And Eoin had taken her to one of these rooms to mark her.

She took Fitz there now, but to a different room. She re-membered exactly which room Eoin had used, and she would never go there again.

He closed the door. It slammed shut seemingly of its own accord, harder than strictly necessary.

"Fitz—"

His hands closed on her shoulders. Reflexively, she closed her eyes, making it not quite so disconcerting when his mouth found hers, hard and insistent. His tongue shoved past her teeth, his body bearing hers toward the wall.

His hand pressed against her lower back, covering the rune. It sprang to life under his touch, hot again, searing along every line. It didn't hurt, though. It was fire, but not destructive fire. His other hand grabbed the hem of her skirt, yanking it up. He shoved his hand under her panties, clasping her buttock.

She opened her eyes, but it was too strange. She could feel his hard body pressed against her, see her own breasts move as they shifted and mounded against his chest, but she couldn't see him. She shoved at him—at the solid air pushing against her—and he relented.

"Fitz, don't."

He pulled her back to him. "It's the magic. I can smell him all over you. It's making me crazy."

"Take off the coat, Fitz. I need to see you."

"If I take it off, he'll know I'm here."

"Eoin? He won't be able to see you. He's in the other room."

"He'll sense me. I know he felt my signature in the rune."

"Then we should go back home."

"No. He tried to wipe my mark when he touched you back there. I have to be sure it's still at full strength."

"At home. We can do that at home." She backed away, trying to get some sense of where he was. "Besides, you said you wanted to talk."

"We're talking." His voice came from closer than she'd expected.

"Fitz, you're scaring me." She was still shaking from the encounter with Eoin, and now Fitz seemed to be taking over Eoin's role. She wouldn't let him control her the way Eoin had. She would kill him first.

She could hear his breathing now, fast and heavy and just a little farther away now. Gingerly, she reached toward him, until her fingertips found the edge of the coat.

"It's this place, isn't it?" she said. "The magic here, and all the sex everywhere." Her fingers slid over the coat's invisible fabric. It had a soft, silky texture, and felt almost as if it were coated with something, a light oil that didn't come off onto her skin. "And you're wrapped in magic. Is it that? Is it all those things coming together to make you crazy?"

"I want you." Would it have seemed less manic, less threatening, if she could have seen his face? He was close again now; she could hear his breathing.

"Not like this." She traced her fingers up the edge of his lapel, feeling the rapid rise and fall of his chest, the erratic beating of his heart under her hand. He stood unmoving.

She let her hand move upward, toward his face, until she cupped the curve of his jaw. She saw nothing under her hand, but her fingers found the vague prickle of stubble against her palm, the thicker sideburn just in front of his ear, the curves and textures of the ear itself. She touched his closed eyes, feeling his lashes, outlined the strong jut of his nose, the rounded plane of his forehead, and then combed gently into his hair. Heat grew under her palm. Living heat, a moving layer of it between his skin and hers.

"Do you feel this?" she whispered.

His head moved under her fingers as he nodded. "Magic."

"Your magic?"

"No. It's yours." His face moved sideways a little, his cheek nestling into the palm of her hand. "Use it."

And just like that, she was in control. Not because she had taken it, or forced it upon him. Because she had asked for it, and he had granted it. He was as much in her power as the man outside had been in the control of the fairy sprite that'd cuffed him to the pole.

She caressed his cheek again, and this time a vague wash of light covered his skin, following her touch. Where the light passed, she could see him for a few moments at a time, as her hands moved and the light faded. The strain on his face was obvious; he was holding back.

"You want me?" she said. It wasn't as strange now, with the light illuminating him, even if only partially, and with the knowledge of her own power, of his willingness to let her lead and control, the trembling of fear was gone.

"You want me?" she whispered again. "Take me."

He grabbed her shoulders and whirled her around, yanked her panties down out of his way. One hand slapped down on top of the rune as he separated her thighs with the other, then penetrated her hard, his cock riding high and hard and all the way inside her.

She clutched at the wall to keep her balance. His hand on her back hurt as he flashed magic into her again. All the lines of the rune lit up in fire on her skin. The fire wrapped around her, pooling between her legs where he slammed in and out of her. Certainly no gentle lovemaking this time, but that was all right because she'd had that already, before they'd come here. He'd shown her that magic—this was something else.

He was taking her, driving into her, because he was crazy with her. That was her power, or part of it. To make him want her this badly. So badly he would toss aside his civilized veneer and just fuck her. Part of it was the magic, she knew, but the rest was pure lust.

And still, it was hers to control. She reached back between her legs and caught him by the balls. He stopped. She looked for a moment at her hand, apparently cupping air, at her own sex, spread wide open because he was still inside her, regardless of whether she could see him. Then she let a trace of magic loose, to cover his skin for a split second, so she could see the base of his cock protruding from her body, see the lump of his scrotum, clasped in her hand.

"The rune," she said. "Is it good? Still strong?"

"Yes." His voice was strained.

"Then turn me around."

He took a long, slow breath, regaining control. She let him go as he drew back, sliding out of her. "Where?" he said.

"On the table."

Of course there was a table. And a futon thing tossed on the floor, and some kind of weird semi-gynecological rack that gave her the willies just to look at it. The table was the best. Sturdy and flat, with some pillows on it here and there.

He turned her around to face him and picked her up, his hands around her waist. She highlighted him with magic, shedding blue light across his wide shoulders, but still she had to clutch at him to reassure herself he was really there, supporting her as he brought her to the table and set her down.

It was exactly the right height, as she'd estimated. Just the right height for him to butt his thighs against the edge of the table and take her as she cocked her legs up over his arms. He flattened a hand in the middle of her back to hold her, and came into her again, not as hard this time. And he kissed her this time, which was strange but hot and soft and hard all at the same time, so she closed her eyes and felt it turn her wet and willing.

When she opened them again, she laid her hands against his cheeks and let the blue light cover the planes of his face because she wanted to see his mouth, his eyes. There was more than lust there, in the pale crystal blue, in the set of his thin mouth. More than a need to ravage her. She'd seen it before, back in her bedroom. It was something achingly needy but also soft and wanting. Love, perhaps, but that was too large to even consider right now.

He kissed her again and let himself move again inside her. She looked down to see the movement of her own body, but nothing of his. His cock had opened her and changed her shape, and she could see that, but nothing of him. The soft, silky material of the coat brushed her face as she pressed her forehead into his chest.

Suddenly he pulled out again. She heard a soft thump and reached out. Her fingers found his hair, the top of his head between her thighs. A moment later she opened up again, pink and slick, and his tongue trembled against her there, in the pink heat. She tipped her head back and closed her eyes. There was no point watching anymore. It was enough—more than enough—just to feel. She needed no other senses, not right now.

His tongue curled around her clit and his fingers dipped

into her, pressing upward, finding the spot at the top of her vagina that made a sharp, piercing dagger of arousal shoot up into her belly. She moaned with it. He sucked at her, pulling and tonguing until she could no longer contain the heat or the arrowing ecstasy as it pounded through her, making her shiver, making her sob as her hands clutched at his shoulders and her sex clutched at his fingers.

He teased her as she climaxed, his tongue coaxing the last bit of twitchiness from her clit, until she pushed his head away, afraid she might implode if he pushed her even a moment further. She heard his small laughter as he rose again between her legs.

Somehow she knew he was coming, and pushed forward to meet his cock, bringing it unerringly back into her body. The sensation was different yet again; this time she was so wet there was almost no friction, and he came into her like a piece of her own flesh being reattached.

He pressed and pulled and pressed again, and she wrapped her legs around his waist, her arms around his shoulders, as he came. His long, shuddering moan of completion vibrated against her ear. She passed magic over him to see his face. His expression was one of spent contentment.

She held him for a time, cradling his head against her shoulder. Finally he stepped back. It disconcerted her. Her hands on his skin had become like vision, and now he was invisible again.

"Fitz?" she said.

"I'm here." His voice came from lower than it should have; he must have sat down on the floor.

"Are you all right?"

It was, perhaps, a strange question, but she sensed something unsettled from him, even now.

He was silent for a moment. Then, tiredly, "I know him."

"Eoin?"

"Yes. I know him. The scar on my leg. He gave it to me."

She absorbed the implications of this. "You've fought him before. Did you win?"

"Is he dead?" This time his tone was harsh.

She tried not to take offense. "No, but neither are you."

There was rustling, and when he spoke again it was obvious he had come back to his feet. A hand brushed her shoulder. "I have to talk to someone about this. We should go back."

She let him help her from the table, wishing she could see his face. A new wrinkle had entered the situation—that much was obvious.

But did that mean they were in more danger now, or less?

# *Chapter Five*

ANNABETH ROUNDED UP HER sisters, and they went back. When Fitz was certain they were all back, and safe, he left the house, silent and still invisible. He didn't shed the coat until he was seated in the car. Then he yanked it off and threw it aside. Clenching the steering wheel, he just sat for a few minutes, watching his hands shake.

His own rage surprised him. Certainly Eoin's identity had caught him off guard, but sheer professionalism should have prevented this kind of reaction.

Fitz had become far too emotionally invested. But how could he not have? He knew too much about what this son of a bitch had done. And not nearly enough about how to stop him.

But now he knew whom to ask.

Finally he peeled his fingers off the steering wheel and started the car. He couldn't do anything else here. Not until he had spoken to Lily.

He was five minutes from home when his cell phone rang. It was Collinwood.

"I have received no report of your progress, Mr. Fitz-cairn." His voice was low and cold. "Would you care to attempt to give me a good reason to continue to finance this inept farce of an investigation?"

Fitz clenched his teeth. "I'll be back tomorrow night, at which time I will see to it that this situation is resolved."

"Very well, then I will—"

But Fitz wasn't done. "You can keep your fucking money, Collinwood. I don't want it."

He hung up before Collinwood could say anything else. As far as he was concerned, the blame for this situation fell squarely into Collinwood's lap. He was as guilty as Eoin. A pity Fitz couldn't just take them both down.

That wasn't an option, though. So he'd have to concentrate his efforts on getting rid of Eoin.

Pulling into a parking space in front of his apartment, Fitz was not surprised to see Lily standing outside his front door. Nor did the drawn, haggard look on her face, the circles under her eyes surprise him.

He got out of the car and went to her, held her. She collapsed into his chest and wept. He stroked her hair for a time and finally said, "Why didn't you tell me?"

"I couldn't. He marked me, too, just like the others."

She drew away from him, wiping her eyes and collecting herself.

"Let's go inside," said Fitz. "We need to talk."

"You sensed the power in me back then, remember? So did he."

"It was dormant then. It still is. Doesn't he know that?"

He set a cup of coffee on the table in front of her. Her hands shook as she spooned sugar into it.

"Yes. He thought—" She stopped, closed her eyes. Her hand stopped in midair, holding the spoon suspended over the coffee cup. "He had some idea he could awaken it. Turn me into some kind of—I don't know—sorceress or something."

Fitz shook his head. "He had no right."

"He thought he did." She tipped the spoon over. A thin, crystalline stream of sugar poured into the coffee. "He's my husband."

She stirred her coffee, laid the spoon down on the table next to the cup. She picked up the cup and coffee sloshed over the rim as her hands trembled. She set it back down.

"If I had known . . ." Fitz trailed off, not certain what else to say. What would he have done, back then? What *could* he have done? If Eoin—John—wanted her, he would have taken her, even if it had meant killing Fitz.

Lily seemed not to have heard. "He finally grew impatient with me. I wasn't what he'd expected. I could give him no power. He had already seeded magic in the Collinwood sisters. They were old enough now to be used, he said."

"So he went after them."

"Yes. When I found out what was happening, what he was doing—" She shook her head. "It's my fault you're involved in this, Fitz. I made sure Collinwood got your name. I knew that if anyone could defeat John, it was you."

Fitz shook his head. "I hope your faith hasn't been misplaced."

"It hasn't. I know it hasn't. You've already taken the first steps, and they've been the right ones. He's so angry with you right now. There's no way he'll ever recover what you've taken from him."

He thought about Annabeth for a moment, her sleek softness under his hands, the latent power. She had great potential as a magic user. He probably wouldn't be the best teacher for her, but anything was better than Eoin. At least Fitz would have her best interests at heart. Maybe. Hopefully.

"Can we defeat him?" He wasn't sure he even wanted to think about that—about what it was likely to cost him, about what it might cost Lily.

But Lily's face was hard, her eyes blazing. "Yes."

Fitz raised his eyebrows, surprised at her vehemence. "Do you know how?"

Lily's mouth curved into a thin smile. "I can tell you everything you need to know."


ANNABETH SAT ALONE IN the library, waiting. Her sisters had all gone to the pool, where they were no doubt engaged in banal conversation. They could sit out in the sun and babble on about fairy sprites for hours. Normally she just tuned it out. Today the very thought of it made her ill.

So she sat in the cool library, reading and waiting.

The rune on her lower back had begun to ache. This was the first time she'd experienced any pain with the mark, and it distressed her. Eoin's mark had never hurt like this. It had burned at first, and later she'd experienced twinges from time to time, usually when her thoughts toward Eoin had become uncharitable. And flashes of pain, sometimes, when Eoin was angry with her. But this steady, dull ache made her tired and resentful.

Why did it hurt? Had Fitz done something wrong, or was the pain some leftover echo of Eoin's influence?

She shifted on the plush couch. It didn't really matter where the pain came from, she supposed, as long as someone could come up with some way to end it.

She wished she knew more about this fairy magic. Unfortunately it wasn't something you could just look up in the public library, or on the Internet. The fairy world, as far as she'd been able to tell, held itself apart and secret as much as possible. So, rather than being able to find anything out for herself, she had to rely on what she was told, and hope Fitz wasn't lying to her.

Annabeth put her face in her hands. The world was suddenly far too large, with too many things in it she didn't understand. She didn't even know what a normal life was like, what it was like to live within the world instead of just outside it. She wondered, sometimes, if there was any hope of ever regaining any part of what her father had taken from her.

And sometimes she wished she were more like her sisters—too dim and self-involved even to understand, much less to care. Instead she had knowledge she didn't understand, thoughts that made no sense, feelings she couldn't explain to anyone, not even herself . . .

She looked up out of the darkness of her cupped hands into the dim light of the library. Someone was here. She wasn't sure how she knew—she hadn't heard anything, and now she could see nothing amiss—but she was certain she was no longer alone.

"Hello?" she said, keeping her voice low. No sense screeching and wailing and alerting whatever portion of the house could hear her. "Is someone there?"

Narrowing her eyes, she scanned the room. Nothing. But still something. And suddenly she realized what it was. "Fitz?"

"Yes." The familiar voice sounded right next to her ear, a near whisper. She closed her eyes as his invisible breath touched her cheek. "Close the door."

She looked at the wide-open library door. A guard stood outside in the hallway. She was so used to seeing them around the house lately she hadn't even registered his presence when she'd come into the room. Now she wondered if the simple act of closing the door might alert him to Fitz's presence.

Nevertheless, she nodded toward Fitz, then strolled across the room to the door. With a haughty look at the guard, she said, "Must you stand there while I'm reading? It's incredibly distracting."

He only looked at her, stone-faced. Apparently he didn't feel it was worth pointing out to her that she'd been reading for quite some time without being distracted by his presence. She glared at him and pushed the door shut.

When she turned around, Fitz was shrugging out of the trench coat. At the sight of him, her heart lurched in her throat.

Yet another thing she didn't understand. Was this relief that her protector had returned? Or was it, as she'd begun to suspect, love?

He draped the coat over the back of a chair. His gaze followed Annabeth as she came back across the room. Wondering why he was still standing, she drew her chair back out and sat. Only when she had settled in the chair did he join her. She laid a hand on the table and his hand came out to cover it, his palm rough and warm against the back of her hand.

"Are you all right?" he said.

She frowned a little. "Yes. Why wouldn't I be?"

"I just wondered."

Then the ache in the small of her back flared again and she winced.

"What was that?"

"Nothing. Just my back."

"The rune?"

"I think so." She closed her eyes a moment, no longer feeling a need to hide the pain. "Why would it hurt?"

Fitz's lips had thinned. "Eoin's mark left echoes. I did the best I could, but there's still a struggle going on there."

The dull ache faded, but tears sprang to Annabeth's eyes anyway. It felt like a struggle, she thought. Like the same kind of struggle an infected wound might harbor. "Make it stop," she said, her voice thin and wavering.

His hand tightened on hers. "I'll do what I can."

She looked into his face, into the clear blue eyes. He was so open, she thought. He hid nothing from her. If she had met him first, experienced this honesty, Eoin never would have been able to bewitch her.

"Do we go tonight?" she asked.

"Yes. And if everything goes right, this will be the last time."

She bit her lip. Surely he didn't mean . . . "You can defeat him? You know how?"

"I have a great deal of information. I know a great deal about him now. More than he knows about me."

"That's a good thing?"

"If I can figure out how to put all the pieces together, a very good thing."

"So what will happen tonight? What will you do?"

He slid both his hands around hers, cupping them gently. For the first time, his touch frightened her. Because she knew, looking at him, into the clear blue honesty of his eyes, that he would ask much of her. Perhaps, she thought, more than she would be able to give.

"I have to use you tonight," he said softly. "I wish it didn't have to be this way, but it's the only way to provoke him. I have to use you to show him and everyone else there that I've taken over his claim. His power. It will provoke him to the point of fury, which leads to carelessness. I don't see any other way. Not if we want to finish things tonight."

She nodded. He didn't need to elaborate for her to understand what he meant. For a split second, as he spoke, she saw in her head exactly what he asked of her. Saw the scene laid out before her mind's eye as if she stood on the sidelines, observing it.

But tonight she would not be an observer. She would be there, in the middle of it, participating.

Strangely, her fear faded. She only nodded. "And after that?"

His smile was strange. Strained, as if there might be tears behind it. "After that—I have spells, knowledge, but I won't know which to use or how to use them until the moment comes. And I'll need you there with me. You and I together, with the right magic—we can take him."

She nodded. "Then we will."

"Yes."

She reached up, trailed her fingers down the crags of his face. "I—" She stopped, realizing what she'd almost said.

"What?"

"Nothing." She cupped her palm against his cheek.

He bent and kissed her gently. "We'll be all right."

Strangely, she believed him.

WHEN THEY WENT THAT night, she again wore a backless dress, and he wore the trench coat until they had passed the barrier into Eoin's lair. Then he slowly took it off, folded it, and set it aside. The five sisters gaped at him as he appeared amongst the group. Annabeth gave him a sad smile, then came to him and took his hand.

"This way," she said, though he knew the way. He squeezed her hand reassuringly and let her lead him.

Eoin's presence lurked cold and invasive, along the edges of her mind, as soon as she exited the portal. The ache in her lower back swelled, bringing tears to her eyes. It felt like something trying to burst out from under her skin, like something that could be lanced and drained, but when she brushed her fingers across her skin there she felt nothing.

She led Fitz across the floor, oblivious of the rutting couples. Humans and fairy sprites gave them passing glances or harsh looks, depending on whether they'd had to leave off fornicating to make way.

Eyes gaped as she stopped in the empty circle at the

center of the wide orgy floor. There she turned to face Fitz, draping her arms around his neck. As always, as if by silent agreement, no one stepped past a certain point, leaving that circle open in the center. It reeked of Eoin, she thought, though she'd never noticed it before. Her lower back throbbed in sick, feverish agony.

She pulled Fitz's face down to close her mouth on his. The warm movement of his lips, the heat as he opened to her, drowned the pain little by little.

*I must use you tonight.* She had, of course, known exactly what he meant. The thought of it had given her a long moment of shuddering anxiety as they had entered the portal, but now they were *here*, in that moment, and she was prepared to do what must be done. He would take her, right here in the circle where only Eoin was rightfully allowed to be. She felt strong suddenly, possessed of a singular power. Had anyone else, once marked by Eoin, ever defied him? She suspected not.

Fitz's mouth had become hard and insistent on hers, his hands pressing against her back, kneading her buttocks. The hard ridge of his cock jutted against her stomach and he rubbed this too, back and forth over her, stroking himself, stimulating his own desire.

In a sudden flash, she was afraid for him. Could he truly handle Eoin? Brutally, she shoved the thoughts back where she could no longer hear or feel them. He could. He had to, or they were all doomed.

His hands cupped her buttocks, pulling her closer. His fingers walked down the curve of her hips to find the hem of her skirt and tease it up, then found her panties and drew them down, until she felt the movement of air against her labia. His fingers slipped between her thighs from behind, sliding into her where she was already slick but not quite ready.

The pain in her back had changed to a pulsing ache, fading and returning, then fading again. The rhythm matched none of her own, not her heartbeat or her breath. It was an alien thing, not part of her. Part of Eoin, she realized. If she could hear his heartbeat, his breath, surely the rhythms would match.

But she heard only her own heartbeat, and then suddenly Fitz's, as the magic of this circle began to work.

If Fitz had known about this place, perhaps he would have marked her here the first time. Perhaps if he had then there would have been no pain.

But this was more than just marking. This was a challenge to Eoin, a threat to usurp his power. The sex sounds faded around them as dumbfounded participants stopped and stared at the woman they knew had been claimed by their master, and the man who dared challenge that claim.

She'd felt Fitz's strength before, but now it came over her in a wave, amplified by the powers of the circle. She was helpless within it. It had been like this with Eoin—she helpless, he aflame with power—but then she had been afraid. Helpless and afraid, as he hurt her. Now she had no fear. She gave her own power willingly into Fitz's hands. And that gave her more power.

If only she had known back then, before it had come to this. If only her father had let her discover this place where strength and surrender merged. But it was not too late.

Fitz's hands gathered her against him, then traced around her, mounding her breasts into her body, his fingers plying her nipples. The power streaming and eddying around them seemed to hold her up, pressing her away from the floor the way a magnet presses up its matching pole in another magnet. A cushion of force supported her. Fitz seemed to have gotten the hang of it, maneuvering her as he worked her body.

She had never been to this section of the orgy floor before—in fact, she'd never even seen anyone else here—so she hadn't expected this odd magic, nor did she know how or why it was here. Probably another way for Eoin to keep his women helpless, unable to control the movement of the magic.

Why had he not marked her here? Would she not have been helpless? Because she could feel the movement and fluctuation of the power, and while she didn't know where it came from, she had some sense of how to manipulate it.

So she did. Fitz lowered his head toward her breasts and she moved on the shifting magic, giving him easier access. He smiled as his mouth found the hard, rounded nub of her nipple. He swirled his tongue around it, then drew back to kiss the swell of her breast.

"You're good at this," he said.

"I haven't been here before, if that's what you're thinking."

His hands slid up her thighs, up under her skirt. "I know. I can tell. You're feeling out the power."

"And you're feeling out me. Don't stop."

He laughed, as if they were in no danger at all, as if they were all alone and the only thing he cared about was her pleasure.

They could have been alone, as silent as the room had

become. Annabeth put the audience out of her mind, focusing totally on the manipulation of the buoyant magic and on what Fitz was doing to her body.

And oh, what he was doing to her body. Her skin was alight and alive, as if he cast magic over it, but the only magic coming from his hands was that of skin against skin and clever fingers learning every millimeter of her body.

He leaned into the cushion of power, letting it lift him up next to her. Finding his buttons, she deftly worked them open, slid her hands inside the cotton shirt to caress his smooth skin, down his sides, then forward to the hair roughened textures of belly and chest. Before, thinking about this moment, she'd been afraid. Now she could feel only a strange surge of exultation. She leaned into him, whispering into his ear.

"Let's show them how it's done."

She unzipped and yanked his jeans open, happy to find him startlingly erect. She wanted to jump right on, but maybe that would be too abrupt. After all, they had an audience. They should think about being entertaining.

She couldn't believe that thought didn't make her clam right up, clench her thighs shut and run for the hills. Instead, it made her wet. Hot. She spread herself open, testing to see if the magic might mold to her, rise between her legs or otherwise stimulate her. A tendril of heat crept up between her labia, drew back. Ah, that was good.

Turning her attention to Fitz, she shifted herself and him, bringing her breasts down to his crotch. He moved with her, pressing his cock into her cleavage. He thrust between her breasts while she bent her head, catching the head of his cock with her mouth each time it rose toward her.

Fitz's body stiffened, but the magic shifted under him to accommodate. Annabeth grabbed his hips, holding him still while she worked her tongue around his glans, listening to his breathing. When it changed from rapid to nearly gasping, she let him go.

"God," he breathed. "Get over here."

She didn't even exert herself—just let the magic toss her in his direction. Gently, though, so she rode it right over onto him. Now was the time to jump on, and she did, taking him slick and hot and easy into her. He rode the power up a little so he was sitting up where he could kiss her. His mouth opened hers and his tongue pressed inside, penetrating her mouth, thrusting as his cock thrust into her clenched, hot sex.

Movement through the air, on the power cushion, no longer disconcerted her. She turned over, bringing Fitz with her, so that she was under him, taking the powerful weight of his body. She was trapped there, completely under his power. Which was what she wanted.

She lifted her hips, drawing him deeper inside her. One hand clutched his back, feeling the straining of his muscles as he rode her. With her other hand, she groped between their bodies, finding her own heat, working her clit between her fingers. His cock slid back and forth, brushing her busy fingers.

He seemed to have lost any concern about going too fast or too hard; trusting her, she assumed, to let him know if anything needed to be changed. But she wanted nothing changed. The jubilant ferocity of his approach made it that much better, that much hotter. She thought she was going to explode.

And then she did. In a great, undulating river of light that filled her whole body, setting every nerve ending alight. Even the cushion of magic beneath her pulsed, as attuned to her climax as it was to the rest of her body.

And as the orgasm plowed mercilessly through her, she threw her head back, screaming her ecstasy right into the face of her nemesis.

Eoin had appeared from nowhere, eyes blazing as he stood outside the power circle, trembling with rage as Fitz plowed into Annabeth as she floated on the cushion of power. Annabeth looked right into his upside down, rage-red, teeth-clenched face and laughed, and moaned with the final, glorious pulsations of ecstasy. Fitz came right along with her—she felt him empty with her laughter.

As their double climax faded, the field of power faded with it, allowing her to shift until her feet were under her. Fitz's hands, still claiming her, helped guide her as she settled to the ground. He caught the edge of her short skirt and pulled it into place before attending to his own dishabille. Then his hand curled around hers. She jumped a little at the shock of this innocent, yet, at the moment, unspeakably intimate touch.

It was more than that, though. More than just the curl of his big fingers between hers. A current seemed to flow between them, hot and palpable. She didn't know what it was, or if it was anything more than her imagination, but as he squeezed her hand she felt suddenly invincible.

Eoin, by contrast, looked as if he were about to drop dead from a coronary. *If only it were that easy*, she thought, and smiled sweetly into his purple, apoplectic face.

"What is the meaning of this?" he spat.

She realized suddenly the pain in her back was gone. And as Fitz lifted his hand, she lifted hers, as well. She knew what he was going to do, knew how he knew to do it, knew what the result would be, all in a hot, blinding flash that seemed to come from the base of her spine.

This was what it should have been, she thought. If Eoin had wanted to nurture her power rather than own it, this is what it would have been.

"This is about misuse of power." Fitz spoke the words, but she did, as well, their separate voices emerging as one, threaded with light and power. "What you have done is unconscionable and it must be stopped."

Eoin had taken a defensive posture, his hands raised as if to ward off a blow he knew was coming. "You can't stop me!" he shouted, but to Annabeth—or to the single, magically powered unit that was Annabeth and Fitz—the words sounded hollow and without power.

"You had such power, right within your grasp, if only you had been willing to let it go so it could grow." Again, Fitz's words came through Annabeth's mouth. It should have frightened her. If it had been Eoin, it would have frightened her. But it was Fitz, and she knew he would let her go when the need for the union had ended. Eoin would have kept her bound to him as long as he could, regardless of her wishes in the matter. But, joined in this way with Fitz, she felt only the glorious surge of her own power.

"Now," Fitz went on, Annabeth speaking in tandem with him. "Now the power you wished to control will destroy you."

Eoin had regained some control by now. His face had nearly returned to its normal color. Still, Annabeth saw fear in the sneer that curled his lips.

"You have no idea what you're dealing with," he said, his voice thin and harsh.

"The same could be said for you."

As the words came out, in that strange, doubled voice, Annabeth sank just a fraction deeper, a moment further into the shared consciousness that had formed between her mind and Fitz's. She heard his quick calculations, the rapid, efficient gathering of power, shuffling the pieces into order. This was the knowledge Lily had passed to him. She knew it now, too, understood the secrets of Eoin's power, and how she and Fitz together could overcome it.

*Earth to Air, Fire to Water. Air. Form Earth.*

Their power rose richly green, loamy brown, granite gray. An elemental force that, to her strangely altered vision, appeared as a sort of opaque cloud, flowing into human form, but never quite holding it. She could smell rich, damp soil, green leaves, rain-soaked stone. The wave of force rolled, lumbered forward.

But Eoin was ready. His defensive spell rose in almost the same moment. A wall of wind, swirling, a man-size tornado in a room full of people. The occupants of the room stepped back, voices rising in fear and excitement. Annabeth was only barely aware of their retreat as Eoin's magic formed and the battle was joined.

It was two against one. Which should have made the outcome certain, but all the mitigating factors put the advantage with Eoin. He was the older, more experienced magic-user. Fitz knew what he was doing and possessed a formidable level of power, but Eoin had been around a long, long time in spite of his apparent youth. He was also not bound in the use of his power by such pointless concepts as fair play and morality. If it came down to it, he would employ any means necessary to ensure victory.

Annabeth's contribution to the confrontation was significant, but when it came down to it, she had no clue what she was doing. Some portion of Fitz's power had to be redirected in order to channel Annabeth's raw energy and make it usable. It was a disadvantage on Fitz's side, and though it should have been two possessors of extreme power easily overcoming another, lone combatant, the balance in actuality proved very different. Fitz and Annabeth together actually presented power levels almost identical to Eoin acting alone.

Annabeth knew all this in a split second. How, exactly, she didn't know, but as she absorbed the raw knowledge she also absorbed some sense of how to even the balance to make the most efficient use of her own power as it rose and merged with Fitz's.

Of the best way to kick this amoral sorcerer's ass.

And the first thing she had to do was get up to speed. Fast.

Control of the power she knew she could leave up to Fitz. She had to concentrate on producing it, and channeling it to him. If they could produce a clean, melded front against Eoin—

And it began to happen. She felt it, almost tangible, like breath flowing out of her body into another's lungs. Mouth-to-mouth resuscitation, but with magic, and it flowed not out of her lungs but just out of *her*. Filling him. And he took it in, gathered it, and directed it at Eoin.

She felt also his sudden surge of pleasure, of pride, as her efforts came with more ease. A smile took over her face as bliss rose within her with the magic. It built and crested, rose, flowed out of her, rose again until it was flowing out of her in pulses, wave upon wave, a huge, crazed, orgasmic exchange of power. It made the sex she'd just engaged in seem inconsequential.

The raw, barely disciplined power seemed not to faze Fitz. Annabeth had very little control over what she passed on to him, but just her awareness of the flow and the rhythms seemed to help. In her mind's eye, where the incomprehensible became comprehensible, she saw Fitz grasping the cords and threads of power, weaving them together, readying them.

But what about Eoin? She realized suddenly she had given him almost no thought over the past several minutes—or was it seconds? Hours? She focused a moment, narrowing her strange, interior vision so she could get a better sense of exactly what was happening.

Eoin was there. Very much so. And, to her surprise, he was attacking.

His power, in its airy, ethereal but steely hard manifestation, continued to flow outward, toward her, toward Fitz, in a column of blue-white flame.

Lightning, she thought, electricity. The manifestations of the power of Air. They lashed and crackled toward Fitz and Annabeth as they held their ground. But the licking tongues of cold fire couldn't seem to reach past a certain point. That point lay only inches in front of Fitz, but it was enough. Enough to keep death at bay. Enough to buy the time they needed to collect the necessary power.

The power surged, green, gray and brown, and suddenly she was inside it, one with it, one with Fitz, as the power of joined minds, hearts and strength burst forward out of them to slam hard against Eoin's no longer sufficient defenses. He had been the strong one, but he was alone. They were two, and had become a single strength beyond anything he could have ever dreamed of conjuring.

She saw the look of utter surprise on Eoin's face as his formidable defenses shattered. The blue and silver of his air-magic splintered, broken by the great column of earth. His protection gone, he himself was crushed. The column of magic slammed into his chest like a battering ram. The last expression on his face was one of wide-eyed disbelief.

It was over. The room fell silent. The massive power Annabeth and Fitz had conjured fell like silver rain, its cohesiveness gone now; it had destroyed its target.

Annabeth's awareness of her own body returned. She could feel her heart slamming in her chest, her taut, labored breathing. Her hand clenched Fitz's, his fingers hard and solid inside the curve of hers.

"What have we done?" she managed. Her voice was thin and shaky.

He turned to her and smiled bleakly. "We've won."

# Chapter Six

I T DIDN'T FEEL MUCH like a victory, though, when Fitz stood in Collinwood's office. It felt like a dressing down. He'd saved the man's daughters, stopped their nocturnal wanderings, and freed Annabeth from a demon-fairy who wanted little more than her soul. Yet here he was, with Collinwood looking down his nose at him in disgust.

"I will be certain you receive your payment," Collinwood said, his voice thin and cold, "though I have my doubts that you deserve it."

"I told you I don't want your money. All I want is for you to understand."

"Understand what?"

"That you did this. None of this would have happened if you hadn't locked those girls up and thrown away the key."

Collinwood's mouth tightened. He looked evil suddenly,

as evil as Eoin. Thin-lipped and thin-faced, his cheekbones knifelike slashes under narrowed eyes.

"I would watch my tongue if I were you. I could make certain you never work again."

Fitz nodded grimly. "You could try."

Collinwood lurched to his feet. "I could have you killed! You have no idea who you're dealing with."

Fitz lifted his hand, palm up, in front of Collinwood. Then he closed his fist. When he opened it again, a flame burned blue in the middle of his palm. Collinwood stared.

"Neither do you," said Fitz, and flung the blue ball of flame against the wall.

Collinwood paled, making his face look thinner, his cheekbones sharper. "What are you?"

"I am the only P.I. in this city who could have dealt with what your daughters were mixed up in. And this never would have happened if you had only treated them like daughters instead of slaves."

Collinwood's mouth trembled. "I didn't want to lose them."

"Well, you damn near did anyway." For a moment he regretted the flare of temper, the demonstration of power that Collinwood would only rationalize and eventually convince himself hadn't happened. Then the regret faded in the immediate need to get through to this cold, hopeless man. "Let them go. Let them live."

Collinwood's lips curled against his teeth. "I won't. I can't."

"You will. Or I'll make things impossible for you."

"I don't think you can."

"I know I can. Legally, magically—you don't want to tangle with me, Collinwood."

"Don't threaten me, Mr. Fitzcairn. I have a great deal of power—"

"Yes. You have all the power money can buy. I have the kind of power you can't touch."

"I'm not afraid of you."

"You should be."

Fitz shoved his chair back in disgust. At Collinwood, but also at himself. He hadn't wanted to resort to crass threats. But threats, with the power to back them up, seemed to be all Collinwood understood.

"The truth is, Collinwood, they're over eighteen. They can leave this house any time they want and there's not a damn thing you can do about it."

"If you take my daughters, I will hunt you down and slaughter you."

Fitz smiled thinly. "I'd like to see you try."


IN THE SUNROOM, ANNABETH chewed her fingernails. Surrounded by green, lush beauty, by the wide, bright blooms of tropical flowers, she could think of nothing but Fitz.

She had no doubt he would come through for them. She'd seen him deal with Eoin—after that her father should be no problem. But after he did what he had to do, after he took them out of this place, this prison, what then?

She knew what needed to happen. But would she have the courage to be sure it did?

So she paced among the flowers and chewed her fingernails. Her sisters had gone to the pool. Catherine had hesitated, just for a moment, before joining the others.

"Will we be all right?" she'd asked Annabeth.

Annabeth had nodded. "We will."

It was the most meaningful exchange she'd had with any of her sisters in a long time. Since before Eoin. In fact, it seemed to her that they were waking up somehow, as if freeing herself and them from Eoin had freed their minds, as well. It seemed like too much to ask, especially after everything that had already happened. But it also seemed to be true.

Not everything was going perfectly. She understood this as soon as Fitz stormed into the room, his face taut, and fists clenched at his sides.

"Get your sisters and get your bags. We're going."

She stood slowly and faced him. Suddenly her anxiety disappeared, replaced with a deep, steady calm. "Not yet. I want to talk to him."

Fitz stared at her. Obviously this possibility had never occurred to him. "Are you sure that's wise?"

"No, but I need to do it. For me."

"All right." He hesitated, looking out toward the pool. "Should I load up the car while you're gone?"

"I think that would be a good idea."

He'd told them to pack their bags as soon as they'd come back, and now they were ready to go. A couple of high denomination paper bills had convinced Bo to bring the bags out to the carport. Fitz hadn't been prepared to put them in his trunk right then; he'd told Annabeth he wanted to at least give her father a chance to do the right thing.

But Collinwood hadn't. Annabeth had hoped to leave the house with her father's blessing. If that wasn't to be, she could at least try to explain part of her heart to him. Not all of it. Even she didn't understand all of it.

As she came to the door of his office, it occurred to her that this was the first time in her life she had not been afraid of her father.

She knocked on the tall, dark, wooden door. Just for a moment she listened to the echo, then opened the door and went in without waiting for her father's invitation.

He sat behind the big, mahogany desk, staring at the wall behind it. A black hole as big as Annabeth's hand had been blown in the plaster. Fitz's work, she surmised. She could only imagine what had prompted it.

When she came in her father swiveled his chair around to face her. His eyes widened briefly. He looked pale, she noticed. Pale and old. Slowly, he came to his feet.

"Annabeth."

She inclined her head. She had never been less afraid of anyone in her life. Except Fitz. But Fitz engendered other feelings. Here, in front of her father, she found it difficult to have any feelings at all.

"Father," she said, and the word seemed like something out of a foreign language.

"I will not allow you to go with this man." Her father's voice was thin and cold, but not as firm as it once had been—as it should have been if he truly believed he could stop her. Fitz had shaken him somehow.

Annabeth shook her head. "You can't stop me, Father. You can't stop any of us."

"Then why are you here?"

She stared at him, suddenly not sure she could say what she'd come to say. She shuddered. She had feared her father for so long. Now she knew there were much worse things in the world. She wasn't afraid of what her father might say;

rather she was afraid of the emotion that might surface if she said anything at all.

"You have no idea what you've done to us," she said finally, her voice taut and trembling.

"I wanted to protect you."

"You didn't." Anger flared, burning away everything else. "If you had only let us live like normal girls, it would have been so different."

Her father said nothing, but ferocious anger hardened the lines of his face.

"You thought you were protecting us, but you almost destroyed us."

"You may not leave," he said, standing, anger shaking every inch of his body.

Annabeth shook her head. Casually, she lifted her hand. Her father sat down as if someone had shoved him back into the chair. He sat staring at her, his eyes wide.

"I may do whatever I wish." She lowered her hand and he blinked in shock. Annabeth backed toward the door. "Remember—if you come after us, and Fitz doesn't kill you, I will."

She left the room, slamming the door behind her. This wasn't the best way to end this, she knew, but it was the only way she had right now. Someday, maybe, she could forgive him. But not now.

OUTSIDE, A SECOND CAR had pulled up next to Fitz's. A woman was helping Fitz load suitcases into the two trunks. Annabeth hesitated, sizing the woman up. She was pretty and about Fitz's age. Annabeth knew in a sudden flash that the two of them had slept together at some point. But it was over, and had been over for a long time. She wasn't a rival.

This, then, must be Lily. So not only was she not a rival, she had been instrumental in saving Annabeth and her sisters. And had been just as much Eoin's victim as they. Annabeth stepped forward, smiling.

"Hi. Lily?"

Lily returned the warm smile. A genuine feeling moved between the two women, surprising Annabeth.

"And you're Annabeth."

Lily held out her hand and Annabeth took it. This, she knew immediately, was someone she could trust.

Fitz watched the exchange approvingly. "Lily's got everything set up for all of you. We'll drive you to her place and you can all get settled in."

Annabeth looked at Fitz and swallowed. Fitz's expression was unreadable. But when she looked back at Lily, she saw only understanding. And sympathy. The older woman gave a nearly imperceptible nod. Encouraged, Annabeth stepped toward Fitz.

"We need to talk, Fitz."

"Okay, talk."

"Alone."

Fitz looked at Lily, who raised her eyebrows. "Okay . . . Lily, the pool's over there. Could you go get the other girls?"

"Yes, of course." She gave Annabeth a last look of encouragement, then left her alone with Fitz.

As soon as Lily was out of earshot, Annabeth crossed her arms firmly over her chest. "I think it's wonderful what your friend has offered to do for my sisters, but I'm not going with her."

Fitz was silent, just looking at her, as if trying to understand exactly what she was saying. The bond between them had become almost tangible. Annabeth's ability to understand her new levels of perception improved daily. So she knew he hadn't quite gotten it yet, and knew when it finally clicked in his brain.

"You'll be safe with her," he said, without much conviction.

"I know. But it's not where I want to be."

He smiled a little, crookedly, not quite hiding the regret in his eyes. "I don't think this is the right thing for you."

"Let me decide that. If there's one thing you've taught me, it's how to stand up for myself."

"Well, I tried."

"You've succeeded."

He shrugged helplessly. "I can't help thinking I'm no better than he was."

"Not even close to the same thing, Fitz." She wanted to touch him, but was afraid that if she did she would just end up grabbing him and shaking him until he acquired some sense. God only knew how long that might take. "He wanted to control me. You want to teach me, to free me. I need that, Fitz."

"You'll still be safer with Lily. In a lot of ways."

"She can't teach me, Fitz." She paused. "And I don't think she'll fuck me, and I need that, too."

Fitz grinned broadly. "She might if you ask nice."

Annabeth laughed. "I want you, Fitz." She sobered. "I love you."

His smile faded, as well, and in his sober blue eyes she saw exactly what she needed to see. "You come with me, Annabeth, and you're staying. And I don't mean that in a control freak kind of way. Because if you come with me, and then change your mind, I don't think I could bear it."

Now tears gathered in her eyes. Apparently the forecast called for strange mood swings. "I won't change my mind, Fitz. This is where I'm meant to be. With you."

He reached out and brushed a finger down her cheek. "Then get your pretty little ass in my car."

She smiled through the tears. "With pleasure, my love. With pleasure."

# Dragons
## and
# Dungeons

TAWNY TAYLOR

# Acknowledgments

Thank you to my editor, Sue Ellen Gower, who has the patience of a saint and an eye sharper than a surgeon's scalpel.

And my husband, David, who may not have eighteen-inch biceps, but he has a heart ten times bigger than your average romance hero.

# *Chapter One*

*K*AYA CORDOVA HAD READ somewhere a long time
ago that the devil was the most beautiful angel
in heaven. That was, before he was booted out
of paradise, of course. At the time—she was probably in
grade school then—the significance of that statement had
been lost to her. But now that she was staring straight into
the eyes of what had to be Lucifer incarnate, she had no
doubt of its validity.

Today the devil had taken the form of a six-foot something, sun-kissed blond, suntanned, muscular god in crisp,
finely tailored clothes that fit him like a second skin. And
unfortunately for Kaya, he had just entered the winning bid
on the one item that she had desperately wanted. Damn.
And damn.

The second the auctioneer acknowledged his victory,
bidder number nine, as he was officially known at the private

auction, gave Kaya a slightly gloating but wickedly sexy smile.

In contrast, she maintained her dignity, although she wasn't above sticking her tongue out at someone who had completely ruined her day, week, month. Naturally, as was her luck, the item she'd just lost to the incredibly yummy Mr. Nine, was the last item left to be auctioned. She'd held out, bidding conservatively on the earlier artifacts, accurately anticipating she'd need every penny of her budget to buy the last item, a piece of a large collection reportedly smuggled into the United States by an ex–United States Marine turned treasure hunter.

Everything she'd seen today was valuable, would potentially bring a small fortune for Kaya's boss, a woman who owned a shop that specialized in rare Asian antiquities. But that last piece, a copperplate imprinted with some form of ancient writing, Kaya had a feeling that was priceless.

Being half-Filipino on her mother's side, the fact that it had been found near the mouth of the Lumbang River in the Philippines by a man dredging for sand, and sold for pennies to the Marine back in the 1980s, made it even more intriguing. How old was the copperplate? What did the inscriptions mean? Was it real, or one of the many fakes that had been offered to Americans with deep pockets and the hunger to own a piece of international history?

Kaya grumbled at her loss as she reluctantly shuffled toward the exit, mindful of the winning bidder's unhurried gait. He strode like a proud peacock toward the cashier to pay for the artifact she wanted so badly her belly ached. If only she'd had another few thousand dollars to work with! Then again, that was probably for the better. Although no longer a novice buyer, she would've been tempted to keep bidding, forgetting what she'd learned ages ago—not to fall in love with something and bid beyond her budget. In this case it had been so tempting.

And speaking of tempting . . .

Her head turned and her gaze glued itself like a fly on flypaper to the man responsible for her temporary discouragement. Never mind what he'd purchased, the man himself was walking, talking temptation right down to his well-shod toes. If not for her strong sense of self-control, she would have done just about anything to run her fingers through those flirty blond curls, trace the line of his jaw with her tongue, maybe even nibble on one of those adorable earlobes. And don't get her started on the dimples! Dimples were her weakness.

"That man is trouble with a capital T." She sighed and forced herself to keep walking, even though she wasn't watching where she was going. After taking only a few steps, however, a high-pitched yelp made her stop.

"Sorry!" She apologized before she turned to look forward. She realized the instant she did that she'd slammed into the petite but friendly looking young woman who'd formerly occupied the seat next to her during the auction. "Oh! I'm so sorry," Kaya repeated, still slightly distracted. For some illogical but frustrating reason, even now her gaze seemed to want to stray to the left where it would find Mr. Nine's slightly mocking smile and blue, blue eyes.

They were bluer than any eyes she'd ever seen. Very striking.

"It's all right. I've taken worse," the woman said, giving Kaya a friendly, not at all mocking smile. So unlike Mr.

Nine's. "I took ballroom dance lessons with my cousin once. At thirteen, he was six-five and a hair shy of two-fifty. He broke two of my toes the first night." She tipped her head and glanced beyond Kaya. "That copperplate was something, wasn't it?"

"Yes it was, assuming it isn't a forgery," Kaya said, trying to hide her disappointment. "Since it hasn't been authenticated yet, I wasn't at liberty to bid any higher. There've been too many fakes coming out of the Philippines lately to risk it."

"I'm new to this sort of thing, so I'm hardly an expert, but that makes sense to me." The young woman offered her hand. "I'm Mary, by the way. Mary Stratford."

"Kaya Cordova." Kaya gave Mary's tiny hand a firm but relatively gentle shake. Standing as close as she was to the pretty, petite woman, she felt like a horse, all big and clumsy. It seemed like all it would take was a wrong move—or even a light breeze—and the little woman might shatter like glass into a gazillion pieces. "I'm not two-fifty, thank God, but I'm no lightweight either. I didn't break any bones, did I?" She motioned toward the foot she assumed she'd stomped on.

"Not a one." Mary followed the line of Kaya's fleeting gaze, from her foot to the cashier. "I'd pay good money to see the smug smile knocked off that man's face if he learned he just spent over twenty thousand on a worthless piece of industrial waste turned priceless artifact."

"For some reason, I don't believe we'll get the satisfaction. Besides, looking at his clothes, I have a feeling twenty thousand is nothing to him."

"Oh well," Mary said on a sigh. "As they say—the rich get richer. Speaking of rich, I've got to get to the airport. I'm off to Chicago to catch another auction. Sorry you didn't get this one, but you'll get the next."

"I hope you're right. Good luck in Chicago." Kaya pushed open the door and held it for Mary.

Mary gave her an over-the-shoulder thanks as she hurried out the door and into the soggy, cold late morning. She shuffled down the two front stairs to the ground level. Kaya followed Mary outside but stopped under the wooden overhang, not exactly eager to dash through the monsoon dumping water from the sky by the bucketful.

Thanks to the downpour, the air had chilled nearly twenty degrees to a crisp fifty-something. Because it had been a lot warmer earlier, Kaya was wearing only a light sweater over her lightweight, short-sleeved dress. That loosely crocheted garment wasn't going to offer even meager protection against the gale-force winds, any more than it was going to keep her dry. "Stupid Michigan weather. I wish it'd make up its mind and decide whether it's winter or summer," she muttered to herself, hugging her sweater around her body. "What's wrong with some transitional weather? Say a nice, comfortable sixty degrees?"

A particularly strong blast of wind that made her shiver and coated her face with a cold mist was the only response she received.

It was then that she decided she had two choices . . . either A—go back inside and wait out the storm, or B—make a run for it. Since she was expected back at the store in less than an hour, and the all-encompassing gloom didn't look like it was going to break before next week, she figured she had no choice but option B.

She just hoped the Dry Clean Only tag on her dress

didn't mean the garment would shrink to toddler-size when exposed to water. She'd had that happen once. And once should have been enough to keep her from buying Dry Clean Only clothes altogether. A grown woman with fairly ample curves wearing a dress that would fit your average four year old was not a pretty sight. Today, she'd have to take her chances.

Preparing to run into an icy-cold downpour was a lot like getting ready to dive into the Detroit River in the middle of January. It required a bit of time, some deep breaths, and a little bit of jogging in place to get the blood pumping, which were all good reasons why she didn't make a habit of swimming in January or making mad dashes through thunderstorms to her car. For one thing, time was something she rarely possessed an excess of. Second, deep breathing made her dizzy and her hands numb. And third, running in three-inch heels was dangerous, especially in slick-soled three-inch heels that tended to slip on wet asphalt.

Thanks to the difficulty in running and a bit of reluctance—Kaya had never been the kind to dive into water, frigid or otherwise. She'd always been more the toe-in-the-water kind of girl—she hadn't made it more than a step or two away from the front door before a big, black limousine swooped around the corner and came to a skidding stop in front of her. Muddy water coated the lower half of her body and she prepared to give the passenger inside a good, nasty glare when the passenger door opened. Instead of some rich snob stepping out of the car like he was preparing to walk the red carpet, only an arm jutted out. A hand caught her dress at about hip level and yanked.

Out of instinct, she jumped backward and tipped her

head to look down in the car, spying none other than sexy Mr. Nine grinning at her from the backseat.

"Hi there," he said, looking absolutely amazing in the dimly lit interior of the car. His dimples were on high beam, his smile too. "I'd like to give you a ride to your car."

She was grateful for the shelter of the overhang as she stood by the side of the car trying to pry her tongue loose from her throat. If she was going to stand there for a while, her jaws snapping open and closed like a possessed mouse-trap, at least she wouldn't get drenched. Then again, the look Mr. Nine gave her, one of the flirty, render-a-girl-brainless varieties, made her so hot she was tempted to throw herself into the biggest puddle she could find for some relief.

After indulging in a sigh that finally knocked her tongue free, she shook her head. "Thanks, but no. I'm just parked over there, not more than twenty yards away."

"Are you sure I can't change your mind?"

*I could think of one or two ways you could.* "No, thanks. Al-though this storm is getting bad, I don't think I need an ark to get there yet. Appreciate the thought, though." She tried to step farther back from the car, fearful of getting her toes run over when it pulled away, but his firm grip on her dress kept her from backing too far. Puzzled, she gave him her best, practiced "what's up?" look.

"Please," he answered. "I'd like to speak to you."

"About what? What could you, the person who obvi-ously got what he wanted, want to talk to me—the one who didn't—about? I don't have anything you want."

Silent laughter making his eyes glittery, he mumbled something incoherent that made her blush then added, "About this." Those two sweet dimples poked into his cheeks as his mouth curled into a naughty smile that made her knees all weak and trembly. He lifted a black case which she assumed held the copperplate.

"Yes, I know you have it. You bought it. What do you need me for?"

"Please. I have a few questions. And I promise, if you're worried about getting into a car with a strange man, I'm not suggesting anything sinister and I've never been convicted of a crime."

"Thanks for clarifying. Yes, I was worried you might be a crazed monster who entices women into your lair during our infamous Michigan downpours and then does unmentionable things to them."

"Wow, you have me pegged already. Want to risk it anyway?" he joked. Those dimples became even deeper.

She chuckled to hide a near-swoon. Charmed almost out of her mind and curious about what he wanted, she looked into those big blues for some sign of subterfuge. What she saw was confusing but not threatening. But before she made her decision, he made it for her. When she reached down to smooth her windblown dress against her legs, he caught her by the wrist and yanked her inside. The door slammed the second she was in the car.

Alarmed, and feeling off balance, her body basically sprawled over his, her chest on his belly, her groin on his thigh, she glared up at him and shook a scolding finger. Funny little tingles and zaps buzzed through her body, like little bolts of static electricity as she warned, "If you try anything funny, I'm outta here." Still not comfortable with the situation, although the position was growing on her, she gathered herself together, settled into the black leather seat, smoothed out her wrinkled dress and tried to fake a casual, confident air. "Hmm. This is cozy. I could get used to this."

"So could I."

So much for her confidence. It crumbled at the sound of those three little words. Then things went from bad to worse. When he winked then glanced meaningfully at her crossed legs, she just about died. Sure her face was as red as a stop sign, she tugged at her skirt, which was slowly inching up her thighs, no doubt the result of the drenching she'd received when the car pulled up. To keep him in his place—or at least attempt to—she gave him her best mean eyes, the ones she used regularly to intimidate any door-to-door salespeople who chose to ignore the "No Soliciting" sign plastered to her front door. "You, behave yourself."

"I'm doing my best to tame the beast, I swear. Here, I'll play polite host. Can I offer you something to drink?" he asked, motioning toward the minifridge.

"No, thanks. Call me silly, but I have this rule. No alcohol before noon." *And no alcohol while locked in a moving vehicle with a man who makes my head swim.*

He glanced at his watch then blinked wide-eyed at her, clearly trying to look innocent. It wasn't working. No sirree.

But it did make him look cute.

"Well, then, we'll just have to wait ten minutes." He pushed the intercom and asked the answering female voice to carry on.

"Carry on? What's that mean?" Kaya watched as the stretch limo did indeed carry on, gliding across the parking lot like it was floating rather than rolling on the road, past her car and onto the street. "Um, where are you taking me? I agreed to a ride to my car, not a tour of the city."

"We're . . . um, taking the scenic route." His crooked smile still firmly in place, he leaned forward and offered his hand. "Name's Jestin Draig."

Whew, being up close and personal to the body that possessed that wicked grin was doing some very interesting things to her, especially the parts south of her waistline. Shockwaves of awareness paraded up and down her spine like a marching band playing a Sousa march, which in turn made her inner girly parts start strutting to the beat, waving flags and tossing batons. "Jestin? Not Justin?"

Despite the parade going on in her body, she hesitated before taking his hand. Surely there was extreme danger in shaking hands with the devil. She'd never been the kind to embrace extreme danger, in any form, male included. Heck, just being in the car with him—a complete stranger—was a first for her. She stared at his hand, trying to decide what to do.

He cleared his throat, an action that naturally lured her gaze to his face. "And you are?"

That had been a good move on his part—making her look at his adorable face. Now, she was practically dumbstruck, again staring into impossibly blue eyes. It only took a few seconds for the playful twinkle in those eyes to melt her reservations almost completely. Her girly parts broke into a chant, *Go, team, go!* and she reached for his hand. "Kaya Cordova."

The instant her skin made contact with his, a blaze of searing heat shot up her arm. Taken off guard, she yanked her hand away, shoved up her sleeve and checked her skin for burns. She saw nothing, not even the slightest tint of pink but she sure felt something. Waves of heat were fanning out from her center like ripples on a pond. Her pussy throbbed as the heat thrust her into near orgasm. "What the heck was that?" She pushed her sleeve back down and tried to silence the rioting crowd inside her by fanning her face. The marching band kicked into high gear, playing a fast staccato. And the chanting girls were doing backflips and carrying on like the football team had just made the winning touchdown.

He answered her question with a couple of raised eyebrows that did nothing to help her suppress the ruckus in her body. Though it did confuse her. If she hadn't been nearly scorched to death by some mysterious electrical charge leaping between his hand and hers, what had that been? And why was she now a throbbing, wet, horny mess?

By his puzzled expression, she guessed it was fair to say he hadn't felt the same thing she did. Not to appear the fool, she pasted on as convincing an "I'm okay honest" smile, fanned her flaming face, and nodded toward his hand. "That's one heck of a grip you've got there, buddy. My, my."

She squirmed as her gaze met his and the heat churning deep in her belly dispersed in another wave. Some of it went down into her groin. Some of it settled at about nipple level in her chest, and the rest rose to her face. She shoved aside the notion of throwing herself on him and instead shed her sweater.

He glanced down at his hand, now resting on his knee instead of where she silently yearned for it to be—on hers, maybe even a little higher. "I didn't . . . did I hurt you?"

"Oh, no. I'm fine. Totally fine. Very fine. Yeppers. Just a little warm." She fanned her face again. "Do you have a thermostat back here? Might want to turn down the heat a few notches. I . . . er, get carsick." She wrinkled her nose, which gained her another brilliant smile from Jestin, which made those adorable dimples deeper, which of course sent the parade into high gear. Marching, cheering, flipping and twirling. "So, um. What did you want to talk to me about?"

He held up an index finger and glanced at his wristwatch again. "Well, what do you know?" His gaze met hers. "It's twelve-oh-one."

"Isn't that something?" she said, trying to sound dry. There wasn't a part of her that was dry, literally or figuratively, except maybe her mouth.

"You'll have a drink with me then." It wasn't so much a question as a demand.

"I have to get to work. I doubt my boss'd be too happy having me come staggering in, reeking of alcohol."

"A small drink." Obviously not the kind to take no for an answer, he poured two glasses of wine and lifted one to her.

She waved it away. "I said, no thanks. Don't take this wrong but I have to ask, what's up with the wine? Do you prefer to talk business with soused women or are you just a control freak?"

"I'm sorry if I seem too pushy. I admit I've been told I have some control issues . . ."

"That's big of you to admit."

". . . but the purchase of this particular artifact means a great deal to me and despite the fact that you were also hoping to buy it, I was thinking you might like to celebrate with me."

"Me? Celebrate with you? You don't even know me. I don't know you either." *But boy, would I like to!*

"If anyone, I assume you know the copperplate's value

and might have a measure of respect for the significance of this purchase." He tried to hand her the glass again.

She shook her head, still refusing to accept it. "I'll give you that, but—"

"And as someone who has a great deal of respect for such antiquities, and a person of character," he added, emphasizing the last part. "I appreciate the fact that you have no hard feelings for having lost." With beseeching eyes, he offered her the glass for the third time. "Please?"

*Who's saying I don't have hard feelings?* "Um . . ." Good grief, he looked so darn sweet, like a little boy begging his mother for a puppy. What woman could resist? "Okay! Okay. Just spare me the puppy dog eyes, would you?" Besides, what would a single taste of wine do to her? A teeny, tiny sip would be safe. And although it broke her "No consuming any drinks she didn't serve herself" rule, she'd watched him pour it right in front of her. He had no reason to do anything crazy, like drug her. Besides, she was a plain-Jane, horse of a girl—so tall and big-boned for a Filipino woman—no way his type. He was just a lonely man, looking for someone to celebrate his victory with. It was kind of sad when she thought about it that way. She accepted the glass and took a sniff. It smelled strong. She wrinkled her nose and told herself it would have to be a very small taste.

Looking very pleased, he lifted his glass in a toast. "To Filipino copperplates."

"Yeah. Copperplates." She touched her glass to his, drank a small sip, surprised by the fact that she actually enjoyed the spicy but incredibly smooth flavor of the wine. Usually, she hated wine.

He watched her drink over the rim of his glass.

Oh, that was good. She smacked her lips, and just to make sure it tasted as good as she thought it had, she took a second sip before handing him the still half-full glass. "Okay. That's enough wine for me. So, if you'd like to get on with things, explain why you dragged me in here, I'd be mighty grateful." Before he set down her glass, she snatched it from him. "You know what? Think I'll take one more sip." She faked a cough and added in a raspy voice, "The dry air in the car's making me thirsty."

"Yes. Dry air." He watched her drink with laughing eyes then took it from her when she finished. "Are you sure you don't want more? This is an extraordinary vintage. I save it for special occasions."

"No, no. I'd better not. Despite my size, I'm a total lightweight when it comes to alcohol. If I drink any more, I'll be boring you with sob stories about my high-school days."

"That sounds rather pleasant, actually."

"Oh, don't get me started."

"Very well. Maybe another time."

Another time? There was going to be another time? That thought put the parade into overdrive. Things were getting real festive down below. Most notably, the fast but steady beat of the deep bass drum was thrumming in her pussy. The girls were doing triple backflips.

"I was hoping, since you had a keen interest in bidding on the copperplate, that you might know an individual who would be able to translate it? I can't even tell what language it's in, wouldn't know where to begin looking for someone."

All he wanted her for was her connections? Bummer! The parade came to a screeching halt, that is, all but the drum. That still beat at a steady pace down below.

Whoever was pounding on that drum was obviously not paying attention.

"You know, you didn't have to get me tipsy to ask for some help," she pointed out, trying not to sound as disappointed as she felt. "You should've saved your expensive bottle of wine for someone else. I'm afraid you wasted it. Whether I wanted to or not, I can't help you. At least not directly. I work for a woman who has a store in Birmingham. She's the one with the connections. I'm just the buyer."

"Hmm. What's the name of the store? Perhaps I should pay her a visit."

"You're welcome to go there anytime you like. It's open to the public, especially someone with . . ." *Gobs and gobs of cash.* ". . . an obvious appreciation for rare antiquities. The name of the store is Kim's Uniques. We're on Old Woodward, just north of Fifteen Mile road."

"Okay. I know where that is. I appreciate your help. Thank you."

"Not enough to let me buy that copperplate off you?" she joked.

"No, I'm afraid not." He reached forward and rapped gently on the window separating the driver from the passenger area, and the limousine turned up the auction house's driveway and into the parking lot.

Kaya shot Jestin a quick glance—who wouldn't? He was so fun to look at—then got out, ducking against the rain. Getting more drenched by the second, she fumbled with the door locks, cursing them for not being automatic. Finally, soaked to her skin, but at least back to normal with the exception of a slight tingle down below, she plopped into the driver's seat, started the car and flipped on the wipers.

The limousine, and its sexy passenger, were long gone.

Jestin watched the woman fumble with her door locks through the window, tempted to jump out, grab her again and drag her back to him, back into the car, back into his arms, back into his life.

Patience, he told himself. You must be patient.

That had been no ordinary woman. Human, yes. Common, far from it. He knew from the moment they'd first touched, from the blaze that had burned in his blood at the joining of their energies. She had felt it too. And her reaction to the wine—a formula that would make all women but one cough and sputter with disgust—had only affirmed his suspicions.

Kaya Cordova was his mate.

With mixed feelings, he told Bridgette his driver to take him home. He had preparations to make.


"I'M SORRY I'M LATE—"

At hardly over four feet, and probably no less than eighty years of age, Kaya's boss, Mrs. Kim, could hardly be described as physically intimidating. But the little frail-looking woman knew how to work with what she had. She could give a person the nastiest glare this side of the Mississippi at the drop of a hat and it was said one of her mean-eyed stares could make grown men twice her size shake in their boots in fear. At the moment Kaya was at the receiving end of one of those stares.

"You know I have appointment every Friday. I had to cancel," Mrs. Kim said in broken English as she polished a tarnished silver picture frame with brisk movements. "To top it off, you come back a mess and empty-handed? What happen?"

"I'm very sorry, Mrs. Kim. It's raining like you wouldn't believe."

"Really?" Mrs. Kim asked, looking doubtful. She glanced out the door then shook her head. "Why you lie to me?"

"It isn't raining now?" Kaya took a look for herself, then, disgusted at the sight of a cloudless, brilliant blue sky that reminded her of a certain set of eyes, said, "I swear it was raining earlier. And regarding the auction, I really tried. I wanted to get one item in particular. A Filipino copperplate I know Mr. Vandenberg would've paid a small fortune for," Kaya said, referring to their best customer, a man whom she'd never met. "But I was outbid."

"Copperplate?" her boss repeated, still scrubbing.

"I couldn't believe my eyes when I saw it. It looked exactly like the one I saw on the net. Same odd-looking inscriptions, everything."

"You did not get it?"

"The price went sky high, higher than the budget you gave me for the entire auction."

Mrs. Kim set down the frame. "I must have it. You must get it for me. You know the one who bought it? Tell me his name. I bet he work for that Mr. Angus."

"No, I know Harry Angus's buyer and that wasn't him. I've never seen this guy before. I chased him down afterward. In fact that's why I was late. I went to him after the auction, tried to talk him into selling the copperplate to me, knowing you'd feel this way." So she was stretching the truth a smidge, but the subject of selling did come up. She had to cover her butt, get herself off Mrs. Kim's shit list. "Unfortunately, even though it seems he has no idea of what he has, he refused my offer."

"Did you get a card? I call him. He listen to me."

"All I have is a name—Jestin . . . something." Kaya anxiously rummaged through her brain, trying to recall his last name. She was bad with names anyway, but with the added distraction of his eyes, and smile, and those dimples, it was a lost cause. Outside of his first name, the rest had gone in one ear and out the other. "I can't remember his last name," she admitted.

Mrs. Kim mumbled something in Korean, something Kaya knew wasn't polite and she took that as her cue to go in the back and get to work on the books. She was less than halfway through the payables when Mrs. Kim came back and parked herself in front of her desk. Kaya mentally prepared herself for a tongue-lashing.

"I give you big reward," her boss said.

"Reward? For what?"

"You get me copperplate. I give you big reward."

"You mean . . . like a bonus?" Mrs. Kim had never given her a bonus. Heck, Mrs. Kim had never given her a raise, not in three years, even though she'd made her craploads of money.

"Yes, bonus. How about . . ." The older woman eyed Kaya shrewdly. "Fifteen thousand?"

Kaya fought he urge to gasp. "Fifteen thousand dollars?" That was a windfall!

Fifteen thousand would pay for her grandmother to stay in the nursing home she loved for almost six months. That was huge, considering just this week Kaya had been trying to come up with a way to explain to Grandma why she had to move. Still lucid, but getting less so every day, Grandma didn't take bad news well. Even learning the evening's dinner menu didn't include chocolate cake caused an uproar.

"The plate hasn't been authenticated yet."

"I trust your judgment."

"That's very kind but I'm certainly no expert—"

"I give you fifteen thousand if you can get it from man Jestin."

"I . . . I'll see what I can do. I'll need some time to find him, since I can't remember his name. Although I did mention the shop. He said he might come here—"

"You must not wait. He will sell it as soon as he discovers its worth. And I can't afford for that to happen. You must find him first." She shooed Kaya out from behind the desk, through the back stockroom, and out the shop's back door. "You go. Find him. I pay up to fifty thousand for the copperplate. No more. Make him say yes." She slammed the door before Kaya could respond.

After gaping for a few minutes at the closed door, Kaya turned and muttered, "Okay." She got in her car, shoved the key in the ignition, cranked the engine to life, then said, "What now?"

And just then, a crack of thunder ripped through the sky and another downpour coated her car.

"Great. Just great. I'm on the hunt for a devil with dimples in the midst of a hurricane." Not knowing what else to do, Kaya pulled out of the parking lot and headed back toward the auction house. "I hope this storm's not an omen of what's to come." She flipped the wipers on high speed.

# Chapter Two

*I*'M SORRY BUT THAT information is confidential," the woman seated behind the cashier's desk at the auction house said in answer to Kaya's question. "You understand I'd lose my job if I gave out our customer's names and addresses."

"Of course. I'm sorry. But I . . . he . . . Jestin asked me for some information about the copperplate he purchased today. I'd call him but he didn't give me a phone number."

"Yes, well, I'm sorry. I can't help you."

Kaya sighed. "Oh well. Hopefully, he'll be able to find someone to authenticate the plate on his own then. I located the gentleman who'd translated the original copperplate at the National Museum of the Philippines."

The woman looked less than impressed. "Is that so?"

"Couldn't you at least give me his last name? He told me but I'm such a nitwit I forgot."

"I'm sorry. No. If you'll excuse me?" Evidently, trying to get away before Kaya harassed her to death, the woman stood and shuffled out from behind the counter. "I have some work to do."

"That's fine. I'll just be going now. Though, if you would do me a tiny, tiny favor?" She didn't wait for the woman to agree to continue. "If Jestin whatever-his-last-name-is happens to call here, or come in for any reason, will you tell him Kaya Cordova from Kim's Uniques is looking for him?"

"Certainly." The woman disappeared behind a door.

Kaya stood in the lobby, the only things separating her from the information she needed—and possibly fifteen thousand dollars—were a four-foot counter and some nerve. She looked to the right. She looked to the left. She looked up, searching for a security camera.

It was mighty quiet. There wasn't a soul in sight. And no camera either. What luck! What crappy security!

*Go for it!* a voice inside her head shouted. *Before the screen shuts off and you have to punch in a password. No time to wait. Do it now.*

Before she had time to rethink her options, or second-guess the wisdom of what she was about to do, she ducked behind the counter and knelt almost under the desk as she ran the mouse over the countertop, activating the computer screen.

Bingo! The woman hadn't signed out.

Kaya skimmed the registration list for Jestin's name, found it easily then repeated, "Draig, 1253 Lakeshore Drive," over and over as she hurried from the building. Luckily, no one stopped her as she made her hasty retreat.

Lakeshore Drive was at least an easy road to find. As its

name suggested, it ran parallel to the shore of Lake Erie in the affluent town of Grosse Pointe Shores. The homes situated on the road were positively palatial. Owned by some of metro Detroit's more well-known bazillionaires, like business owners, descendants of Henry Ford and professional athletes, they were giant, beautiful, and intimidating.

Jestin's house was no exception.

A home that had to be the size of Kaya's house times five, it was enough to take her breath away. A redbrick fence enclosed the house and surrounding land, an iron gate the only way onto the property. Naturally, it was locked.

Kaya pulled up to the gate's column and pushed the call button. A man's voice—not Jestin's—answered. "May I help you?"

"Hi. My name is Kaya Cordova," she said into the little metal speaker box. "I'd like to see Mr. Draig."

"One minute please."

Kaya toyed with her key ring as she waited for the man to determine whether or not she warranted a visit to the handsome and obviously extremely wealthy Jestin Draig.

Moments later, the gate swung open. Assuming that was an invitation to enter, Kaya drove up the tree-lined drive to the house, parked and walked the short distance to the front door.

If ever Kaya Cordova—humble buyer who very rarely rubbed shoulders with the rich and famous—felt out of place, it was the moment she stepped into Jestin's foyer.

She swallowed back a sigh of amazement, forced her gaping mouth to close before something unfortunate happened, and nodded as Mr. Gibs, the elderly gentleman who let her in, motioned her to follow him into a dark, cozy study.

She took a seat in a huge leather chair and waited for Jestin to join her, thanking Mr. Gibs before he left.

"What a pleasant surprise." Jestin's deep voice, smooth as satin and warm as hot chocolate, caressed her raw nerves.

Almost feeling at ease, she twisted her body to greet him with a big smile. "I was in the neighborhood and thought I'd stop by."

He had a pleasant smile on his face too. So pleasant, in fact, that her heart did a funny little hop in her chest and her cheeks flamed hot. "Glad you did." He took the chair next to hers, throwing a casual arm over the back. "Would you like a drink? Some more wine perhaps?" he asked, his eyes glittering with challenge and mischief.

"No, no thanks."

"Very well." He sat back and eyed her sharply for a moment. She couldn't help squirming under his assessing gaze. Not only did it make her feel exposed, but also incredibly turned on. Like grab-the-man-and-jump-his-bones turned on. As she struggled with the urge to either give in to the temptation or run like a great big chicken, he asked, "Would you care, then, to tell me the real reason you're here?"

"I have a feeling you know," she practically stuttered.

He leaned forward, looked her dead in the eyes and said, "Indulge me."

Her breath caught in her throat at the double entendre. The more liberal parts of her psyche and anatomy prepared to do just that as her mind screamed, "Whoa, Nelly!"

"I . . . I came to make you an offer on the copperplate," she said.

"Oh, that." He donned a reasonably convincing pout. "I'd hoped your visit was of a . . . more personal nature."

*Me too.* "I'm sorry to disappoint."

"No, no. Don't be sorry. I'm not. However, I will tell you I am not interested in your offer to purchase the plate. At least not at this time."

"I'm prepared to offer you a great deal of money."

"Which I appreciate."

"Thirty thousand."

He waved the figure away. "You must understand something about me."

"Okay, thirty-five."

"I do not do business with people I don't know personally. It's a practice I inherited from my father. My father was a very successful man," he added, meaningfully.

"I understand. Forty?"

"And so," he said, crossing his thick arms over his chest in a show of iron will. "I'd say you have two choices. Either you can give up trying to purchase the plate from me and leave now, or you can spend the evening with me and get to know me personally."

"Personally? Wait a minute," she drawled, wagging a finger at the suspicious glimmer she saw in his eyes. "Something sounds fishy here. You want me to get to know you personally?" She scooted forward in the chair, planted her hands on her hips and gave him a challenging glare. "Are you sure you're not just trying to get me to sleep with you?"

He had the nerve to laugh at her! "As I said, I do no business with strangers, and I assure you, many of my business associates are men. Would you make the same assumption if you were a male?"

She shrugged, trying not to look worried about the fact that she was rapidly losing control of these negotiations. She couldn't afford to do that. But it was so hard to keep her mind on track with so much wicked temptation staring back at her. Especially when he kept showing off those dimples. "I might. For all I know, you could be homosexual."

"I assure you I'm not homosexual." He gave her one of the most sinful grins this side of Hades.

Her cheeks burned and her knees melted to the consistency of molten marshmallows. Worry stiffened her spine, reinforcing it, but only slightly. There was too much at stake here to be allowing a smile, a set of the cutest dimples on earth and a few naughty suggestions to mess with her mind. *Get it together, girl! You're about to let the charmer wearing designer duds and a pair of killer dimples win round two.* "Then you aren't telling me I have to sleep with you to buy the plate?"

"No. If you decide to sleep with me, it will be because you want to, not because you are coerced," he said in a voice that had her almost ready to throw up the white flag in surrender. "I don't have any respect for a man who must trick or force a woman into sleeping with him."

For some reason, his last comment didn't ease the worst of her worries. She'd learned a long time ago that sex and business didn't mesh. She couldn't afford to blow this deal, yet she wanted to sleep with him like she'd never wanted to sleep with a man before. And he hadn't done anything more than bat his eyelashes, flash an occasional smile and toss a couple of suggestive comments her way. "Even so, this is an extremely unusual request and frankly, I don't think it's—"

"I would like to assure you that whatever we do—or don't do—tonight would not be held against you in our negotiations. Along the same vein, sleeping with me will not make me lower my price. And so, the choice is yours. Spend a pleasant evening with me, and have some chance of buying the plate, or refuse and have none." He sat back and waited, his unwavering gaze on her face making it mighty difficult to think about anything but jumping into the nearest bed with him.

"Let me make sure I've got this straight. You want to spend the evening with me. Yet, anything I do during that time won't help me. Nor will anything I refuse to do hurt me."

"In a nutshell, yes."

"Any catches—er, besides the obvious?"

"None. Oh, that is, unless you have a problem with being honest."

"Oh?" She felt her cheeks flaming for the umpteenth time. She didn't remember ever blushing so often in such a short span of time.

"I value honesty above all else, in both business and personal relationships and I intend to test your integrity tonight. No matter what question I ask, you must answer it truthfully."

"All this to do a single deal?"

"That's right."

"And you expect complete honesty? Always?"

He nodded.

She swallowed a lump the size of a bowling ball in her throat. While she wasn't one to lie constantly, she'd always been a firm believer in the benefits of the occasional white lie. This was especially true when it came to dealing with men, and in business. "I don't know. Like I said, this is highly unusual. I need to think."

"Take all the time you need." He looked down at his watch.

Mrs. Kim's promise of fifteen thousand dollars echoed in

her head and she dropped her gaze to the floor to give herself some room to think. Would it be so bad to spend an evening with a rich, handsome man? Maybe even—gasp!—sleep with him just for the fun of it? It had been so long since she'd had sex, she'd almost forgotten what it felt like. And she'd never slept with someone who looked like Jestin, or someone who possessed such an air of restrained power before. There was some kind of invisible force around him. She could practically see it.

She could get around the lying thing, she was pretty sure. Besides, he wouldn't know if she was lying. He couldn't read minds. No one could do that.

She nodded. "Very well. Only one evening?"

"Yes. Tonight. You will have dinner with me." He glanced at his watch again. "I prefer to dine early. Three o'clock."

"That's fine. I didn't have any lunch." She didn't add the reason why she'd missed her lunch break—specifically because he'd insisted on taking her for that little car ride.

"Excellent. Afterward, I always enjoy a spell in the steam room and then a massage. You will join me." Again, that was no question. It was a command.

His tone rankled her a bit but his expression did much to counteract its more unpleasant effects. Once more, she found herself fanning her heated face. Her spine felt soft, her insides flitty and fluttery.

Then, the thought of sitting in a hot steam room with a nude Jestin, the only thing between her body and his a few feet of terrycloth, skipped through her mind and her fluttery insides went all ascurry like leaves blown in a storm. A wave of hot shivers buzzed up and down her spine. Heat pooled in her groin, her empty pussy clenched.

No sooner did the words, "Very well," come out of her mouth than she was being led, her hand in his, up a flight of grand, sweeping stairs to the most opulent bedroom she'd ever seen.

She looked from their joined hands, to his handsome face, to the mammoth bed and muttered under her breath, "Ho boy. I have a feeling I'm in way over my head here."

"Only if you don't appreciate the more refined pleasures of the flesh," he whispered in her ear, his words and the caress of his hot breath on her neck sending a blanket of goose bumps down the left side of her body. Just before completely melting Kaya into a puddle of goo by whispering any more smoldering words in her ear, he turned, strode across the room and opened the door to a large wardrobe. "I think you'll find everything you need in here. Perhaps you'd like to freshen up before dinner?"

Kaya stepped up behind him to take a look. Hanging on padded pink satin hangers were frilly, lacy garments of every color, some skimpier than others. "I see you've done this before. You're better stocked in lingerie than any woman I know. But my mother always told me not to wear another woman's undies. Ew."

"You'll find that none of the garments have been worn. They all still bear their sales tags. I had to guess your size. I hope they fit—"

"You bought all these for me?" She tugged at a long, white satin gown, ran her fingers down the smooth fabric, measuring its weight. It was pricey, not doubt about it. "After what? A ten-minute ride in your car? Doncha think that was just a smidge premature?"

"I knew you would come."

"My, my, my, aren't we full of ourselves?" she asked, sifting through the other garments. They were all absolutely gorgeous.

"No, I knew you wanted the plate. Besides, the security officer at the auction house called. If you had any aspirations of getting into the spy business, I suggest you consider something a little safer instead, preferably that doesn't involve keeping secrets, stealing information or performing any other covert operations. To put it bluntly, you stink at it."

She dropped her hand and lifted her guilty gaze to his face. "They saw me?" Her cheeks flamed hotter than they already were. "Why didn't they stop me?"

"Because I told them to let you go." He reached into the wardrobe and pulled out an ankle-length, white terrycloth robe. He handed it to her as she stood gape-mouthed, still trying to respond to his answer.

Finally, she opted to just close her mouth and nod.

"Have you ever had a massage?"

Still unable to speak, she shook her head.

"You may keep on your underclothes if it makes you feel more comfortable. And you may choose between a masseur or masseuse."

"I'm easy. Whatever. Just make it someone who's blind, if you could. That way they won't see anything that'll crack them up."

"I assure you anyone in my employ is a professional and would never laugh at any of my guests."

"Okay," she said reluctantly. "I'll take a woman then. A big-boned woman like me who has real boobs . . . and cellulite. I don't want a mannequin with a twenty-two-inch waist and perfect hair."

"I can manage that."

"Good. That makes me feel better." She waited for him to speak, but he simply pointed at the robe. "Oh! Do you want me to undress now? Before dinner?" She stood holding the robe to her chest, not sure if he expected her to shed her clothes right there on the spot, with him watching. She had no intention of doing so, if that was the case. Nor did she intend on wearing any of those sexy numbers he'd had the gall to buy for her. What . . . what nerve!

Nerve like steel. Muscles like steel too. She liked steel.

"You can change now if you like. I will be. I prefer to be comfortable when I eat. Also, I want you to know that even if you wear none of these tonight, I wish to give them to you as a gift. You will take them with you when you leave. I admit, I have a weakness for buying lovely things for women, particularly women who spark my interest as you have."

She sparked his interest? Big-boned Kaya Cordova? "I . . . I . . ."

"I will leave you to your preparations. There are some personal items in the bathroom, if you need them." He motioned toward the nearby door. "I will return in a half hour."

"Okay."

The second he closed the door behind him, she made a mad dash for the bathroom. She stripped nude and turned on the tub's tap then sat on the tiled deck and hung her legs over the side to give them a quick shave. Continuing north, she shaved her way up to her armpits, making sure she left every inch of skin silky smooth. Then she coated herself with the scented body lotion he'd so kindly supplied, put on a pair of clean, black lace undies and the matching bra—the man had guessed her sizes perfectly. She wasn't sure if that was a good thing or not—and shrugged into the robe. After brushing her teeth, fixing her makeup and fooling with her hair, she returned to the bedroom.

He was waiting for her. He greeted her with a quick visual assessment and a smile that left her knees wobbly.

# Chapter Three

$\mathcal{S}$ITTING IN A CHAIR with only a teeny, tiny towel wrapped around his hips, one arm curled over the top of the chair, the other draped over the padded armrest, Jestin was once again living, breathing temptation. Kaya's gaze flitted over his broad shoulders, wide chest and muscled stomach like a butterfly hopping from flower to flower. Finally, after skidding down his smooth-skinned legs, also corded with muscles, it found a resting place on his face.

"I trust everything is to your liking," he said.

"And how."

"I wasn't sure if you preferred any particular brands of lotion, shaving creams or toothpastes."

"Oh, that." Her face heated again with embarrassment. "No, I'm easy. Don't care much what brand it is, as long as it does the job."

"Very good. Are you ready?"

"Yes. But . . ." She let her words trail off. Surely he meant to put some clothes on before they went down to dinner.

He raised his eyebrows in question as he stood his full six-foot-something.

"That's what you call comfortable?" She motioned to his naked torso. "I mean, don't get me wrong, I appreciate comfort as much as the next girl, but most people prefer wearing clothes when they eat."

"I don't. In fact, normally I'd eat completely nude. I'm forgoing that pleasure for you." He offered his arm to her. "Shall we?"

She took a split second to admire the way the thick ropes of muscles of his arm flexed as he moved, before curling her hand around his forearm. "Okay. I just hope you don't spill anything hot on yourself. You could end up with a wicked burn."

"Wouldn't be the first time," he said with a twinkle in his eye. He led her down the main staircase to the ground level of the house, across the humongous foyer and down a hall to a grand dining room with deep burgundy walls and rich swathes of fabric dressing a line of windows along one wall. In the room's dead center stood a massive rectangular table fashioned out of dark wood that had to seat at least thirty people.

It was the most bizarre, most fascinating table she'd ever seen. In the place of legs in the four corners were four wooden sculptures of dragons. Their mouths were open, their hands holding opaline globes the size of softballs. Their tails curled up around their bodies to provide additional support to the tabletop that had to weigh a ton. Along the center of the tabletop ran a deep burgundy runner with a continuous line of unlit candles.

Jestin led her across the room, past the table to a door at the rear. They stepped into a smaller, more intimate room with gold walls, a single window and a round pedestal table. The only light in the room came from the five candles in the candelabra sitting in the table's center. Right away, Kaya spied the two place settings, complete with filled stemmed glasses and plates with those metal covers on them to keep the food warm.

Every cell in her body was aware of Jestin's nearness as he pulled out her chair for her. The sensitive skin at her nape tingled when his breath brushed oh-so softly against it like feathers. Stifling a shudder of cold-heat, she scooted her chair in and watched Jestin sit.

The soft candlelight did amazing things to his hair, turning it into a burnished golden color. It also made his face look harder. Deep shadows slashed under his cheeks, eyes and mouth, making him look mysterious, dangerous, despite the smile pulling at the corners of his lips.

He lifted his glass in a toast, and mesmerized, Kaya mirrored his action. "To new acquaintances," he said, gently tapping his glass to hers.

She nodded in agreement then stole a single sip of the wine. It was very similar to the last one she'd tasted with him, in the limousine.

He set the glass on the table then nodded at someone or something behind her. His gaze was above her head level. Before she could turn around to see who it was, an arm reached around her side.

Startled, she jumped, lunging sideways.

The hand, which was attached to a black suit-bedecked arm, which was attached to Mr. Gibs, lifted the silver cover on her plate. Then he stepped away silently, rounded the table and did the same for Jestin.

After she was relatively sure she wouldn't have another surprise, for at least a little while, she glanced down at her plate.

The strange-looking food, which was totally foreign to her, was arranged in the deliberate manner she'd seen on those food shows on cable television. It looked like a little sculpture rather than something she'd want to eat. Not exactly eager to take a taste—she preferred plain old comfort foods like mashed potatoes and extra-crispy fried chicken— she lowered her head slightly to take a whiff.

Fish. She hated seafood.

"Is something wrong?" Jestin asked.

She jerked upright, blinking innocently. "No, no. Nothing's wrong." She tried on a convincing grin for size. Clearly it didn't fit.

Jestin's brows bunched together over the bridge of his nose. He eyed her speculatively, which made her squirm. "Are you certain? Do you have an objection to something on your plate?"

"No . . ." she said, not wanting to be rude. Her mother had always told her it wasn't polite to complain to your host about the food.

Jestin's eyebrows rose. His gaze followed, lifting to where she assumed Mr. Gibs was standing behind her. "Gibs?" he asked.

Mr. Gibs answered. "I am afraid she is lying, sir."

"As I feared." He gave her a martyred look. "As I said, I

expect complete honesty, Kaya, or we are wasting our time."

Kaya twisted her torso to give Mr. Gibs a look. When Gibs responded with nothing but an empty stare, she turned forward again. "What's he? Your lie detector-slash-butler?"

"Among other things. Gibs has been in my employ for a long time. I trust his judgment." He added meaningfully, "A wise man knows who to trust."

"You really have a thing about trust, don't you?"

"I have my reasons. A man in my position must know who he can trust and who he can't."

"A man in your position? Are you like a spy or something? Would you have to kill me if you told me what you do?"

"Maybe." He winked. "No, I'm not a spy. But you could say I'm in the security business."

"Ah." She nodded. "Are you like a personal bodyguard to someone famous or more like a mall rent-a-cop?"

"Neither, actually. My work is a little more complicated than that. So," he said, forking a morsel of green stuff with yellow sauce into his mouth and chewing, "would you care to tell me what your objection is to the food?"

He wasn't going to let it rest, darn it. "I was trying to be polite, you know."

"Which I appreciate."

"And I can appreciate your need to determine who is trustworthy and who is not but I'm of the not-all-lies-are-equal mindset myself. When it comes to something insignif-icant—like my dislike of seafood—I think there's nothing wrong with telling a little white lie." She turned her body so she could give Mr. Gibs another look. "It certainly doesn't mean I'm not trustworthy, at least not in my book."

"That may be so, but then you would walk away from my table hungry and that is unacceptable." He nodded to Gibs and the butler left the room.

Alone with Jestin at last. That realization gave birth to a flurry of contradicting emotions, along with a few stuttering heartbeats and a smattering of goose bumps. Why had he asked the butler to leave? Was he going to do something good? Or bad? She positioned herself so she was facing Jestin straight on again.

"You do not like sushi?" Jestin asked.

"Oh, for heaven's sake. It's only food. Why are you getting so obsessed?" When he didn't respond, she added, "If I'm not mistaken, sushi's not just fish, but raw fish." She stifled a grimace of outright disgust and tried to paste an impassive expression on her face. "Eating raw meat of any kind is dangerous. I won't touch meat that isn't thoroughly cooked, even steak," she said with a level voice.

"How unfortunate." He slipped another forkful of the icky food between his lips. She watched as he slowly drew the fork's empty tines from his mouth. He chewed slowly, visibly savoring the food's flavor. His tongue darted out to lick away a bead of moisture clinging to the center of his bottom lip. She felt herself unconsciously mirroring his action. She even swallowed when he swallowed. She had to admit, he made raw fish look absolutely sinful. "Have you never tasted a steak cooked to perfection—still pink on the inside, seared and spiced on the outside?" Jestin asked.

"No. I prefer my steak with no pink whatsoever."

"But a rare steak is so tender . . ." he said as he stared into her eyes and she felt a few of her muscles getting soft, ". . . juicy and flavorful."

There went a few more muscles. Pulverized to mush. She whimpered.

Gibs snatched away her plate and replaced it with another one. He silently lifted the lid, revealing a thick filet and baked potato with the works. She looked up at Jestin's face.

He smiled and motioned toward the plate. "Better?"

"Yes. Thank you, but I hope it wasn't too much trouble. I wouldn't have said anything if you hadn't made me."

"No, no. Don't worry. Just enjoy." He watched as she cut a small piece, checked to make sure it was cooked through then put it in her mouth.

A parade of spices marched over her tongue as she chewed. She felt herself smiling. She'd never tasted a steak that delicious. Never. It put her favorite steak house to shame. "Oh. Wow."

"Is that a good wow or bad?" he asked.

She swallowed and cut another piece, quickly filling her mouth again. "Definitely good. Very good," she said around the steak. Swallowing first, she added, "This is the most delicious steak I've ever tasted. I don't suppose you'd give me the recipe?"

"It's a family secret," he said, looking mysterious and amused and sexy. He leaned forward, his gaze riveted to hers, and murmured, "I'm afraid I'd have to kill you if I told you."

She giggled as she finished her dinner. It wasn't easy eating when her innards were tied into knots and her throat felt like it was swollen shut from nerves. But she managed to eat a respectable amount. Gibs took their plates away and replaced them with small bowls of ice cream. Chocolate therapy.

She loved this man, consumer of raw fish or not.

Jestin ate the ice cream in the most provocative way possible—tongue licking, lips smacking—and she swallowed a guffaw, instead wagging her finger at him and shaking her head in a show of disapproval.

"You are bad," she scolded.

"You have no idea how bad I am," he said in a low voice that hummed in her belly and made her feel all girly and soft. He stood and reached for her hand. "Shall I show you?"

She looked up into his sparkling eyes and nearly threw herself at his feet, shouting, *Hell yes!* Instead she gave him a light punch in the gut and stood. "You behave yourself, Mr. Naughty, or I'll tell Gibs to send you to your room for a time-out."

She caught the low rumble of Gibs's laughter and turned her head to look at him. He wore a severe poker face.

"I heard you," she said to Gibs. "You laughed, and before I leave tonight I'll make you pee your pants you'll be laughing so hard."

"I," the butler said with a less than enthused expression on his face, "look forward to seeing you try."

"Ha!" Jestin laughed. His face shone with such boyish delight, her knees nearly gave out. To keep herself erect, she gripped his arm and hung on. Naturally, the skin-to-skin contact only made things worse. A wave of warmth washed over her body as she tried to distract herself with thoughts about Gibs and how she'd make good on her promise. He was clearly a tough nut to crack.

Unfortunately, her efforts didn't help much. Feeling all jittery and girly, she let Jestin lead her up the stairs and down the hall. They passed through what looked like a workout room, but with some gear she'd never seen before, into a smaller area. A glass door on the back wall opened to the cedar-lined sauna room.

It was blazing hot in there, so hot, her face burned after only a few seconds. Knowing she wouldn't be able to stay in there for long, she glanced at Jestin as she took a seat on a towel-covered wooden bench.

He looked as cool as a proverbial cucumber, even as sweat poured from every pore of her body, making her feel slick and slimy. He smiled. "The heat rejuvenates me, gives me energy."

"It's draining mine. I'm afraid if I don't leave in a few seconds you'll be carrying me out."

"Just a minute more. Do you know all the health benefits of dry heat?"

"No."

"Heat helps keep your heart healthy, aids in weight loss—"

"Are you trying to tell me something?"

"Absolutely not!" He gave his head an emphatic shake. "It also helps keep your skin youthful by cleansing toxins."

"Great, so you're telling me I look old and am fat," she teased giving him the eye. "I'm dying here. I think I'd rather carry a few extra pounds and bags under my eyes than sit in this miserable heat for another minute." Barely clinging to consciousness, she watched him close his eyes. He looked so peaceful, so comfortable, so in control. Not even his hair seemed to be touched by the heat. The flirty curls were the same, silky and shiny. His golden skin didn't even look pink. It was as if the heat didn't touch him. "It's not fair. Looks like you haven't even broken a sweat yet while my makeup's melted off my face and my hair is a limp, sticky mess."

When he opened his eyes, she caught a strange violet flash in them, like a bolt of static in a darkened room. Then he stood and pushed open the door, taking her hand in his to lead her from the heat into the chill of the workout room.

"Follow me."

She followed, eyeballing the workout gear as she walked. "What is this stuff? Is it for Pilates or something? I don't see any weights."

"Not exactly," he said with a chuckle.

Now extremely curious, she stopped in front of a tall thing with what looked like Velcro wrist straps dangling from it. "Oh! I get it. They work on some kind of pulley system." To test her theory, she reached out and gave one of the wrist straps a sharp yank. It didn't budge. "Wow. You must be strong. The tension is set awfully high. I can't get it to budge even a little."

"Well, should you decide to put any of this equipment to use, I'd be glad to make some adjustments," he said, laughter making his voice uneven. "However, I think I should explain one thing to you. This equipment isn't for your traditional workout."

"My point, exactly. I'm hardly keen on the latest gym gear. I admit I avoid the gym like the plague, but this stuff doesn't look like anything I've ever seen in a gym before."

"That's because it isn't supposed to be in a gym."

"Huh?"

"This is a dungeon."

"Dungeon?" She took another look at the room and its furnishings. "First of all, didn't those go the way of dragons and princes on white stallions, eons ago? And aren't they supposed to be down in the bowels of the basement? Dark, spooky places where prisoners are kept? Why would you have a dungeon next to your bedroom?"

"It's not the kind of dungeon you're thinking of, though I was fond of those as well. They bring back such pleasant memories." He sighed.

"You've lost me."

"This is where my clan role-plays. This is where we play sexual bondage games."

Kaya felt her jaw drop but lacked the wherewithal to pull it up off the floor. Shock slammed through her body, reaching her brain last. "Bondage games? As in BDSM?" On the wake of shock rode profound fascination.

He nodded.

She felt his gaze on her as she hesitantly approached the same piece of equipment she'd touched earlier. It was tall and reminded her of stocks, or a cross. "What's this one for?" When he touched her shoulder, she shuddered, but not because she was scared. She was far from frightened.

"A slave would stand either facing the wall or this way," he eased her around until she was facing him and her chest was pressed against his solid bulk. "Would you like to try it?" At her silent response, a wide-eyed head-nod, he lifted her right arm and wrapped the strap around it then did the same with her left. "As you see, the slave is now powerless to stop me from giving her any sort of pleasure I might like to. Like this." With no warning whatsoever, he tipped his head and slanted his mouth over hers. His lips feathered soft kisses on each corner of her mouth before hardening, making her heart skip a few beats and stealing her breath. When she opened her mouth to draw in a gulp of much needed air, his tongue dipped inside to stroke hers.

Instantly she found herself dizzy and weak with need. Her pussy throbbed with each pounding beat of her heart. Her knees softened. Her body tensed. And her self-control snapped. Just like that, she realized she would sleep with him. Tonight.

His kiss was hot and demanding and thorough and she quickly lost herself in it, in his flavor, in his spicy, masculine scent, and in the emotions they stirred in her. She felt such joy, such hunger, such need to relinquish all control to him, body and mind. The feelings swirled round and round inside her until they were all mixed up and she couldn't tell what was what anymore.

His tongue stroked hers, twisted, thrust, tasted. Drowning in swelling need, she met his fire with her own heat, silently pleading with him to take her. Her arms still tied out to the sides, leaving her hands useless yet itching to touch him, to pull him closer, she groaned in agony into their joined mouths.

She was going, going, gone. Her heart was pounding so hard, it was bound to leap from her chest. Her lungs were screaming for air she didn't have the ability to draw in. Just when she thought she'd die, he broke the kiss and pulled those wonderful lips, that magical tongue from her.

And she thought she'd known what agony was!

In those seconds, while she struggled to keep herself vertical, she thought back to all the times she'd done the safe thing, stuck her toe in the water to test it rather than just suck it up and dive in. What had her playing-it-safe, take-no-risks attitude gotten her? Had it spared her any pain? Maybe a little. Had it also stolen her chance to find even fleeting bits of happiness? Of experiencing everything life had to offer—both good and bad?

It had! Her fears had been more powerful bindings than anything she'd find in a dungeon. They'd made her a prisoner. They'd caged her more effectively than any cement walls, or bars, or cell ever could.

It was time to break free, take a chance, live life. It was Jestin who had helped her see that.

"We're going to miss our massage," he said.

She puffed up her chest, pushing her breasts forward, and lifted her chin. "To hell with the massage."

The fingertip of his right index finger traced her jaw then slid lower, along her neck to her breastbone. It stopped where the deep V-shaped opening of her robe closed. "Then you wish to be here with me? I will say this again because I want you to be sure. You do not have to sleep with me if you are not certain it's what you want."

"Believe me, there isn't a part of me that isn't certain."

"Very well." Jestin looked as pleased as Kaya felt as he unfastened her wrists. Kaya shook her arms and rubbed her wrists when they were unbound. "We will go into the bedroom now."

"We will?" She took another look around. "But this place has promise and I'm intrigued, thanks to that sneak peek you gave me." When he gave her one of his trademark lifted-eyebrow "really?" looks, she amended her position. "Okay, okay, it's a little scary too. Maybe too scary. You don't get into pain or anything, do you?"

"Nothing you can't handle." He reached forward and raked his fingertips over her right breast through the rough cotton robe. Her nipple tingled and puckered, the reaction making her gasp in surprise. No man had ever stirred such overwhelming wanting in her body before. He smiled at her then caught her arms in his fists and dragged her closer until all her soft curves were pressed against his hard angles. He tipped his head and found the sweet spot on her neck. He nibbled and kissed in between words. "You're not quite ready for the dungeon yet, don't have a respect for what it means to be here with me. But that doesn't mean things won't get hot. In fact, just in case I go a bit overboard, we'll have to come up with a safe word before we start."

"Safe . . . word?" She let her eyelids shutter out the visual distractions and concentrated on the fire he was churning in her body with every touch and kiss. Goose bumps erupted over one side of her body as mind-blowing need pulsed through her veins. Her pussy burned to be filled, her body burned to be possessed, her spirit burned to be complete. Complete with this man, a man she hardly knew.

"Yes," he whispered. His hand slid into the opening of the robe and traced the cup of her lace bra. Her spine arched, pushing her breast into his palm. "Hmmm." His voice rumbled through her body like thunder on a still summer night. "Give me a word you would not normally say during lovemaking, something easy to remember and say."

Say? Talk? Think? How could she do any of those things with his hand closed over her breast, kneading it and grazing her sensitive nipples until she wanted to scream. And his mouth . . . the things he could do with his mouth. She was sure her neck would never be the same. "Like . . . ice cream?"

He unfastened the front clasp of her bra then closed his hand over her bared breast. His touch was like a brand, so fiery it left her reeling. "Yes, like ice cream," he murmured. As if he wanted to illustrate, he dropped to his knees, untied the belt of her robe and parted it. Then he ran his velvet tongue over her nipple as if he was licking an ice cream cone. Over and over until she swore her blood was on fire and her legs shook with the effort of standing. He scooped her up into his arms and carried her toward the door. "If I do something you don't like and you want me to stop, say ice cream and I'll stop."

"Okay," she whispered, wrapping an arm around his neck.

His soft hair tickled her arm as he turned his head to see where he was walking. But that was nothing compared to the other sensations her body was being pummeled with while he carried her.

She felt weightless in his arms. Small and powerless yet safe. There was something, some kind of energy that buzzed around him, humming just slightly in her ear. The sound seemed to seep into her pores and buzz through her bones like a low vibration, making her pussy throb until she thought she'd weep.

*How are you doing this to me?*

He opened the door to a huge, opulent bedroom with a bed that put a king-size bed to shame. It was giant, the size of a smaller bedroom all in itself. Low, it sat on some type of pedestal she couldn't see. It looked like it was hovering above the floor on air.

He lowered her onto it. The mattress was extremely soft and she sank into it, making her feel like she was lying on a cloud. When he climbed over top of her, she shivered.

Her body tight and ready, her pussy wet, burning for his touch, she didn't want to wait another second for him to fill her. "Please," she whispered. "Take me now."

In response, he silently helped her shed her robe. When she met his gaze, she swore she saw red and gold flames in his eyes, sparking, dancing, whirling.

*Who are you? What are you?*

She lay on her back, mesmerized by the sight of those flames until he pulled off the towel hiding his erection. Then her focus definitely went south.

His cock was huge, and quite clearly ready. It stood fully erect. Her fingers itched to trace the rim of the head. She ached with the need to take it into her mouth and taste him.

As if he could read her mind, he shook his head and pressed down on her shoulders. Then he scooted back toward her bottom and dropped his fiery gaze to her mound. "Open for me," he commanded, his tone resonating like a gong through her trembling body.

*How are you doing this to me?*

"You will have your answers soon, my sweet," he murmured. He used both hands to gently pull her bent knees apart until her pussy was open and exposed.

She once again shuttered out the world by closing her eyes, hardly able to sift through the intense sensations he stirred in her body through the other four senses. His touches left her skin aflame. His voice made her insides thrum. His sweet, spicy taste still lingered on her tongue. She drew his scent into her nostrils. It too was sweet and spicy like her favorite Thai food, and she couldn't get enough. She eagerly drank it in, breathing in deeply over and over until she was dizzy.

"I'm going to taste you now," she heard him say. But so lost in the rapture of those overwhelming sensations and the joy they brought, she hardly comprehended them.

She felt him push her knees back farther, until they were so wide apart the muscles of her inner thighs burned with the stretch. His soft curls tickled her skin as he lowered his head. Then he touched her. One fleeting touch to her labia and she was nearly out of her mind with wanting. He parted her swollen lips and found her clit, flicking his tongue over it. She heard herself cry out. Each flick of his tongue was like the lick of flame. Balls of white light danced behind her closed eyelids. She shivered with fever as his tongue danced over her clit, carrying her closer to release with every stroke.

And then she was there, her body coiled tight like a spring, at the pinnacle of orgasm. She writhed under him, her pelvis gyrating with every thump of her racing heart. He stopped his oral onslaught on her pussy, traced a burning path up to her throat with his tongue and positioned himself over top of her, his hips between her thighs.

"This is the test," he whispered in her ear as he pressed the head of his cock against her empty pussy.

"Test?" she said, gasping for her next breath. She blinked her eyes open to stare up into his beautiful face.

"If your spirit is strong enough and you are able to accept what most people believe is impossible, then when we join, you will have your answers. You will see me as I truly am."

Despite being nearly blind with need, she reached up and ran her fingers over the smooth skin of his shoulders. It was cool under her touch. Soft as satin. "I don't understand."

"Whatever you see, you must not be afraid. It is me and I will not hurt you. Not ever. Do you believe me?"

A little scared, curious and overwhelmed, she looked

into his eyes, searching their sapphire depths for answers to her doubts.

"Take my strength, draw from it if you must, if you feel yourself being overcome. I want you to." And with that, he pulled back his hips and then drove his cock deep into her pussy.

A primal roar burst up from her chest, shot out her mouth at the raw joy and wonder of their joining. As he thrust in a second time, it felt as though she'd been thrown into a blaze, a giant inferno that licked at her skin but didn't burn her. Words that weren't hers, thoughts she hadn't thought, feelings she didn't have coursed through her, binding themselves to her soul. They echoed in her head and pulled at her heart. Joy, sorrow, pain, elation, hope, fear, they churned inside her, growing stronger with every second that ticked by until hot tears seeped from her closed eyes and burned her cheeks.

"That's it, my love. Accept me. Accept all of me and we will grow together. You must trust me, open yourself up to me," she heard him say as his body drove hers to the edge of bliss. Fingers pulled and pinched at her nipples. Teeth grazed the skin of her neck. His cock filled her completely. She pulled her legs back farther and tipped her hips up, changing the angle of his thrusts until she found just the right position.

She felt his weight lift from her body, felt the chill of the air on her skin. Then felt the pressure of a fingertip on her clit, drawing tight circles over it until her mind was numb and her body screaming for fulfillment.

Once more she was there, on the verge of orgasm. Her chest and stomach warmed, her insides tied into tight knots.

Her hands clenched into tight fists, reaching for him. She wanted to feel his weight and heat as she came, needed to feel it pressing against her. Her arms trembling, she reached up, pulled him down until his chest was heavy on hers, and gave herself over to release, letting it sweep through her in a furious blaze.

When the heat eased, she blinked open her eyes.

And sheer terror shot through her body. "Ice cream! Ice cream, ice cream!"

# Chapter Four

THE AIR OVER HER body shimmered and for a brief second or two, the man who had formerly looked like the epitome of California hunk was now about ten feet tall, red—as in red like the color of an Irish setter—and covered with scales. His—no, *its*—face was like a lizard's, with a long snout and sharp teeth the size of her pinky finger, pointed ears and the most bizarre eyes. They were still blue but instead of round pupils, the centers were oblong and vertical like a cat's. A puff of smoke billowed from its nostrils as Kaya let out a full-blown scream.

The air shimmered again, like she was looking through sparkling water and the monster vanished, replaced by Jestin's scrumptious bod. She shook her head, rubbed her eyes and blinked several times. All that did was clear her vision a smidge, allowing her to watch the image shift back and forth several more times from man to monster, monster to man with crystal clarity. What the hell was going on?

Then, as her pussy spasmed, she realized he was still inside her. That . . . whatever he was. She glanced down, following the wide line of his chest and abdomen to where his body met hers. Even now, his gigantic cock was thrusting in and out of her. For a brief instant, his body was coated in scales. That sight made her scream again. She jerked away from him, crab walking backward.

*Look into my eyes, Kaya,* his familiar voice echoed in her head. *Remember what I said? It's still me, Jestin. Your spirit is strong if you're seeing me as I truly am. I would like to mark you now, if you will let me.*

She shook her head against the words rumbling through her body. "You're not marking me with anything until I know what the hell is going on. Is this some kind of joke? Because if it is, it's not funny." Her fingers found the edge of the mattress and she spun around on her bottom, flung her feet over the edge and jumped to her feet. She snatched up a throw from the floor, and in a wild sprint for the door, wrapped it around herself. The second she burst out into the hall, she ran smack dab into Gibs, who didn't look surprised to see her.

"Looks like I didn't have to work hard to get that laugh outta you, did I? Joke's on me. Har-de-har-har. I'm outta here. You and Jestin can have your laugh now. Sick bastards!" She shoved her way around Gibs, heading toward the bedroom where she'd left her purse and clothes.

Unfortunately, Jestin followed her. He stood in the doorway, still morphing back and forth from man to beast, watching her gather her things in her arms. The only thing stopping her from leaving was his body blocking the doorway. "No, Kaya. This is no joke. This is real. I am real. Touch me and you will know the truth."

"Nuh-uh! I'm not getting any closer to you than I have to. I'm not strong and this is insanity. I can't be seeing . . . what I think I'm seeing. You can't be— I can't be— Oh hell! Just let me leave."

The man-monster didn't move. It stood very still, still changing back and forth from one form to another, as she slowly backed away. Her heart pounding so hard she could hear it, she checked the room for another exit. But her gaze kept leaping back to Jestin, taking in every detail of its alternating gorgeous and hideous forms. In its latter state, it sported short arms, hook-shaped digits with long claws, powerful rear legs and tail. The only thing that even slightly resembled the man she knew as Jestin was the beautiful golden mane of hair running down his neck and back. And in a blink he was back to being the beautiful man she knew.

"Trust yourself if you cannot trust me. Believe what your heart is telling you," he challenged.

She ran to the window to see if she might risk jumping. She was only two stories up, but couldn't get the window to open. "What the fuck?" she said, her back turned to him while she continued fighting with the window. "Are these windows nailed shut? Shit! If this is what I get for deciding to cut loose a little and take some chances, then I think I was better off hiding in my cave, watching everyone else take all the risks."

"You don't believe that."

"Wanna bet?"

Once again, he changed into the monster. *I would like to*

*ask you a single question. If you answer honestly, you will have no choice but to see the truth.* The monster took one step toward her. Thanks to his huge size, that one step left her cowering in the corner, nose to chest with it.

"If I answer your question, will you let me leave?"

The monster nodded its giant lizard head. A forked tongue jutted out of its mouth, wagged up and down above her head a couple times like a snake's tongue then disappeared back in its mouth. *If that is your wish.*

She shuddered. "Fine. Ask away. I want to get the hell out of here." *Hell* was for sure the operative word, since she figured that thing had to have escaped the very bowels of it somehow.

"Are you lonely? Have you been searching for something—someone—to fill a void in your life?"

"Yes, but I was thinking about getting a dog. Dogs don't break your heart. They don't cheat on you, or act like they can't live without you one minute and then like they couldn't give a shit whether you lived or died the next. Dogs are loyal and trustworthy and love you even if you forget their birthday. You feed them, you take them for a walk and they love you. End of story."

"Are you afraid to trust? Afraid of me?" it asked, its lips curling back, displaying a single row of razorlike teeth. It bent its neck so its face was inches from hers and his hot, sulfur-smelling breath burned her cheeks and nose.

"Heh, yeah. You look like something out of a sci-fi film," she said, her gaze fixed to those teeth. When it wagged its tongue in front of her nose again, like a lizard looking for its next meal, she said, "Are you going to eat me? Please don't eat me. Oh God." She searched the tiny bit of space between it and her, frantically looking for a clear escape route. Her breath sawed in and out of her lungs in quick, shallow pants and her heart thudded in her ears. Her knees turned to marshmallow and she wondered if she'd be able to make it across the room if she tried to run.

"No, I'm not going to eat you. Remember what I said about my strength?"

Hot tears burned at her eyes but she blinked them away. "Yes, but—"

"Take my hand." It lifted a giant claw-tipped paw.

"No." She shook her head. There was absolutely no way she could touch that . . . thing. That monster, uglier than anything she'd ever seen in a horror flick.

"Please." It nodded again. Light shimmered around it like an iridescent cloud, red and gold and blue. "Take my hand and conquer your fear." Slowly, it reached toward her, its digits curling and uncurling as its paw drew closer, closer to her hand.

She stood frozen like a deer caught in headlights, unable to budge from blinding panic. Then his scale-covered skin brushed against hers and instantly she felt a charge of electricity zap through her body like thousands of volts of pure, raw power. It buzzed up her spine, through her head then down to her toes. She briefly thought about yanking her hand away but something stopped her.

*Take my strength, draw from it if you must. I will not hurt you.*

Her hand shaking, she closed her fingers one at a time around one of his digits and drew in a slow breath. A single eye blink later, a warm sensation seeped up her arm and spread through her body, slowing her racing heart rate. Her trembling stopped. Her knees returned to normal.

"Very good," he said.

As she watched, a mist swirled around the creature like a fog caught in a brisk wind. As the cloud cleared, she saw Jestin, the man, had returned to her and by some miracle she wasn't so anxious to run like a scared ninny from the house. In fact, for some in inexplicable reason, she felt eager to get closer to him.

*This is insanity!*

Why did it feel like she'd never take another breath if she couldn't take it with him? Why did she want nothing more than to mold her body to his, sink into his embrace and shut her eyes to the monster she'd seen him become? She'd never been so forgiving in the past when it came to men. She'd dumped men for much more trivial matters— like a love of seventies classic rock music. Ozzy Osborne? Gag! Why was she now not only able but willing to accept Jestin, despite the fact that he either had played the nastiest trick on her ever, or was some kind of freak of nature?

Maybe it was because he'd trusted her enough to show his ugly side to her, instead of putting on airs and pretending he was perfect, like people usually did when they started a new relationship. Or maybe it was because of the power she could practically see shimmering around him and the way it made her feel—safe, cared for. Then again, maybe it was because she was mentally unstable.

Blinking back tears of confusion, she reached forward and reluctantly caught a lock of golden hair in her fingertips. "Was it a trick?"

"No."

That almost made her feel better. At least he hadn't tried to scare her on purpose, though that left only one frightening option. It was real. "Which one is really you—the monster or the man?"

"They both are. Although you alone can see me in my true form, and only when we are most open to each other—at the moment of climax."

"I don't understand. How could this be? Giant lizards don't exist. At least not in Michigan." Shaking, she released the curl and wrapped her arms around herself.

"Come to me. Let me explain." He drew her into his arms. She fought him for only a second then gratefully fell into his embrace, thankful for the small measure of comfort she found there. Confused, scared, she pressed her cheek to his chest and listened to the slow, steady thump of his heart and the soft whoosh of his breath. He walked her to the bed, sat and positioned her on his lap, capturing her chin in his hand and forcing her to look into his eyes. "I am from an ancient bloodline, one humans think had gone the way of dinosaurs eons ago. In truth, despite their efforts to kill us off completely, we have survived, and continue to increase in strength and number, because we are superior to humans."

"You speak of humans like you're not one," she said, stating the obvious.

"I'm not. I'm an Immortal. What most humans would call a dragon."

"A dragon," she repeated, not sure if she should check herself into the nearest hospital for some major drugs or accept what she'd seen as something more than a hallucination. If she hadn't seen it with her own eyes, hadn't seen the monster that looked exactly like the dragons in the Asian artwork she'd studied in art school, hadn't smelled the scent of sulfur on his breath, hadn't felt the hard ridges of his scaled skin with her own hands, there was no way she'd believe it. As it was and since her senses had never deceived her, she had no choice but to accept the impossible and believe him.

Those adorable dimples poked into his cheeks as his lips pulled into a warm, encouraging smile. His eyes sparkled. "You have passed the second test, have proven yourself strong enough in spirit and thus worthy to be my mate."

"I have," she said, not sure if she was happy about that or not. There was something, she supposed, to being married to a powerful dragon-man who was gorgeous, would live forever, knew how to make her melt like an ice cube on asphalt in July, and had enough money to feed a small nation. But . . . but when she imagined her dream man, scales, a forked tongue and a six-foot-long tail had never been among the attributes she'd visualized. "This is very fast. Like I said, I was thinking about buying a puppy, not finding a 'mate'."

He stroked her thigh while he held her. "I understand your ambivalence." He kissed a tingly, tickly trail down her shoulder and arm, making it increasingly hard to remember why she wasn't so sold on the idea of becoming his mate. "I will give you as much time as you need to make your decision."

His promise of patience eased some of her worries but she was still bothered by the truckload of questions rumbling through her brain, not to mention all the tingles and hot flashes his strokes and kisses were birthing. She gently lifted his hand from her thigh. "Thanks. For not pushing me."

"I would never force you to make a decision you're not ready for."

"I appreciate that. In fact, I wish everyone thought that way. I dated a guy once. We were going out for oh, maybe six months and then he threw the 'M' word at me."

"'M' word?"

"Marriage. Then he proceeded to give me a deadline and told me if I didn't have an answer by that deadline, we were done."

"And?"

"I told him I didn't need any more time to think about it. And I left."

He chuckled and she marveled in how deeply she felt the gentle rumbles in her belly, and how the sparkles in his eyes made her all happy and warm inside. Those feelings almost shoved away the lingering doubts, but not entirely. She was never one to make a decision of any kind based on emotion. That was plain foolish.

Facts. She needed facts. Lots of them.

Still, that didn't mean there was anything wrong with having a little innocent fun while she gathered facts, she reminded herself. She could do both concurrently. She was a very adept multitasker. She released his hand, letting it go about its business making her all tingly and hot again. It dutifully carried on.

"I'm not saying I'm agreeing to anything. But I do have some questions," she said. "Like would . . . would we have children? And would they be . . . like . . . you?" she asked, tipping her head back so he could get the sweet spot right below her ear. Oh yeah, that was the one. She shivered, and not because she was scared anymore, and completely forgot what she'd been saying. "This isn't fair," she mumbled, not trying to stop him. "You're using your sex appeal to your advantage. And it's working . . . and here's the kicker, I know you're doing it and I'm letting you because I like it."

"Then I will stop." The hand that had been on her thigh swooped up her body, resting on her tummy while the other one rested at the side of her face. He traced her bottom lip with his thumb. "Yes, you would carry my children. And the pregnancy would be normal, our babies will appear human at birth. There will be only the slightest birthmark to reveal their true nature. Female offspring remain in human form all their lives. The males, however, go through The Change during adolescence, in their late teens."

She was slightly disappointed that he'd taken her half-joking comment about his sex appeal seriously, but also relieved, since she was now a little more capable of thinking, comprehending the facts he was providing to her. "And even though I'm human, the children would be immortal like you?"

"Yes. They are immune to the effects of aging beyond adolescence as well as to all human diseases." He combed his fingers through her hair, capturing a lock and pressing it to his lips. That familiar naughty glimmer sparked in his eyes.

"I see." She squirmed in his lap. Although his words were confusing and her brain felt like it had been scrambled and fried in a pan over high heat, there were other parts of her that seemed to know on a gut level that this was right and that she belonged with Jestin Draig, the dragon-man. "I hate to sound self-involved or shallow or anything but what about me? You and our children would remain young and healthy and I'd become an old hag. I mean, why would you want a stooped old biddy for a wife?"

"With the completion of our Joining, you would become somewhat immortal."

"Somewhat?"

"As long as I remain alive, you would not age. However, you could still die from other causes."

"Interesting. I could live with that, but one last question."

"Go ahead."

"Are there any other Mrs. Jestin Draigs running around the world? I mean, you say you've lived a long time and I'm not so naïve to think you haven't had other women, what with that setup down the hall. But I'm so *not* interested in being a member of a harem. Heck, I can't handle sharing a bathroom with another woman, let alone sharing a man."

He released the tendril of hair and rested both hands on her shoulders. "No. There is no other Mrs. Jestin Draig. Not any longer." His fingers walked up her neck to slide around the back of her head. He traced her lower lip with his thumb. "I was Joined once before. A very long time ago. But my mate died . . . in a tragic accident." Deep pain darkened his eyes.

Wishing she could comfort him but knowing she couldn't, that there was nothing she could say or do that would lift the weight of his sorrow in the slightest, she laced her fingers through his and whispered, "I'm very sorry."

"I wanted to die with Anelise. A part of me did, which was why, up until now, I never considered taking another mate."

Not knowing what to say, wanting to ask him why now and why her but afraid to, she nodded and ran her hands up and down his arms, following them to his shoulders. She leaned into him again, resting her head against his chest.

"I will explain one other thing to you, so that you have all the information necessary to make your decision."

She nodded against him.

"Our people are Guardians. That is our role in the world. Much like in the fairy tales you probably read as a child, we protect things—not usually princesses in high towers—but magical artifacts that would threaten any of the Immortals. There would be some danger—"

"Danger? But you are immortal. What could threaten you?" she asked, suddenly worried for his safety. She straightened up and waited anxiously for his answer.

"Each species has its weakness. They can be destroyed. For the red dragon, my people, it takes the spell spoken by a powerful mage. The spell has been lost to the humans for centuries, so at the moment we are safe."

She wanted to sag against him with relief. The thought of him being destroyed, even if he was scary in his other form, it was simply too much for her to imagine. "That's good to hear. But you said each species. There are other types of immortals?"

"Many different bloodlines, yes. There are the Lamiae, commonly known as the muses, several different clans of vampires including the Ancient Ones and Wissenshaft, and a variety of shapeshifters."

"I thought all those things didn't exist."

"They exist. And as my mate, you will likely meet many of them, which is why I wanted to mention them to you."

"I . . . see," she muttered. She felt like she'd walked into the *Twilight Zone*, or fallen through a hole and landed in a different world, a world she'd never known existed, with strange beings and bizarre rules.

"Of course, the biggest danger to you would come from your own, from humans. And that is if they were to ever learn of my true nature. Even if they could not destroy me, they would try. And their methods would be deadly to you and to any other humans who happened to be in the way."

"Is that what happened to your wife . . . how she . . .?"

"Yes." He blinked several times then continued in a softer voice, "Fortunately, the only way any human would learn what I am is if you told them." He caught her face between his palms, forcing her to meet his gaze. "So again, I challenge you to search your heart. If you make the wrong decision, a great many lives, including your own, could be at stake. I shouldn't have told you so much and I've put my clan members at risk by putting our secrets in your trust so soon."

"I swear I won't tell a soul. Not even my priest."

"You see now why trust is so important to me?"

"I do. But you will give me time to think about this whole mate thing, right? I mean, this is a lot more complicated than deciding what breed of puppy to buy and that's taken me months. Even now, it's a draw between a cute little cocker spaniel or an Irish setter."

"I vote for the Irish setter," he said with a grin.

"Why did I know you'd say that?" She gave him a soft slug in the belly.

"Seriously now . . ." He let his hands fall away from her. "Take as much time as you need. Also, understand that the process of taking a mate isn't a simple one. There are several stages. If you were to change your mind, you could do so at any point up until the final Joining."

"Okay."

He eased her to her feet, stood and helped her find her clothes, then strode past her. "I will leave you to make your decision." He opened the door and stood in the doorway again. "Gibs will help you carry your clothes to your car."

"Okay. Thanks for the beautiful gifts. I never expected . . ." She paused. "But one thing I was hoping for—" She hesitated for a moment then continued, "I hate to bring this up now, after everything that's happened. Everything we've talked about. What about the plate? You said you would consider selling it, if . . ." She let her words trail off again.

"Yes, I did." He looked pained as he nodded slowly.

"If it means someone or something is threatened by your selling it, you don't have to."

"No, no. I must keep my word. But will you give me the same consideration I have given you? Will you come back tomorrow? Spend another evening with me? Give me a chance to consider my terms for the sale?"

Give him the same consideration? Oh, this guy was good. Nothing like heaping on the guilt to make her walk away empty-handed even though he'd told her he would sell it after only one night. "Sure. I'll play along for one more night. After tonight, I'm anxious to see what other surprises you have in store for me. A little scared, too."

"Thank you." He gave her a gentle kiss on the lips that made her insides melt like warm butter. "'Til tomorrow. Seven?"

"Yes. Seven'll be fine." She left later with a car full of sexy lingerie, a brain full of confusing thoughts and no plate for Mrs. Kim. Yet, she was in good spirits.

Unfortunately, Mrs. Kim didn't share her sunny outlook

when Kaya returned to work the next morning and let her know she'd found the buyer and was close to cutting a deal with him for the copperplate. Although Mrs. Kim allowed Kaya to remain at work for the day, she badgered her with a zillion questions about who the buyer was, where he lived, what kind of demands he was making. Kaya kept her answers as vague as possible and kept busy until quitting time. She left, making Mrs. Kim a departing promise that she'd return the next day with the plate in hand or not return at all.

Finally, Mrs. Kim seemed pleased.

Now the pressure was really on. Not only would she lose out on the biggest bonus of her career, but her job as well. She had to do whatever it took to convince Jestin to part with the copperplate. Anything.

Or become his mate tomorrow. A dragon's mate. An Immortal. After having known him for maybe thirty-six hours. Faster than it had taken her to pick out the paint for her living room.

"FORGIVE ME FOR SAYING this. You've made a terrible mistake, sir."

Jestin sighed as he ceased pacing for a second before resuming the useless motion again. It wasn't like it would bring her back to him any quicker. Yet he couldn't bear to stand still. And sitting at his desk and concentrating on his work was damn near impossible. "Gibs, you must trust me," he said with confidence he didn't feel.

"As I recall, that's not in my job description."

"Neither is nagging me, but you do that often enough." Jestin gave his servant and dearest friend a smile to soften the blow of his words. "You know I'd be lost without your nagging, my friend. Promise me you'll never stop."

"You have my word. But what will you do if the woman does not come back? You told her a great deal more than—"

"I had to. She was scared senseless. She will be back. I am certain."

"Is that so? You are certain? Then you are pacing to get some exercise? I give you thirty to one odds she doesn't show."

"Thirty to one? You're mad, but who am I to not take advantage of a madman?" Jestin accepted the wager with a handshake. "Don't you see? She is the one. I thought I could keep things casual, not go through with the final Joining. But now . . ."

"Then God help you."

Jestin purposefully ignored his friend's jab. "I didn't want this. I didn't want another mate. You know how I was after Anelise died. Yet now that I have seen Kaya, talked to her, tasted her, I cannot fathom the idea of existing without her. I know I am right. She drank the wine with no ill effects, she saw me in my base form. Two tests passed and the third—"

"She lied," Gibs pointed out.

"About fish. She answered the most important question truthfully, the one about being lonely and needing someone in her life. Thus she has passed the third test and must merely accept my true form to move to step four."

"I do not think you should've told her everything. She knows too much. You gave her too many reasons not to return."

"Which is wise. When she does come to me, I will know she has done so knowing everything."

"Nearly," Gibs corrected.

"Nearly. I only left out a minor detail."

"She may not find it so minor."

"I will deal with it when the time comes. She wasn't ready to hear it. But tonight when she comes to me, she will have passed the fourth test—having embraced my nature freely. That leaves only two tests remaining. She should be more ready by then."

"You are going too quickly. This should take time— weeks, even months. What if she fails to take the final step? You know the risk to yourself, your people, all of the Immortals. She could reveal your secret, lead your enemies to you. Think what would happen if they found the treasures you have locked away here. With the copperplate alone, they could destroy all the Guardians, which would mean the end for all the Immortals."

"I am aware of that. She could destroy us, yes. But she won't. I'm confident she'll keep our secret. Besides, I'm not convinced she knows what mysteries the copperplate holds, or even has the means to have it translated to find out what they are. But if she does, I have faith she'll return it to me."

"The risk is too great. Anelise was a different sort. She was steadfast, loyal from the beginning. And she was strong."

"And so is Kaya. She will prove so tonight."

"I hope you're right."

"I know I'm right."

"How can you know someone you met just over thirty-six hours ago?" Gibs shook his head. "I will go make the final preparations for your dinner."

"Just make sure her steak is cooked well. She will need a full stomach tonight to face what I have in store for her."

"Too much information, sir." Gibs disappeared through a doorway at the end of the hall, leaving Jestin to pace in peace.

When she didn't arrive at seven on the dot, he told himself she was probably being held up in traffic. When she didn't arrive at five after, he told himself there was probably an accident somewhere causing her delay.

When she still hadn't arrived by five-to-eight, he had no choice but to accept the fact that she wasn't coming and when he did that, he realized exactly how disappointed he was. His mood darkened to the shade of coal. Familiar darkness coiled inside of him, snuffing out the small flickers of light Kaya had ignited the night before. The light he had sworn he'd never again enjoy.

At five after eight, Gibs entered the room with a glum expression that suited Jestin's mood perfectly.

"Why would you look so down, my friend?" Jestin asked. "You were right. You won our wager."

"She has arrived. She is waiting for you in the dining room."

Jestin really had to work hard at not giving loose with a mighty whoop that would echo off every floor, wall and ceiling in his massive home. How much respect would his mate have for a man who shouted like a gleeful boy at her arrival? Instead, he cleared his throat, straightened his tie and smoothed his pant legs. "Very well. Thank you, Gibs. I will join her shortly. As soon as I conclude my business here."

Gibs took in the empty room, clear desk and phone resting quietly in its cradle, smiled slightly and said, "As you wish, sir." He left, closing the door behind him.

Jestin made her wait fifteen minutes before he joined her in the main dining room for dinner. It took every one of those minutes to get his racing heart to slow down, his palms to dry and his breathing to find its natural rhythm. She looked uneasy as he entered. When he stepped near, the sharp tang of her fear stung his nose. She was afraid, yet she came back. He respected her for that. It was a sure sign of strength.

Looking very small in the high-backed dining chair, she tilted her head to look him in the eye. The angle made her eyes look enormous, her heart-shaped face adorable, her thick lashes a mile long, her lips full and tempting. "I apologize for being late. I didn't get out of the store until almost six-thirty and then there was an accident on I-94. Traffic was backed up for miles."

"No need to explain." He scooped up her hand in his, lifted it to his mouth and, staring into eyes the shade of ebony, pressed a kiss to the back of her hand.

She blinked and a hint of pink touched her cheeks. When she dropped her gaze to the salad sitting before her, he released her hand and took his seat next to her, at the head of the table.

"I'm afraid your steak is probably as tough as shoe leather by now," he said after forcing himself to take a bite or two of salad. Vegetables were far from his favorite. Not to mention the fact that the food wasn't moving through his system as it should, thanks to his insides being tied into knots. There were so many things he wanted to share with his Kaya. His mate. Would she let him? Would she get over her fear and learn to trust him?

"That's okay. It's my fault for being late. To be honest, I'm not really hungry. I ate a snack at the store before I left."

"Neither am I," he admitted. "Would you like to retire to the study?"

She looked relieved as she nodded. "Yes. That sounds great. But I'm not insulting anyone by not eating, am I?"

He stood, took her hand in his and waited for her. "Absolutely not, as long as you tell me you're not hungry."

"Believe me, eating is the last thing I have on my mind at the moment," she said as he led her down the hall.

"Hmmm. And if I asked what is foremost on your mind, would you answer truthfully?"

"I would if I knew. Can't say my mind's exactly clear at the moment. It's kind of bogged down with a bunch of things."

"That answer is truthful enough for me." He pushed open the study's door and held it for her, following her into the room and closing the door behind him. He went to the small bar at the rear of the room. "Drink?"

"Just water, thanks."

He poured two glasses of ice water and handed her one, joining her on the settee. After he emptied his glass, he took hers and set them both on the side table. His gaze settled on her lips, tinted an iridescent, glossy pink that reminded him of the roses in his garden.

"I'm . . . I couldn't stop thinking about you last night," she said meekly.

His insides did a few somersaults yet he forced himself to maintain a sedate expression. "Is that so?"

She blinked as she lowered her gaze to her hands, which were sitting restlessly in her lap. "I came here yesterday wanting to buy the copperplate, and I still do. But I also want to know more. About you."

"Are you certain?"

"Yes. The whole dragon thing was a little hard to deal with at first but after a few . . . oh, hours or so . . . I think I got over it. Mostly."

"You are still afraid."

"A little." Still looking down, fiddling with the hem of her top, she nodded.

He lifted her chin with an index finger until she met his gaze. He read so many things in her eyes—indecision, fear, curiosity, to name a few. The others were too vague to identify. "Yet you came here tonight."

"I didn't want to. I mean, I was scared poopless, but honestly I had no choice."

"And I have no choice but to do this." He leaned in, molding his body to hers, and kissed her until his cock ached with the need to plunge into her sweet wetness. She kissed him back with equal heat, her tongue meeting his every thrust with one of her own. Her fingers dug into the flesh of his shoulders, the slight sting of her fingernails a welcome addition to the already overwhelming flurry of sensations battering him. Sounds, tastes, scents, touches. Sweet, hot, soft, tantalizing. They swirled around inside him like a maelstrom. He felt his control crumbling, quickly. His cock strained against his pants, his balls tightened until the skin of his upper thighs burned. Flames licked every inch of his body as overwhelming need blasted through him.

No woman had ever done that to him with just a kiss.

His heartbeat an irregular stutter in his ears, his every muscle a tight knot, he broke the kiss and fell backward against cushions almost as soft as Kaya's gentle curves. "If you are to be with me, and I believe you want to be, you will accept me as your Master."

She looked back at him with heavy-lidded eyes. "I don't know what that means. This is all so confusing. I'm not sure I'm ready."

"Would you like me to explain? Would you like to learn?" He waited for her answer, unable to draw in his next breath until she spoke.

"Yes," she whispered.

"I will show you then. We will go as slowly as you need." So happy he swore he might jump up and down and give a mighty whoop, he stroked her cheek with the back of his knuckles. Her skin was like fine silk. "First, you will address me as Master."

"Okay. Master." The words sounded stilted, awkward coming from her mouth. She grimaced slightly.

"Very good. It will take some time to get used to all this, I understand. But I want you to try. I promise, you'll be pleased with the results."

She gave him a weak smile. "Okay."

"And this is important," he continued, encouraged by her response. "I know it'll be hard, but it's vital. When we are in the dungeon, you must promise to respect me, to always be honest with me, and to trust me, from this moment on. Can you make those promises to me?"

"That's a lot. I mean, I can try. I'm not sure . . ." Her gaze darkened then dropped to the floor. "This is so strange . . . complicated."

Wishing to soothe her, to take away every one of her fears, he ran his hands down her arms. "And I promise to protect you, cherish you and trust you with my very life. Always. No matter where we are."

She didn't speak for a long time. Seconds passed with

the unsteady thump of his heart. One, two, three. Finally, she lifted her gaze and looked him in the eye. "Please. Teach me. What do I do first?"

"Kneel before me like this." He gently coaxed her to kneel with slight pressure on her shoulders. "This is how you show me you are ready to listen, to do my bidding." She looked up at him with wide eyes for a moment then lowered them in a natural show of subservience that made his heart swell. He would serve this woman, his mate, Kaya Cordova, for the rest of his days. He would show her the joy that came from conquering her fears and make her every fantasy come true.

"That is very good." He scooped her into his arms and carried her to his dungeon. The training would commence. Immediately. "Now you will see what it means to relinquish complete control."

He felt her slight shudder as he entered the dungeon.

"You will trust me," he said, setting her on her feet.

"Okay."

"Master," he said firmly. "Remember, you must address me as Master when we are in the dungeon.

"Yes, Master."

"Obey me and you will receive rewards beyond your wildest dreams."

"I . . . I will?"

He gave her a slow nod. "Undress."

# Chapter Five

*I* WANT YOU TO UNDERSTAND what will happen before we get started," Jestin said as his steamy gaze followed her motions.

Getting hotter by the second, despite the couple of reservations that stubbornly refused to release their chokehold on her, she peeled off her top first then pushed her skirt down over her hips. Her heart was beating so fast she swore it was about to explode, and her hands were shaking so bad it was almost impossible to use them.

She'd spent all last night reading, thinking, struggling to understand her feelings. She'd come to a couple of conclusions. First, the easy one. She had to get the plate from him because it was what her boss needed, it was what she'd promised. It would save her job, no matter what happened between them. And second—but somewhat unrelated to the first—she'd explore what it meant to be a dragon's mate.

Despite her natural inclination to rebel against another person's attempt to control her, there was something about Jestin, about this, that felt right. Natural. Exciting and fulfilling, too. By the end of the night, and after reading so much, she'd grown bleary-eyed, she'd become convinced she was about to learn a great deal, about Jestin, about dragons, but also more important, about herself. That made her both nervous and excited at the same time.

"I've . . . never done anything like this." She fumbled with her clothes, dropping them on the floor.

"I understand." He swept up the dropped garments and set them aside then closed his warm hands around her upper arms. "I will show you some patience. However, you won't want to push me by being impertinent or mocking. I know how you like to joke and tease. And I adore you for the carefree, joy-filled, independent woman you are. But this isn't the place for auditioning a standup routine or engaging in a battle of wills. To do so would bring terrible consequences. You would be mocking my feelings for you, my affection for you, and commitment to making you happy and keeping you safe. I will not tolerate it." He released one arm so he could unfasten the front hook of her bra. Then he used both hands to slide the shoulder straps down her arms before closing a warm palm over her breast. His gaze still locked to her face, he said heavily, "Remember—a reward is far more enjoyable than punishment."

"I understand, Master." Between her jittery nerves, the promise she caught in his voice and the way his fingers pinched and pulled at her nipple, she was already close to dropping at his feet. She nodded.

"Your panties. Take them off but leave on your stockings

and shoes. I am pleased with your choice of thigh-high stockings over those wretched pantyhose. For that, you will receive a reward as well."

Every cell in her body jumped up and down with glee. "Yes, Master." She pushed her panties down over her hips and let them slide down her thighs until they dropped to her feet. She was about to kick them off when he shook his head.

"You will bend over and take them off properly. Knees straight. Feet shoulder-width apart. Your ass this way." He positioned her so her rear end was right in front of him and he had a clear view of her most secret places when she bent over to tug the bit of lace off her ankles. She managed to get them off without falling over—a real feat considering both her position and nerves. Feeling quite proud of herself, she tried to stand up, but he stopped her with a firm hand on her back. "You will remain like this until I return."

"Yes, Master," she said, not particularly comfortable in the position he had left her in—it hardly brought light to her more favorable assets—but not wanting to displease him. A reward sounded a heck of a lot more fun than punishment, although she'd always found the idea of being spanked sexy. She hoped he'd spank her sometime.

She couldn't see him leave but she heard him. She also heard the squeak of door hinges as he opened and closed a door. Had he left the room? Left her bent over like a jogger stretching for a run? A soft shuffle of feet on the wood floor suggested otherwise. And the prickles of awareness skipping up her spine when he returned to his position behind her confirmed her suspicion. Evidently, he'd only opened a closet or bathroom door.

A heartbeat later, two warm, large hands cupped her ass cheeks and kneaded them until her pussy simmered and slickness coated her inner thighs. She heard him inhale deeply. "Very nice. I can smell your desire and that pleases me. You may stand now."

Her head swam a little when she straightened up. She wasn't sure if her dizziness was the result of the position she'd been in or from the pleasure he'd given her already, with only a gentle massage of her ass.

"Turn around, slave," he commanded in a soft but firm voice.

She did as he asked, puzzled by what he was holding. It looked like a gold, bejeweled collar, like the kind the rich and famous in Hollywood might buy for their little froufy dogs from some overpriced specialty shop. While the collar was pretty—the thing had to have a bazillion diamonds and rubies on it, along with several little silver rings—she wasn't sure what the heck she was supposed to do with it.

Was it for her future pet? That had to be it. A collar for her soon-to-buy Irish setter. How thoughtful! Although it was quite large around for a puppy and certainly a bit glitzy for a setter. They were more sporty dogs than fussy in her opinion.

"This is for you." Looking quite pleased with his gift, he unfastened the buckle and dodged her lifted hands to wrap the collar around her neck. "You will wear it whenever we are in the dungeon." He fastened the buckle.

"Oh! It's for me? Not a . . . oh, my." She lifted her hands to her neck and fingered the facets of the jewels. "I'm . . . gee, thanks. It's . . . er, lovely."

"You are my slave. We would not want to have any of my

fellow clan members mistaking you for a free woman. I will admit, and I don't expect you'd be surprised to know, I've brought free women to my dungeon in the past. But never again."

A twinge of jealousy tied her insides into a knot, even though she knew she had no right to feel that way. What he did in the past was in the past. She knew he was no virgin. "No? Um . . . can I ask? Your clan will be here? In the dungeon?"

"I will explain this only because you are new to being a slave and I care about you enough to want you to understand." He traced the line of the collar then let his finger drop lower to the valley between her breasts. "My fellow clansmen do come here. And they would devour you if they had the chance. Literally."

She shuddered as a half dozen images, each one more bizarre than the next, flashed through her mind. "Oh."

"And now you will show me your gratitude for my gift, which is an outward sign of my love for you."

"Love?" She stood frozen as her mind tried to wrap itself around that word. How could he love her already? After only one day? "Love?" she repeated again.

"Love is not a feeling. It is a decision, a commitment. And I have decided I will love you as my slave, my mate," he explained, pushing gently on her knees until she was facing him, kneeling. "With my love comes the promise that I will always put your needs and feelings before my own, to always treat you with respect and caring, to be faithful and kind.

Her kneecaps ground into the hard wood floor and she grimaced slightly.

"What is the matter, slave?"

"Sorry, Master. Floor's hard on the knees. I have bad knees."

"This way." He took her hands and pulled until she was standing then led her to a thing with two low, narrow pads close to the ground and a higher one in between. "This is a prayer bench," he explained. "Kneel here." He pointed at one of the low pads, "Facing me."

"Um . . . like this? I'm not joking. Is It time to pray? Now . . . er, Master?" Although it was awkward getting into position, because her feet tended to hit the other low pad, she was surprised by how soft the cushions were. She clasped her hands together in front of her chest.

"Better?" he asked.

"Yes. Much better. Thank you, Master. Will you be leading the prayer or me?"

"Neither." He pulled off his shirt and she watched, marveling at the beauty of his body, the lines of developed muscles coating his shoulders, arms and chest. When he moved, those scrumptious muscles bunched and stretched. What a lovely sight! It certainly inspired her to say a few words to whatever god had created him. "Would you like to serve your master and receive great rewards in return?"

Great rewards? He'd made a lot of promises of rewards today. She was sure ready to see what that was all about. Tingles skittered up her spine. She imagined him parting her legs wide and pushing his cock deep inside her pussy. A lump completely closed off her throat.

"Kaya, have you ever wanted to be tied up? Forced by a dark stranger?"

"I don't know. I never thought about it."

"What are your darkest fantasies?" His fingertip traced

the line of her throat then continued lower. He pinched her left nipple and gave it a sharp tug that made her gasp. Her empty pussy clenched, warm juices dripping down her inner thighs. "You will know, the beauty of being a slave is in both the giving and in the receiving." His other hand cupped her chin and lifted it. Her gaze snapped to his eyes and froze there for a moment then slid south to rest on his broad, smooth chest. She ached to reach out and trace the lines of his pecs, to feel his satin-smooth skin under her fingertips. "Like I said before, when you please your master, you receive pleasure beyond your wildest dreams. I will make your darkest fantasies come true." When he didn't continue, she glanced up. His smile was more wicked now than it had ever been. She trembled, her whole body tense with expectation. He licked his lips then continued, "I'm guessing you'd like to be bent over and fucked from behind. That way, you can touch yourself and come over and over. Is that true, Kaya? Would you like me to bend you over and fuck you from behind?"

"Yes," she whispered.

"And just before you come, would you like me to push my finger into your ass?"

"Oh, yes." Almost ready to come before he'd done more than pull on her nipple, she trembled. "Please."

"You will show me your gratitude first." He unbuckled his belt and unzipped his pants. "You will take my cock in your mouth."

"Yes."

"Would you like to do that?"

"Oh, yes, Master." She could barely remain upright thanks to the trembling his naughty talk was causing. Knowing herself, she'd always held the notion that her mind had as much to do with good sex as her body. Jestin was clearly a master of brain-stroking. She'd never been so ready with so little actual foreplay.

He removed both his pants and underwear, standing before her in all his glory. His skin was deeply tanned all over and smooth-shaven like a swimmer's. His cock was very large, erect. His balls hung heavily behind it.

He gripped his cock in his fist and gave it a couple of strokes and she nearly crumpled over, boneless and weak. Did he have any idea of what he was doing to her? "Open your mouth, slave. Take my cock in your mouth and show me how grateful you are for my gift."

She thrust her tongue out first and took several shy swipes across the head as Jestin held it to her mouth, his hand still wrapped around the base, sliding up and back. She licked round and round then opened wide to take him into her mouth. His flesh felt hot against her tongue. It tasted sweet and spicy, wonderful. As he pulled out, she caught a droplet of pre-come seeping out with the tip of her tongue. Then he plunged back in, fucking her mouth with shallow in-and-out thrusts.

"Touch yourself," he commanded. One of his hands was in her hair, holding her head still as he pumped his delicious cock in and out of her mouth. The other slid up and down the shaft of his cock. "Damn it, you feel good. Touch yourself."

She reached between her legs with one hand and found her clit. It was supersensitive and she gasped at the first stroke. She reached up and laid her other hand on Jestin's lower belly, just above his cock. She felt the muscles under his skin trembling and moaned around a mouthful of cock. She quickened the pace of the circles she drew around her clit until her stomach coiled into a tight knot, too.

Jestin abruptly pulled his cock from her mouth and demanded gruffly, "Turn around."

She stood up and knelt back down, resting her stomach on the high cushion. She felt the heat of his thighs against the back of her legs, even though his skin didn't touch hers. She moaned as he parted her labia with his fingers and pressed two inside. His knuckles scraped against the sensitive upper wall of her canal as his other hand alternatively slapped and kneaded her ass.

"You are such a good slave, Kaya. You are learning so quickly. You deserve a lifetime of rewards, each one greater than the last. I know you will serve me faithfully, and you have my promise that I will live my life dedicated to giving you every pleasure you desire." With his sweet words still echoing in the room, he thrust his cock deep inside her.

The first stroke sent bliss sweeping through her body. Her pussy stretched to accommodate his size then gripped him tightly, increasing her pleasure. The second stroke took her breath away. The third sent her careening toward release. She groaned and tossed her head from side to side.

"Have you ever let a lover push you to your threshold then pull you back, over and over until you couldn't take it anymore? Let him take complete control?"

"No," her answer was a pleading whisper. "Please." She shook all over, so close to orgasm she could feel the grip of release tightening deep in her belly.

He stopped moving inside her but didn't pull out. His

hands stroked her back. Sweet butterfly kisses coated her shoulders, giving birth to a flock of goose bumps. She was shivering cold and hot at the same time and ready to lose complete control, to hand it over to Jestin, the man whose words caressed her mind with as much tenderness and raw sensuality as his hands did her body.

She was there with him, not a single cell in her body wanting anything more than to share this bliss with him, to join him in an intense release that she suspected would shake her to her very soul. Her fear was gone. Her reservations burned away by the blaze consuming her body. "I will give you your release in a moment," his rough voice shook as he spoke, suggesting he was as close as she was to losing control. "Trust me."

"I do. In all ways."

"You are not afraid anymore?"

"Not of you."

He pulled his cock from her and pulled on her shoulders, easing her around to face him. "I know I promised you I would fuck you the other way, but I will give you the choice. Would you rather face away from me, or toward me? As before, when I climax, you will see me as I truly am."

"I will see the dragon?"

"Yes."

"I wish to face you."

His smile was so brilliant it brought tears to her eyes. He led her to another piece of furniture that looked a lot like a weight bench and lowered her onto her back. "Kaya, you make it so easy to love you." He eased her knees apart and with his fiery, heavy-lidded gaze fixed to hers, buried his cock deep inside her again. His lips parted slightly as a soft sigh slipped between them. Overcome with joy, she smiled and let her eyelids shutter out the distraction of sight, wanting to relish every touch, every sound, every scent until they found release and the dragon reappeared. He left her there in the dark world filled with the soft thwack, thwack of his groin striking her with every inward thrust, with the combined scents of man, dragon and desire, with the bliss of his intimate strokes inside her body. "Come for me. Take your release."

Tense pleasure gripped her body, pulling it into tight, shuddering coils. Her heavy breaths sounded hollow in her ears, muffling but not completely drowning out the sweet words Jestin continued to whisper to her. And then she was there again, and before she could say a word, she gave herself over to it, to the climax that pulsed through her body like waves on the sea. She gasped and jerked as the waves battered her, over and over, until they slowly subsided to little ripples. Hot tears streamed down her cheeks. She cried out, "Jestin!"

"I'm here, baby."

When she opened her eyes, the air before her shimmered and the dragon stood before her, mighty and powerful and beautiful. In awe, she stared until a moment later Jestin was back, smiling at her, his face and chest flushed.

"Next time. I promise," he said between heaving breaths.

"Next time?"

"You will have it your way."

"What are you talking about? I just did."

He gathered her into his arms, and their bodies still

joined, he held her in a tight embrace that made her feel strong and safe and loved. This was right. She was ready to take the final steps, to become Jestin's mate forever.

AFTER LYING IN BED for hours with Jestin, she eventually looked at the clock. It was late, or rather, early. Early morning. She had little more than an hour to get ready for work.

"I should get going."

"Stay here with me." He hugged her tighter to him.

"I have to go to work. No one's going to pay my bills for me." She unenthusiastically peeled his arm off her and sat up. He watched her dress from the bed, all rumpled and sexy and tempting. It took every ounce of willpower she possessed not to jump back into bed with him and go for round three, or was it four for the night?

Once she was fully dressed, she reluctantly brought up the one subject she'd avoided all night. "I need to ask you about the copperplate."

"Yes, I said I would consider my terms and I have. I will sell it to you for what I paid, not a penny more."

"You will?" Kaya couldn't believe her ears. She hadn't even told him yet that she had made her decision, that she would be his mate forever.

Would there be a hitch? There was always a hitch. Would he tell her she couldn't give it to Mrs. Kim? Would he ask her to hide it? "You'll give it to me and I can do what I like with it?"

"Yes," he said, sounding slightly defeated. "In fact, I trust you to make the payment later and will have Gibs bring it down to your car. You may do whatever you like with it."

"That's it?" she repeated, wanting to make sure she understood. "You're going to give it to me just like that?"

"Yes, you expected me not to?"

"I expected something, some terms. A word of caution, maybe."

"I will ask for only one thing—you deliver the payment to me personally tomorrow. Those are my terms."

"Those are terms I can agree to." She didn't know whether to shake his hand or hug him. She opted for a hug and was extremely glad she did the moment he pulled her to him.

Bazillion-year-old fire-breathing dragon or not, the man knew how to hold a woman.

# Chapter Six

KAYA WASTED NO TIME getting the copperplate back to the store, and to the relative safety of Mrs. Kim's built-in safe. The case tucked under her arm, she raced into the building, shut and locked the back door and shuffled down the back hall toward the front of the store. She heard Mrs. Kim's voice up ahead and the rumble of a man's voice. Just before she reached the back entry to the store, she halted when she heard Mrs. Kim say the word "plate."

"You must get it, no matter the cost. Have you no idea what it holds?" The man's voice rose slightly with anger. "It holds the key to the most powerful spell on the planet."

"Yes, I know. I sent Kaya with offer. I expect her to return with the copperplate today. She promise."

"You should have taken care of this yourself. It is too important and if the gentleman knows what he has, he will not part with it easily."

"But if he is not mage, what could it do for him?"

"If he is one of the red dragons, he will protect it with his life. The spell would strip all his people of their human disguises and they could then be easily destroyed. In their dragon forms, they are easily killed."

Kaya gasped and looked down at the black case snugged under her arm. Why would Jestin hand over the one thing that could mean the destruction of his entire race? Was the man wrong? He had to be.

Still, she wasn't about to take that chance. She whirled around on her heel. Unfortunately, she bumped into the swinging door as she turned. A quick look over her shoulder told her both Mrs. Kim and the man had heard her.

And a man running toward her at full speed told her he'd seen her, too.

Not taking the time to think, she did what came naturally—she ran. Zigged and zagged around boxes of antiques lining both sides of the narrow hallway to the back door. The man was on her heels within seconds.

Then the deadbolt on the back door did her in. It stuck, as usual. And before she could get it to twist open, the man snatched the case out from under her arm.

"Why were you running?" he asked in a powerful voice that suggested he knew the answer.

Still trying to disengage the lock, she shrugged her shoulders. "I just remembered I'd left my lights on. Don't want the battery to go dead."

"So it had nothing to do with this?" He held up the case.

She finally unfastened the lock and turned to face him. "Oh no. Not at all." She aimed for nonchalance in her expression. "Thanks for holding it for me so I could get the lock."

There were a lot of things Kaya had done in her life, like go to college, buy her own home and pay her taxes. But there were a lot more things she'd never done. She'd never risked life and limb for anyone. She'd never gone parasailing, bungee jumping or white-water rafting and she'd never broken the law.

She figured she was about to do at least a couple of those in the near future. Kaya Cordova would play it safe no more!

When Mrs. Kim lumbered up and spoke to the man she called Mr. Vandenberg, Kaya took advantage of his shift in attention, snatched the case which still rightfully belonged to Jestin and barreled through the door. With a shouting, furious, very large and intimidating man on her heels, she dashed to her car, locked the doors, started it and burned rubber out of there.

She even ran a red light to make sure she wouldn't be followed, and thus she did at least two things on that list in the span of only a few minutes.

There was only one place to go—back to Jestin's house.

Thanks to her nerves being wound tighter than a coiled spring that was ready to snap, it was hell driving the speed limit. But because she couldn't be sure whether Mrs. Kim had called the police or not, Kaya didn't want to take any chances at being pulled over. As a result, it took her over an hour to get to Jestin's. By the time she was sitting at the gate, buzzing to be let in, she was shaking from head to toe.

After being let inside, she parked the car, clutched the case to her chest and ran to the front door. It opened before she reached it. Mr. Gibs gave her a friendly smile and said, "This way, please. Mr. Draig is in a meeting. He wasn't expecting you quite so soon."

"Could you please tell him it's urgent? I need to talk to him."

"Very well." He motioned for her to take a seat in the library. She felt very warm and safe in the huge leather chair. "Can I get you something to drink while you're waiting?"

"No. Thanks. But if you could, please tell him it's important."

"Yes, miss." Mr. Gibs left, leaving her to shake and panic all by herself, not a good thing. Her mind jumped from one horrific thought to another: What if that man did something to Mrs. Kim? What if they called the police and reported her as a thief? What if she went home and was greeted by a SWAT team?

By the time Jestin strolled into the room, looking cool as a cucumber, she was an absolute mess.

She couldn't wait for him to wander his way across the room and so she jumped up and ran to him, the case still in her arms and thrust it at him. "I can't believe you gave this thing to me! Why? Why'd you do that? Are you suicidal? I don't get it." She resisted the urge to clobber him with it when he didn't take it from her.

In answer, he lifted both eyebrows.

"That's it? You're just going to look at me like I'm nuts?"

"Why have you returned this to me? Isn't it what you wanted?"

"It was until I found out what the copperplate says."

"You found that out already? From whom? What did you learn?"

"There was a man at the store, talking to Mrs. Kim when I came in. He said it had some kind of spell on it, a spell that would mean the destruction of the red dragons. That's you. That's your people. Was he right or did I just do something stupid that probably cost me my job, maybe even my freedom?"

"He was right. Was his name Vandenberg?"

"Yes. I've never met him before but he's purchased a lot of things from us."

"Yes, I know. He is becoming something of a threat to the Immortals although this is as close as he'd gotten to gaining possession of something that could've done some serious damage."

"Well, aren't you going to stop him? What if he comes after me? What if he gets the plate?"

"There's still no guarantee he has the power to invoke the spell. As a Guardian, I must do my job but I must do it quietly—under the radar, so to speak. I will continue to watch him but I will not do anything covert to stop him. As far as I know, he merely has a collection of relatively powerless trinkets. Nothing of real value."

"But you almost handed over something that could've caused real harm. You don't know how powerful the man is."

"True."

"Why then? Why did you do it?"

"I had no choice. I had to put my faith—and my life—in your hands. It is the next step."

"Yeah well, here. Glad I passed. But now I have some madman collector after me and I am probably jobless. Do those count as steps of some kind?"

He smiled.

"Don't tell me. Losing one's livelihood is step, what? Six? Seven? I've lost count."

He gave her a few innocent blinks. "We do seem to be clocking a new record. Only one step remains." He pulled her into the kind of embrace she'd come to expect from him. Warm, protective, gentle but firm.

Her knees turned to marshmallow and her fiery rage cooled.

She tipped her head up to give him a half-hearted dose of mean eyes. "Will you at least tell me what the final one is so I'm not caught by surprise again? And what will I do about my job? My bills? My criminal record? My grandmother! The poor woman'll be out on the street faster than the jury can say, 'Guilty'."

His laughter rumbled through her body making her insides tingle. "I will consider telling you. However, I believe you are overreacting. You won't have a criminal record because you didn't break any laws—at least none that I know of." He kissed her nose. "Did you?"

"I ran a few lights."

"That's nothing."

"Nothing! I've never gotten so much as a parking ticket before."

"Ah, but you're no longer that fearful—"

"Law abiding."

"—overly cautious woman you once were. I'd say you are uniquely qualified to work for me. The next items I need to buy are being auctioned in Chicago. A spear and a harp that can be used to destroy the Lamiae. What do you say?" His hands slid down her sides until they rested on her hips.

He pulled until her mound was pressed firmly against his leg. "I cannot possibly attend all the auctions throughout the world. Will you be my representative? Help me locate artifacts and attend auctions on my behalf? I promise the pay's good—at least double what you were making at your last position." He moved his leg so it rubbed her pussy through her clothes, making her all weak and warm.

Double? Double! That would give her plenty to live on plus pay her grandmother's nursing home bills. Thrilled beyond words, she said, "Wow! I don't know what to say. That's a very generous offer." She added, meaningfully, "Will I get benefits?"

"Absolutely. But I warn you, you must learn your place in my organization. I will not tolerate your stepping out of ranks." He winked. "At least not during business hours." He glanced at his watch, twisted the itty-bitty knob on the side. "Gee, look at that. It's exactly six-oh-one. Quitting time already."

"Wow, where did the day go?" she teased.

He took her hand in his and led her up the stairs and down the main hallway. He opened the door to the dungeon and said, "I don't have to tell you the consequences of insubordination."

She clapped her hands in delight then sobered her expression. "Oh dear. I suppose calling you my hunky, spunky dragon-boy would be considered stepping out of ranks?"

"It certainly would."

"And the punishment?"

His grin literally reached from one ear to the other, bringing back the California-boy beauty she'd admired so much the first time she'd met him, at the auction. Two deep dimples poked into his cheeks, making her all warm and weak in the knees. "Well, since we're still on this side of the doorway it'll be slight. How do you feel about . . . floggers?"

"Never met one personally, but I have an open mind, my widdle dragon-poo."

He gave her an exaggerated sigh and martyred look. "And thus your training continues. First rule, which you seemed to have forgotten already, you will call me Master."

"We're not in the dungeon yet," she pointed out with a smile.

He led her into the room and straight to the kneeling thingy, eased her down until she was on her knees and bent over, her stomach and chest resting on the raised part, her rear end up in the air. "Naturally, for your insolence, you will feel the sting of my flogger on your bare flesh."

"Yes, Master," she said, not bothering to hide the shudder of delight rippling through her body.

He reached up her dress, flipped the skirt over her back, and yanked down her panties. He tugged her knees wide apart so that her bottom was exposed, her pussy open wide. Her breathing came fast and ragged as her spine tensed in anticipation of the first strike. He walked away, strolling slowly toward a cabinet in the far corner of the room, and she tipped her shoulders to watch him.

"You will remain in position, head down, Kaya, or you will taste the sting of my wrath." His tone was firm but far from terrifying.

"Yes, Master," she said, lowering her shoulders.

He returned a moment later. She felt him near her, even though in her position she couldn't see him. It was the way the air crackled, like static electricity, all around him. The little snaps made her skin tingle and gave her goose bumps, too, both very delightful effects.

"Did I hear mocking in your voice?" he whispered.

"Oh, no, Master. Not mocking. I remember what you said. I would never dare to mock you. Not in here."

"Good." In reward, she received a light smack from the flogger. The fringes struck her bare bottom with a slightly stinging whap that made her yip in surprise. Oh, she had no idea how sexy and exciting being spanked could be. Her pussy was already burning with the need to be filled. She arched her back, thrusting her rear end up as high as she could, hoping he'd do it again.

The second strike was slightly harder than the first but equally pleasurable. And the third and fourth made her whimper with need.

"What you do to me," he murmured.

The kisses that followed were soft, gentle and incredibly erotic. They cooled each of her burning cheeks. Then, she felt his fingertips as he pulled her ass cheeks apart. One finger delved into her crack, sliding slick up and down until just the tip pressed into her tight hole while another slid down to her pussy. Barely able to remain kneeling, thanks to her trembling muscles, she groaned.

"Shall we go for the final step tonight, love? Will you join with me for eternity?"

Thanks to his intimate strokes, the kisses he trailed down her spine, the heat he stirred in her body, it was easy to tell him she'd made her decision. "Yes, oh yes."

She wanted to be his, in all ways, to learn to submit to him sexually, to fall asleep in his powerful arms at night, to stand by his side as Guardian, to live life as she'd never done before.

"Show me how to please you, to make you as happy as you've made me," she begged.

"It will take time, my sweet. I will show you as you are ready. For today, learn this—I will always do what is best for you because I cannot do anything else. I wish for you to trust me, always." As he spoke the last word, he pushed two fingers into her pussy and one into her ass simultaneously, making her see stars. With increasingly swift strokes, he brought her to a swift but mind-blowing climax that left her breathless and dizzy and aching for his cock.

He gently helped her up and led her to what looked like a chair suspended from the ceiling. After gently securing her legs and arms in position, he removed his pants and wedged his hips between her thighs.

"After tonight, we will become one in every way. We will breathe for each other, laugh for each other, cry for each other and live for each other. Your body will become mine, mine will become yours and you will know no more loneliness, no more fear, no more doubt. But it is painful."

"You never mentioned pain. Pain like a little spanking or pain like shoving bamboo under my fingernails?"

"You must surrender your soul to me. You must die."

Her heart skipped one, two, three beats. "Die? But I thought I would become immortal."

"Yes, you will. But immortality comes with a price. You pay with your mortality, with your life. But as I've said before, nothing will happen until you are ready. I will wait for your word. Until then, we will learn about each other, share in each other's bliss. It is as it should be." And then in a single thrust, he drove into her, stealing her breath and mind. All that existed was him. His cock moving within her, his fingertips digging into her thighs, his breath warming her chest, the sound of his breathing and gentle words in her ears.

This time, as she climaxed, she opened her eyes and marveled in the sight of him shifting back and forth from man to beast. He awed her. Such a powerful, beautiful creature. And he had chosen her, the woman who had, until she'd met him, lived as a slave to her fears.

The woman who had been afraid to take any risk now had the courage of ten women. As she was swept away on the waves of passion, she cried out without the slightest bit of fear, "Yes, my love! Yes! I am yours. Join with me."

"And so you will be." Jestin tipped his head and pressed a hot kiss on her chest, several inches above her left nipple. Instantly white-hot flames seared her flesh, leaping and churning through her whole body. She trembled and cried out against jagged blades of pain scissoring along her spine, making her weak. Her senses dimmed until there was nothing but silent, empty blackness. And then an explosion of colors blasted at her eyes. Scents so strong her nose burned shot up her nostrils, and touches so intense they felt like punches battered her skin. Her lungs burned for air and she dragged in a deep breath, blinked her tearing eyes and cried out, "Oh God!" The taste of sulfur soured her mouth.

*It is done. You are mine now, and I am yours. We are bound by the soul.* His thoughts echoed in her head.

Slowly, she found her way out from under the mountain of sensations to look at him. Although the colors, scents and touches didn't return to their normal state, they eased to at least the point of no longer being excruciating. She still heard even the smallest sound as clear as can be. And her vision was sharper, colors brighter. Scents pummeled her nose and she inhaled, trying to sort them out. And as her body adjusted, she realized with joy that something else had happened in that moment when they'd fused.

She could feel him inside. Could hear his thoughts as he worried about her. Could feel his emotions as he struggled with guilt, fear and bliss. He was a very real part of her now, and she him. The best part yet—she would have an eternity to share his joy and pain. And he hers.

She'd made a deal with one golden-haired devil and would never again face anything alone, not fear, nor joy, nor sorrow.

Her very own devil with dimples.

*The End*